Finn slipped an arm around her shoulders to draw her closer.

"I don't mean to give you mixed messages, but I liked having you and Emmie here. I haven't liked anything as much since I came to Barren. I don't know what to make of that, either, but maybe I should stop trying and just try...this."

His mouth angled to touch hers in a warm kiss that took away the cold night, the falling snow, and turned it into the heat of a summer day.

She kissed him back. She'd dreamed of being in his arms, never thinking it could happen. But where could this lead? He'd made his position clear. He hadn't recovered from the tragedy in Chicago and his belief in the future. In Barren he might care for Emmie, even care a little for Annabelle, but...

Her thoughts battled with the growing need inside for something more, something lasting and, if she were being honest, for Finn.

Dear Reader,

By the time you see this, I will have moved from Tennessee, where I've lived for quite a few years, to Arizona! As I've learned all over again, a new start can be exciting but also a bit scary.

That's certainly true for my heroine in *Her Cowboy Sheriff*, the fourth Kansas Cowboys book, even though Annabelle Foster is more than ready to move. When she's finally free of her family's diner, she plans to find a new career and travel far and wide.

But when Annabelle abruptly becomes the temporary mom to her cousin's vulnerable child, she soon learns little Emmie could steal anyone's heart. And then there's Finn Donovan. She's had a crush on him ever since he came to town.

Finn tries not to notice. After tragically losing everything in Chicago, he only wants to bury himself in his work as the new sheriff of Stewart County. But he can't resist Emmie—or Annabelle.

Getting these two wounded people together takes some doing, but nothing good is ever easy (just like a move from one place to another). I hope you'll like their story and come back for more.

The fifth book in this series isn't far behind! If you missed the first three, check out *The Reluctant Rancher*, *Last Chance Cowboy* and *Cowboy on Call*. They're still available, and they'd all love to have you visit their hometown.

For more information, please hop over to my website, leighriker.com, where you can also sign up for my newsletter.

And once again, happy reading!

Leigh

HEARTWARMING

Her Cowboy Sheriff

———

USA TODAY Bestselling Author

Leigh Riker

Recycling programs for this product may not exist in your area.

ISBN-13: 978-1-335-51051-8

Her Cowboy Sheriff

Printed in U.S.A.

™ www.Harlequin.com

Leigh Riker, like so many dedicated readers, grew up with her nose in a book. This award-winning, *USA TODAY* bestselling author still can't imagine a better way to spend her time than to curl up with a good romance novel—unless it's to write one! She's a member of the Authors Guild, Novelists, Inc., and Romance Writers of America. When not writing, she's either out in the garden, indoors watching movies funny and sad, or traveling (for research purposes, of course). With added "help" from her mischievous cat, Daisy, she's now working on a new novel. She loves to hear from readers. You can find Leigh on her website, leighriker.com, on Facebook at leighrikerauthor, and on Twitter, @lbrwriter.

Books by Leigh Riker

Harlequin Heartwarming

Kansas Cowboys

The Reluctant Rancher
Last Chance Cowboy
Cowboy on Call

A Heartwarming Thanksgiving
"Her Thanksgiving Soldier"
Lost and Found Family
Man of the Family
If I Loved You

Harlequin Intrigue

Agent-in-Charge
Double Take

Visit the Author Profile page
at Harlequin.com for more titles.

To my dear Chattanooga friends, Laurie, Kelle and Carol. The guest room is waiting!

CHAPTER ONE

FINN DONOVAN CRADLED the small child in his arms. The little girl couldn't be more than three years old, and her cries went straight to his heart, to the memories that were both happiest and darkest.

"Where's Mama?" she kept wailing.

Finn hated accident scenes.

The pile of nearby wreckage had once been a car and a pickup truck, the now twisted metal gleaming in the dark each time the flashing lights from the ambulance and his cruiser strobed the area. The hash of red and blue made the whole scene appear purple, and the noxious smell of spilled gasoline hung in the air. Hands down, this was the absolute worst part of his job.

Finn had hoped to leave all that behind in Chicago—the tragedy and loss—but his move to Barren, Kansas, apparently hadn't changed that after all. He'd thought as the sheriff of sleepy Stewart County he'd rarely have to deal with such scenes. This was his first here, and part of him wished he could hand the child off to his nearest deputy.

The little girl clung, arms tight around his neck, face buried in his shoulder as if she already trusted him to keep her safe. *"Ma-maaa!"*

Her tears soaked through his cotton shirt. Finn could feel his heartbeat drumming in his chest, his ears. *Get away*, he thought. *Put her down.* At the same instant, he pressed one hand against her skull, his fingers in the fine silk of her hair. The pint-size blonde sweetheart, who wore only a light cardigan over a T-shirt with a Disney character on it and a pair of tiny jeans, made his heart ache. Her miniature sneakers were the kind with lights that flashed like those of the ambulance. She shivered in his embrace, and Finn's pulse caught. Cold. Except for a few scrapes she hadn't been hurt in the accident, but the mid-October night had chilled. Was she going into shock? So small, so helpless…but she shouldn't rely on him.

She needed a warmer place and a quick removal from the frightening views all around them. On his way to his cruiser, Finn passed the paramedic who'd been breathing life back into the driver of the car. She turned to him, shaking her head.

"It's bad, Sheriff," she whispered.

Another EMT was now loading the stretcher onto the ambulance. Finn turned away enough to shield the child from the sight—shield himself, too. The open doors, the harsh light inside and the sight of the gurney, the woman's body no more than a still lump under the blanket, unnerved him. To his relief the child he held hadn't even tried to look, but at least her earlier cries had subsided into whimpers.

The paramedic's gaze met his. "Anyone we know?"

Was she asking about the woman? Or the little girl he still carried?

When he'd pulled up to the scene, Finn had run the victim's plates, her driver's license.

"Wyoming ID." He didn't supply the name. "Twenty-nine years old."

He shook his head, saddened by the obvious severity of her condition. As the ambulance doors closed, she didn't move a muscle. In contrast, the little girl squirmed in his arms, making Finn fear he might drop her, and the crack in his heart opened wider.

"We'll find your mom," he promised, not that the task would be hard.

There were only two choices, and he prayed—though he wasn't much prone to prayer these days—that it wasn't the woman in the ambulance. Finn glanced toward the victim's car. "What's your name, sweetie?"

She was shaking. "Em-mie."

"Can you tell me your last name, Emmie?"

Silence. Maybe she didn't know. When he spoke at day care centers or visited the local elementary school in Friendly Cop mode, he tried to impress on teachers and aides how important it was for children to know their contact information or to carry it with them. This was why. Had the girl been riding with the woman in the car or in the truck that now leaned in the ditch on the other side of the road? The other, elderly driver had already been taken to the hospital, but Finn hadn't arrived at the scene in time to try to talk to him. Was he Emmie's grandfather? Maybe her mother had stayed behind tonight.

He took Emmie to his car, dug in the glove compartment for one of the toys he kept there—this one a stuffed lamb wearing a pink ribbon—then signaled Sharon Garcia, his deputy, to stay with her. But the child refused to let go of him, and he couldn't talk in front of her, even when he guessed his deputy had more information to share.

He'd take a peek in both vehicles—then he'd know.

Still carrying Emmie, he crunched through broken glass to the side of the road. In the tilted pickup, he saw no clue that a child had been there. Which proved nothing. Maybe the older driver didn't believe in child seats, but then Emmie would have been injured in the crash. Finn moved on, sidestepping part of a front quarter panel in the road. With one hand cradling Emmie's head against his shoulder, he leaned over to peer inside the car.

At the instant she said "Hart-well," he glimpsed a child's car seat in the rear.

His stomach dropped into his shoes. Finn had his answer.

And, in silence, he swore. He would have to notify the next of kin.

FINN DONOVAN.

Seeing his reflection in the window, Annabelle Foster glanced away. She (reluctantly) ran the diner on Main Street that had been named for her—and that she had inherited from her parents. She'd turned to put her back to the for sale sign beside the front door when Finn had suddenly appeared behind her.

The sign's bright red letters on white plastic announced her intention to leave this place, and Barren. Tomorrow would be good for Annabelle, though she doubted that might happen. In this small town there wouldn't be many prospective buyers, and her Realtor had yet to show the place, though it hadn't been for sale long.

Annabelle didn't have time to appreciate the fact that at least she'd finally made, and implemented, what would be a life-changing decision. Free at last. That was what she'd be, and she could all but taste the first of her new opportunities in the air, except—why was Finn here?

"Annabelle," he said, and like the shy child she'd once been, she flushed. She always did around Finn, who had walked just now out of the dark, wearing his usual jeans and, tonight, instead of a traditional sheriff's tan shirt, a Henley pullover that stretched across his broad shoulders. Which, in a way, was his uniform.

"Going somewhere?" he asked with a

pointed look at the sign. If she remembered right, Finn hadn't stopped by since the sign had gone up. And where Finn was concerned, she would remember.

"Anywhere," she said a bit stronger than she intended. *Everywhere.* At last she would put the diner and this town behind her. Finn, too, and her hopeless crush on him, which wasn't as happy a prospect for Annabelle as the rest would be.

His gaze slid away. "Not just yet," he said. Finn shifted his weight. "Sorry to ruin your plans, but I have something to tell you…"

He hesitated for another instant while Annabelle's pulse sped up and she thought, foolishly, *Maybe he's here to ask me out.* Which would be a miracle. Her silly daydreams of a relationship with Finn would end when she finally left town. Besides, the only time she ever saw him was when he stopped at the diner to order a cup of coffee or a burger, often as takeout because he was on his way to a possible break-in at Earl's Hardware store—where the old alarm system had most likely gone off again for no reason—or to a traffic stop for someone who'd run the only red light in Barren.

Whenever he did stay long enough to eat

a meal, he sat in the last booth on the right side of the room, his back to the wall. What was he expecting? A replay of the Saint Valentine's Day Massacre?

In any case, Annabelle always had a fresh pot of coffee waiting, brewed strong and black just the way he liked it, and hurried to fill Finn's cup, determined to quell the blush that would surely show in her face. If they talked, it was about some neutral topic, an upcoming local event or his preference that day for apple over cherry pie. But now she didn't have the protection of the glass carafe in her hand like a wall between him and her stubborn awareness of him.

Then she realized from Finn's sober expression that he'd come by tonight in his official capacity as sheriff, not as an improbable—unlikely—boyfriend. She shouldn't be surprised. He'd said *tell* not *ask*. What could be wrong? She hadn't run the one red light in town and never drove above the speed limit.

Finn widened his stance. "You know a woman named Sierra Hartwell?"

Annabelle froze. She had no family in town now but… "Yes, she's my cousin. Why? What's happened?"

"There's been an accident," he said, not

looking at her. But then, he rarely did, or if he chanced a glance at Annabelle, he tended to look faintly off-balance with a kind of polite indifference in his hazel eyes. At least that wasn't like her parents who'd so often expressed some criticism or issued a new command. *Clean those tables now, Annabelle*, or, *Don't even think of leaving early for some high school football game. No one there will miss you.* As an adult her motto was *If I'm nice, as perfect as can be, I won't get hurt again.* But even with her parents gone, she was still trying to suppress the pain their unkindness had caused.

Her mouth went dry. She could barely ask the question. "Sierra's hurt?"

Annabelle tried to envision a minor fender bender, but he wouldn't look as serious about that. Finn touched her shoulder, so briefly she wondered if she'd imagined it, but even his warm hand couldn't penetrate the ice forming inside her. The growing horror. Was Sierra...*dead*?

As if she'd spoken aloud, he shook his head and said, "I'm sorry—her condition looks pretty serious. It was a bad accident."

Annabelle tried to process the news, but all she could say was, "Where?"

"About a mile outside of town she collided with Ned Sutherland's pickup. We don't know for sure which driver was responsible. Your cousin is on her way by ambulance to Farrier General."

Annabelle glanced inside the diner half-full of patrons even this late in the evening. Ned, who owned the NLS Ranch, was getting up in years. His granddaughter was her friend, and Annabelle knew she worried about him. "I didn't think he was even driving since his stroke. That's terrible. About Sierra, too. I admit, I haven't seen her in years—"

She broke off. Once, she and Sierra had been as close as sisters, but in their teens, they had drifted to occasional phone calls. And even those had stopped. Except for one, much more recent, Annabelle remembered with a pang of sorrow. So why had Sierra been close to Barren?

"Did you know about her little girl?" Finn asked.

"Yes, Sierra sent me a text when she was born, a little over three years ago, I think, but that's all I know. She hadn't picked a name yet."

"It's Emmie," he informed her.

Annabelle's throat closed, and something tugged deep at her heart. *Emmie.* Sierra's daughter was still hardly more than a baby. Now her mother was in the hospital and this child Annabelle had never met had become real. "Is *she* okay?"

"Scared, as you'd expect, but unharmed physically," he said. "Which is a miracle."

Annabelle looked away from Finn's dark hair, which under the streetlights appeared brushed with gold. How inappropriate her thoughts of him had been only minutes ago. He had no real interest in her. A relative newcomer to the area, he'd already been labeled a loner.

She shivered but not from the cold. During that last phone call with Sierra a few weeks ago, she hadn't mentioned Emmie, and when she abruptly hung up, Annabelle's questions about her had gone unanswered.

With a slight frown Finn eyed the goose bumps on her arms and she rubbed her bare skin. "I only stepped out for a minute," she said. To see the for sale sign—to pinch herself that, at last, her dream would become real. "My customers are waiting for me. But I'll have to close the diner."

"I'm sorry, Annabelle," he said again. "I

didn't mean to be blunt, but I'm not good at giving news of this kind. In fact, I wish it wasn't a part of my job. You must be upset. Let me give you a ride to the hospital."

She couldn't quell the thought that flashed through her mind. *Upset* didn't begin to cover it, and she wasn't a selfish person, but the timing of this couldn't be worse. She was a blink away from freaking out, yet anything she might say would make Finn see her in a bad light. And with that, another bolt of guilt shot through her. For now, she couldn't dwell on her plan to leave Barren before she knew if Sierra would be all right. As for the little girl…

"Where's…Emmie now?"

"With one of my deputies at the station. Is there someone else I should contact?" Finn asked. "A husband? Or boyfriend? I thought not, since you were listed as the next of kin on the card in her wallet."

That was a surprise. Another shock, really. She and Sierra hadn't seen each other in a long time and they hadn't parted on good terms. "As far as I know, I don't think she's ever married. I wouldn't know about any boyfriends. I'll take that ride to Farrier General, thanks," she added. "I know I'm not good to drive right now." She needed to see Sierra for herself, see that she wasn't in as bad a condition as Finn had said. But that wasn't all. "What will happen to her little girl—to Emmie—tonight?"

Finn squared his shoulders. "Maybe you can tell me. Either she goes home with you," he said, "or I turn her over to child services. I like the first option better."

CHAPTER TWO

AT THREE O'CLOCK the next morning, little Emmie woke up shrieking.

Bleary-eyed, heart instantly in her throat, Annabelle jerked upright in bed, ears alert to the sound of tears from across the upstairs hallway. This wasn't the first time Emmie had stirred, and Annabelle was already at her wit's end. "I know nothing about taking care of a small child," she'd told Finn earlier.

Yet there was no way she would have let the State take over tonight. Emmie was Annabelle's, what, first cousin once removed? Second cousin? She wasn't sure of the proper term. Anyway, a relative, and with Annabelle's parents gone, Sierra and her daughter were the only—if estranged—family Annabelle had left. Even more, Emmie had witnessed a terrible event last night, and she was a vulnerable child. Without her mother, she must feel utterly alone and obviously frightened, not that Annabelle had seemed able to comfort her fears before. *What should I do?*

She slipped out of bed and reached for her robe. The night had cooled even more, probably another ten degrees, and her heat wasn't on yet for the season. The last time Annabelle checked on Emmie, the child's feet had felt like ice cubes. *If she stays more than a night or two here…* Annabelle would have to get the HVAC system going.

But surely this arrangement would be brief. She padded across the hall, cracked open the door then eased into the spare room, taking care not to let the hinge squeak—which it had for her entire thirty-one years.

She was simply the babysitter until other plans could be made or Sierra got out of the hospital, *not that I know what I'm doing.*

As she crossed the bedroom, Annabelle dragged her growing guilt like a ball and chain. Certainly, for reasons of her own she hadn't been that eager to take Emmie in. Just hours before Sierra had called a few weeks ago, Annabelle had paid the first half of her own tuition to attend a two-week course at a well-regarded academy in Denver that would train her to be an international tour director, a first commitment to the future she wanted for herself. Weeks before that she'd sent in her registration fee and a hefty first deposit, using part of the money her parents had left her. Annabelle tried not to feel guilty that she was using her inheritance to escape the diner. And when Sierra had mentioned coming for a visit after so many years, claiming she had *loose ends to tie up in Barren*, Annabelle had told her not to come. If Sierra had listened, she wouldn't be here now lying in a hospital bed.

Emmie lay almost buried under the covers. Only her eyes showed, glowing in the near darkness, looking suspicious and confused. Annabelle had left a night-light on the nearby bureau for her, but obviously Emmie couldn't sleep. So neither could Annabelle.

"Hey, punkin." She heard a shuddering intake of breath. "It's all right."

Annabelle ventured closer to the bed.

At the hospital she'd asked Finn about a crib for Emmie. "At three she's probably done with that," he'd said. "Kids climb out then start roaming. They can fall and hurt themselves."

How would Finn know? He was reportedly single—much to the delight of many other women in town—a fact helpful for Annabelle's fantasies. As far as she knew, he had no kids.

Uncertain if he was right about the crib, Annabelle had decided to improvise. Her parents had long ago donated her baby items to charity. Two straight-backed chairs now served as a barrier to keep Emmie from tumbling out of bed and hitting her head. Rubbing her eyes, Emmie cried out. "Want my mama!"

"I know, sweetie, but she's not here right now."

Emmie didn't buy that weak explanation, but Annabelle couldn't tell her the truth. Again, the child burst into tears.

Annabelle tried her best—which apparently wasn't enough—to comfort her. Earlier, at the hospital while she and Finn waited for an update on Sierra, neither of them saying much, Emmie had been with Finn's deputy at the station. By then, Sierra was in surgery. Later in recovery, looking pale and horribly bruised, with tubes snaking everywhere and monitors beeping, she'd still been under the effects of the anesthesia and couldn't talk. She seemed much worse than Annabelle had expected, and Annabelle had Sierra's daughter to care for—or try to—tonight. As for tomorrow…what if Sierra didn't survive?

Finn had driven them home from the sheriff's office, Emmie in the back seat clutching her stuffed lamb while Annabelle crooned to her without quite knowing what to say. The little girl had finally relaxed in the car seat Finn had provided, and by the time they reached the house Emmie's eyelids were fluttering.

Annabelle thought of Finn standing by the bed when he'd put a then-sleeping Emmie on the clean sheets, a slight—even wistful?—smile on his lips that made Annabelle feel weak in the knees. Finally, he'd said, "It's late."

When he turned from the bed, panic streaked through her. "You're not *leaving*?"

She didn't know what else she wanted then, except not to be alone with Emmie, but another blush bloomed on her cheeks. "I won't know what to do if she wakes up."

Her heart kept clanging against her rib cage, but Finn had only touched her shoulder as if to say *you can do this* then left the room. Ever since then Emmie had slept fitfully, waking every hour in this strange house, probably wondering where she was, to call out for her mama, sometimes pushing Annabelle away.

Emmie's rosebud mouth puckered in the dim light now. "Where Mama go?"

Annabelle drew a breath, then said, "She had to stay somewhere else tonight, sweetie. She asked me if you could sleep here."

Emmie shoved two fingers in her mouth, a built-in pacifier. Not wanting to leave her, Annabelle moved a chair aside then sat on the bed. The soft, silvery light of a full moon filtered through the room's gauzy curtains, and in the hallway her parents' old grandfather clock ticked in the stillness. It reminded Annabelle of all the terrifying time-outs she'd gotten, her punishment for doing something wrong, listening to the minutes march by until she would be freed. To this day she avoided that now-locked closet under the stairs.

She smoothed a tentative hand over Emmie's blond hair, wishing she had some other means of comfort to offer, but even though Emmie needed an adult's reassurance Annabelle had little experience. "It'll be okay," she kept whispering, though she wasn't sure of that. Seeing Sierra in the recovery room hadn't been encouraging, and Annabelle's dreams tonight had been as troubled as Emmie's must be.

Annabelle felt all at sea. She liked children, but she didn't have any of her own. Still, she often gave kids treats at the diner and loved hearing their laughter. At Christmastime, for her smallest customers, she made Santa cookies with red-and-green sprinkles, but that was the limit of her contact with them.

Annabelle was happy to hand out cookies or give a pat on the head, but for now children were at the bottom of her priority list. Yes, she yearned for a good marriage someday, a family of her own, but not before she was ready. At the moment she had no prospective husband in sight—despite her feelings for him, she couldn't count Finn since he barely knew she existed. And what if she screwed up her children as Annabelle's parents had *her*? Annabelle still bore the emotional scars from that closet. No, it was better to focus first on seeing the world beyond Barren. On escaping her past to make that new future for herself. She had waited long enough.

And wouldn't Emmie's father, whoever he was, be a better choice to care for her? Was he a part of the little girl's life? Emmie had

Sierra's last name, not his, and Sierra hadn't been carrying his contact information in her wallet. But once she woke she might fill in the blanks.

Or maybe—Annabelle could hope—Sierra would soon be out of danger and on the mend, well again before Annabelle packed her bags to fly to Denver. She'd booked her flight with a hard lump of anxiety in her throat yet a wild feeling of exhilaration. This would be her "maiden voyage," including the first plane ride of her life, and from there, once the diner did sell...the whole world would, at last, be hers.

"Mama?" Emmie's small voice sounded panicky again.

And here came the guilt once more, creeping in to overwhelm Annabelle. Emmie must feel terrified in this unfamiliar house with this strange woman who didn't know what she was doing, just as Annabelle had felt in the closet that had terrified her as a child. She'd been small and frightened then, huddled in the dark, trembling with fear, alone. Abandoned.

Acting on a maternal instinct she hadn't known she possessed, she drew Emmie closer. "Baby, you'll see her soon. Let's try to sleep."

Annabelle would open her diner by six o'clock, as she did every day, and even sooner than that her prep cook would be in the kitchen slicing onions and peppers for the ever-popular western omelets, mixing buttery biscuit dough and cutting fresh fruit for breakfast. The daily routine was so deeply ingrained in Annabelle that she wondered if she'd ever truly get it out—or stop feeling unappreciated.

She'd never had to think about a three-year-old child. *What about diapers?* she'd asked Finn, following him into the hall hours ago.

"My deputy tells me Emmie's potty trained."

Frozen in place, Annabelle had heard his footsteps along the upstairs hall as he'd departed, his steady tread drowning out the sound of the clock. Feeling more alone than she'd ever been in her life, she'd listened to the front door open, then he was gone, leaving her in charge. If that meant baking a cherry pie or brewing a pot of rich Ethiopian coffee, the diner's special blend this month, that was what she knew. It was all she knew for now. Until the plane took off for Denver.

But a small child to care for? Emmie was counting on her, and she finally nestled against Annabelle as she had in the car, as if she knew they were each other's family. Or maybe, half asleep, she'd confused Annabelle with her mother.

Yet as sympathetic as she felt to Emmie's needs tonight, she didn't *want* another person counting on her just when she was about to turn her back on Barren, Kansas, and everything it represented.

FINN COULDN'T GET the images out of his head: the flashing red lights, the siren, Emmie Hartwell crying in his arms. It was always this way and he'd feel gritty eyed in the morning, which at four was almost here. He wondered if Annabelle was sleeping now or if, like him, she was lying awake.

She'd stayed close to Emmie on the way home, just as he had at the scene, and her heart appeared to be breaking—like his. But at the same time, Annabelle had clearly wanted to hand off the responsibility for Sierra Hartwell's child to anyone else. Including him. That wouldn't happen. Annabelle *was* the best option for Emmie.

Finn didn't know much about Annabelle. Didn't want to know, he told himself. Finn had his life here, such as it was, and with the exception of his dog, snuffling in his sleep at the foot of the bed, that didn't include getting close to someone again. Whether that meant the little girl he'd held at the accident scene...or Annabelle Foster, he didn't have the heart for it.

Sure, he'd noticed her—had seen the flash of awareness in her eyes, too—but Finn refused to dwell on that. It made him feel... disloyal.

She certainly tried to hide her attractiveness with plain clothes, including that everpresent apron, and carried a coffeepot at the diner as if to announce she was unavailable except to work. But she had rich, brown hair that shone like glass. Her pretty eyes could turn from brown to almost green depending on the light—and on her mood, if she had any variation in them. She was cheerful, relentlessly so. Tonight was the first time he'd seen her look shattered. He'd often wondered: Did she really like being tied to that diner, as if the popular local restaurant had

apron strings, too? The for sale sign tonight
told him no, like the sometimes *not-quite-
here* look in her eyes.

Still, unlike Finn these days, she'd always
seemed to be a happy person, as well as un-
failingly kind. More than once he'd watched
her pocket someone's unpaid check then put
the money in the drawer herself because she
knew they couldn't pay.

Earlier tonight, for the first—and probably
last—time, he'd been inside her house. Finn
had noted the overstuffed living room furniture with faded chintz upholstery, and the
tired-looking floral wallpaper that made his
apartment seem like a showcase of good de-
sign. Her place reminded him of his grand-
mother's home until he'd caught a glimpse
of the bright posters tacked to her bedroom
walls. Venice, Paris, Barcelona...holdovers
from her girlhood? Her teens? Maybe she
just liked pictures of pretty places, and he
was reading too much into the decor. Or
were those posters an announcement of her
intention not only to sell the diner but to get
out of town?

Giving up on sleep, Finn got out of bed.
Whether she left or stayed didn't matter to
him. He had paperwork about the accident to

finish, and that wasn't his only concern. The fate of a local cattle rustler, Derek Moran, had been churning in his gut like a lousy fast-food meal. Finn's part in the case was done, but sooner or later Derek would step out of line again, and Finn would be waiting. In his view Moran was a bad actor who reminded him of someone else.

Eduardo Sanchez. He tried to block out the other man's name but it zapped his brain with all the force of a taser. All Finn wanted was to see him in handcuffs, see justice served as it would be for Derek Moran.

For now, even as sheriff he couldn't do anything about either of them. Instead, Finn wanted to take another look in Sierra Hartwell's car. She was something of a mystery to him, one he also hoped to bring to a close.

He padded over to his bureau and yanked open the second drawer. A sudden burst of memory assailed him. *More flashing red lights, another siren, two innocent people lying in pools of blood. The members of the Chicago gang that called themselves The Brothers getting away with murder.*

Like the rest of his past, the top drawer was his personal no-go zone.

SOMEONE WAS CRYING.

In the bed beside her, Emmie sat up, weeping before Annabelle had cleared her mind of her latest bad dream. Sleep continued to be hard to come by, and at four-thirty, when Emmie had stirred again, Annabelle finally carried her from the guest room to her own bed.

She yawned and stretched. Apparently three-year-olds got up early. Neither of them, she supposed, had gotten much rest.

Emmie was cranky. But then, so was Annabelle.

"Mama, I hungry."

Annabelle didn't try to correct her. For these first few minutes awake maybe Emmie thought she was in her own home. "Then let's find something to eat, sweetie."

What did little girls like? Holding Emmie's hand, trying not to take her wary expression personally, she walked downstairs to the green-tiled kitchen. With a glance out the window, she noticed her car, which she'd left at the diner, parked in the driveway. Finn must have delivered it sometime during the night. Yawning, Annabelle decided on cereal for breakfast.

She took milk from the fridge—the same

GE model that had been here since she was Emmie's age—and a box from the pantry. All Annabelle could face right now was a cup of strong coffee. With an encouraging smile, she set the cereal bowl in front of Emmie, but as she turned toward the coffee maker, she caught a flash in her peripheral vision of Emmie's fine blond hair, in tangles this morning. Without warning, Emmie's arm swung out, and the bowl flew through the air. It landed on the linoleum floor and shattered. Cheerios and milk sprayed everywhere, provoking more tears from Emmie.

They didn't last long before, to Annabelle's further shock, Emmie suddenly grinned and her big blue eyes sparkled as if she were proud of what she'd done. Emmie had deliberately spilled the cereal, probably wanting to see Annabelle's reaction—which was to drop to her knees and wipe up the mess. And count to ten. Twice. This was definitely not her wheelhouse.

She straightened with the soggy sponge in her hand. Okay, no Cheerios then. On her feet, she poured a glass of orange juice, but as she started to put it on the table, she saw Emmie already scowling.

"Don't like juice," she said, pouting.

Annabelle yanked the glass out of reach. She didn't own any plastic ones, and there was no sense in causing another mishap to start the day off worse than it was. "What *do* you like?" she asked, trying not to grit her teeth.

"Doughnut."

"That's not a healthful breakfast," Annabelle said, which produced another now-familiar wail of protest from Emmie. *Why didn't I bring home yesterday's leftover blueberry coffee cake*? Better than a doughnut, made of organic flour, and with fruit.

"Mama knows!"

"Of course she does." The morning was threatening to become a full-blown disaster. How to explain? "But your mom didn't feel well, and um, the doctor is fixing her. She'll be fine, Emmie," she added.

Another tiny frown creased Emmie's forehead. She didn't mention the accident but asked, "Where the man go?"

Annabelle thought for a second. "You mean Finn?"

She nodded. "Nice man."

"He's probably at his office. You may see him later."

At dawn, Annabelle had punched the answering machine beside her bed and heard a message from Finn who wanted to see her at her convenience. But how, with Emmie in tow? Annabelle was used to going everywhere alone. Obviously, she'd never needed a sitter, and this wasn't a young-family neighborhood. She ticked off several options, but her closest neighbor was on a cruise through the Panama Canal this week, which Annabelle envied. The elderly woman across the street might be willing to help, but she'd broken her ankle and was on crutches. Annabelle had delivered a lasagna to her only yesterday. Really, neither woman would be able to keep up with Emmie—from Annabelle's now limited experience. Leave Emmie at the diner then, while she was at the sheriff's office? Her staff would already have their hands full with the breakfast crowd. What if Emmie wandered off, out the door and into Main Street? Or threw a fit at being left?

Her pulse stumbled. More to the point, Emmie was traumatized—perhaps one reason she hadn't even brought up the accident, as if her brain had suppressed it. Annabelle wouldn't leave her alone. For a day or two, in Sierra's place, Annabelle would be second best. For now, she was all Emmie had.

She would have to take Emmie with her when she went to see Finn.

CHAPTER THREE

HIS HAND NOT QUITE touching her back, Finn guided Annabelle into his office. His dog, a rescue mutt, part German shepherd, part Labrador with maybe a touch of golden retriever in the mix, lay sprawled on the wooden floor in a square of sunlight, blocking the chairs in front of Finn's desk. He gently nudged him with one boot, cutting off the dog's snore. With a start, Sarge raised his head. "Move over, pal. Give the lady some room."

"I didn't know you had a dog."

Why would she? He and Annabelle barely knew each other. They weren't even friends, and his awareness of her was Finn's to ignore. If Annabelle felt drawn to him too, that was her problem. The less she knew about him, the better for Finn.

"Saved him from the pound over in Farrier a month or so ago," he said. "We're still in the adjustment period." They watched Sarge come to life again, blinking, before he managed to stand, rearrange his bones then shuffle closer to the window. "The sun's better there anyway, bud," Finn told him and pulled out a chair for Annabelle.

"That was nice of you," she murmured, "to give him a home."

"Sarge is kind of the office mascot." He gestured toward the chair. "Take a seat."

Finn looked toward the outer room where Emmie had been placed on a desk. She was swinging her feet plowing her way through a doughnut with sprinkles and chatting with Sharon, his deputy, whom she'd taken to last night. "How did it go after I left your house?"

"As well as it could, I suppose. We ended up sharing my bed." Annabelle told him about an incident with some cereal at breakfast. They shared a brief smile before she said, "I couldn't leave her at the diner and I didn't know what else to do but bring her with me."

"Because all cops like doughnuts?" Finn couldn't resist teasing her if only to see her blush.

She actually laughed, then sobered. "Why did you want to see me?"

Finn looked away. Annabelle's pink cheeks

made her seem more than appealing, like the innocent look in her eyes as if she didn't quite get his joke. Never mind, he thought. His solitary life suited him, and with luck would help him forget Chicago, as much as he could. It allowed him to focus on what mattered most—nailing Eduardo Sanchez's hide to the wall, even from a distance—and he had no room for Annabelle. Or, for that matter, little Emmie. The very thought of holding her last night at the accident scene made him sweat, made him remember...

Finn pulled a form from his desk drawer. "I need your statement. Any information you can supply about Sierra." He searched for a pen then began to fill in the basic stuff. Time, date, interviewee's name... "I never understand why people don't wear their seat belts," he muttered, half to himself.

Annabelle blinked. "Sierra wasn't wearing hers?"

"No," he said.

"She never did like doing things that were good for her—at least in my parents' opinion. Whenever she spent summers with us, she drove them crazy. To me, she was a hero for daring to challenge them."

It sounded as if Annabelle herself never

had. Finn stopped writing. The few times he'd heard her mention her family, Annabelle got that tight sound in her voice and looked past the person she was talking to. Maybe he wasn't the only one with issues to avoid. He wouldn't let himself think about that drawer in his bureau, wouldn't probe his memories like a sore tooth.

"Sierra was thrown from the car," he told her. "Ned Sutherland's life was saved by his seat belt." Finn frowned. "But his granddaughter was right. He shouldn't have been behind the wheel of that old pickup. In fact, when he took off last night she tried to stop him. Ned's not talking yet this morning, but—" He cleared his throat. "Annabelle, how well do you know Sierra?"

She studied her hands in her lap. "As girls we were inseparable into our teens, but as adults we've had almost no contact. Why?"

He tapped his pen against the desktop. "Number one, her driver's license, while still valid in the state of Wyoming, has an address that's no longer hers and I suspect hasn't been for some time. No forwarding one with the DMV there. Wherever she lives now, she should have changed her license. Most states have reciprocity."

"Wyoming?" Annabelle bit her lip. "Actually, I don't know where she lives. Sierra's a corporate events planner—or she was the last I heard—and because of her job, she travels around a lot."

That seemed to interest Annabelle but didn't help Finn now. "Second, in Sierra's glove compartment I found several notices from the court in a different state, but Missouri doesn't seem to be her home base either. After she failed to appear, they issued a warrant for her arrest."

Annabelle leaned forward. "A warrant?" she repeated, as if he'd spoken in a foreign language. "Well, maybe she didn't pay some parking tickets…"

He had to admire her quick defense of her cousin, but his mouth tightened. "The warrant isn't for parking violations. It references a felony for fraud and embezzlement. I'm waiting for further details from St. Louis." The distressed look on Annabelle's face threatened to melt his resolve. For an instant he wanted to reach across the desk, cover her hand with his. Trying to refocus his attention, he glanced at Sarge who was snoring again in the sun, his once dull coat now a glistening brown, tan and yellow. Thanks to a better diet, his liquid dark eyes were also bright, or would be if they were open. "If Sierra was on the run last night, fleeing from Missouri, feeling desperate—"

"You think the accident was her fault? Not Ned's?"

"We're still processing the scene." Finn offered a theory she probably wouldn't like. "But consider this: Sometimes a child in the rear seat cries, throws a temper tantrum, a parent gets distracted while driving—"

"Not in this case." Annabelle sat back in her chair. "Sierra wouldn't jeopardize her child. I know my cousin."

"Really? You haven't seen her in quite a while," Finn pointed out mildly.

"And you don't know her at all." Her eyes clouded. "Sierra couldn't possibly be in legal trouble like that. There must be some mistake."

THE NEXT MORNING, as soon as Annabelle slipped into Sierra's hospital room, her steps faltered. Annabelle had hoped to find Sierra awake, to ask her about Emmie's father. She'd visited twice now and found little change in her cousin. All around monitors beeped and buzzed, but the information on the displays next to Sierra's bed might as well have been written in Greek. Annabelle's brief stop at the nurses' station hadn't provided much information beyond the fact that, although she'd been moved from ICU last night, Sierra was still listed as critical.

What if she *didn't* survive? What would happen to Emmie?

Her throat feeling tight, Annabelle stood beside the bed then took Sierra's limp hand. It was like touching, looking, at a stranger. Her blue eyes were swollen closed, her blond hair, usually so like Emmie's, instead looked dull and stringy and she didn't move at all. Harsh cuts and bruises covered her face and neck, and a bulky bandage slanted across her forehead. *She was thrown from the car*, Finn had said.

Annabelle's spirits sagged. It was a good thing she hadn't brought Emmie with her. Until Sierra looked better or wakened, the sight of her mother like this might be too much. Emmie was getting to know the staff at the diner so Annabelle had left her there for an hour, giving her fat crayons and a book to color at the counter.

"Oh, sweetie," she murmured, fighting tears. She tried to warm Sierra's hand, but after her talk with Finn she had to wonder.

The interview had been difficult for her. Annabelle hadn't cared for his comments about Sierra, but did she really know this woman in the bed anymore? She hadn't told him about Sierra's troubled teenage years because they hadn't seemed relevant. Sierra had since turned her life around, and yet…

She applied slight pressure to Sierra's hand, hoping she'd wake up, and to her relief Sierra's eyelids fluttered once before they drifted shut again. And Annabelle took heart. "You're going to be fine," she said, remembering summer nights together when they'd stayed up late and giggled, played tricks on each other…until her parents had abruptly put an end to Sierra's annual visits. "We'll straighten everything out. You'll see. I won't let you down again." As she'd done when she'd meekly accepted her parents' command not to mention Sierra again and on the phone not long ago. There would be time later for Annabelle's full apology. Time to ask about Emmie's father.

"YOU SAID YOU HAD something for me." Finn cradled his cell phone against his shoulder and tried to stifle his growing resentment at his former partner, who was on the line from Chicago. Finn envisioned Cooper in the squad room, the top button of his uniform shirt undone, one hand running through his surfer-boy hair.

"I'm only human, Donovan. I've spent most of my free time since you left town hunting that gang…and, *sorry*," he said in the sarcastic tone that Finn knew well, "but every one of them has dropped off the face of the earth."

"Not likely," Finn muttered. None of this was Cooper's responsibility, but Finn still hoped he would help bring Finn's most personal case to a close. "When you called, you said you had an update so I thought—"

"Didn't mean to mislead you. But, frankly, there's not much more I can do here. I guess that's the heads-up—the something—I had to give you."

Finn refused to be deterred. "The gang'll resurface. We only need to wait."

"Listen, my friend. If I kept taking those little side trips to follow a lead from my snitches—all of whom have now dried up—I'd be looking at disciplinary action." He added, "That should resonate with you."

Finn came from a family of cops, and in Chicago he and Cooper Ransom had always toed the line. As a kid Finn had learned that from his uncle Patrick. The opposite of Finn's father in temperament, with gentle good humor and lots of one-on-one time while his dad was all about The Job, Pat had guided Finn off the dangerous path he'd walked in his teens onto the straight and narrow again—until years later when that Chicago gang known as The Brothers struck close to home. Because of them, especially Eduardo Sanchez, Finn no longer had a wife he loved, a son he adored. A family.

Justice for them had become his chief concern—his obsession.

"I wasn't fired," Finn said. "I quit."

"In the nick of time." Cooper blew out a breath. "If you'd gone any further in your private quest to send those thugs to prison for the rest of their lives, the department would have taken your badge, your uniform, your gun—and hustled you straight into Internal Affairs. Then where would you be?"

Finn's mouth hardened. "Free to pursue the gang—full time."

This was an old argument, begun the day Finn had lost everything. He heard the metallic clang of a desk drawer being slammed shut, and it reminded him of the no-go drawer in his bedroom. Of Sanchez. Cooper's voice lowered. "If I hadn't talked you out of turning into some vigilante, you'd be in jail."

Or lying dead on the South Side pavement. Finn would have traded his life then for one shot at the gang's leader. He still would but he wasn't there. Now he just tried to get through each day without his thoughts of the tragedy overwhelming him to the point where he couldn't do his job here. "So, instead, I took your advice—and you promised to find them for me."

He could almost see Cooper shaking his head, his gray eyes somber. "I wish I knew what else to do. I hate to disappoint you, Finn—but maybe you need to focus now on being sheriff of Stewart County."

Finn heard a wistful note in his voice. Cooper had grown up near Farrier, a few miles from Barren, on a cattle ranch. He was the cowboy Finn was not and had no aspirations to be. Finn didn't like horses, and he'd never been around cows. But when cattle prices had plunged years ago while Cooper was in his teens, his family had been forced to sell out. He claimed he was still trying to adjust to life in the city, but for whatever reason he'd never come back home. He'd sent Finn here instead.

"Being sheriff is a lot less dangerous than Chicago PD. I write a few parking tickets, stop a speeder here and there…oh, and there was a break-in last week at the hardware store. Somebody stole a few bags of pet food."

He could sense Cooper's smile. "Not the Foxworth kid again?"

Finn nodded, almost dislodging the phone from between his neck and shoulder. "He's my chief suspect. Think I'll go easy on him, though. His mom's been having a rough time since her husband died. Money's tight and Joey loves his dog more than he likes to obey the law. But he's a good boy. Community service seems the right 'sentence.'"

"And you'll pay for the dog food."

Finn didn't answer that. "I like my job here," he told Cooper instead. "There's no gang activity in Barren or the other towns in my jurisdiction. So thanks for that tip about the election." The old Stewart County sheriff had been running unopposed, giving Finn the opportunity he'd needed at the time to get out of Chicago and save his sanity.

Cooper said, "My mother's distant cousin.

Eighty-two, and his wife was worried about him. Competition in the last election nudged him to give up his badge and move to Florida, just what he needed."

Finn owed Cooper for that and maybe he hadn't seemed grateful enough. Hoping to mend the breach between them while they talked more shop, he filled Cooper in on his one real active case, Sierra Hartwell's accident and the outstanding warrant in St. Louis.

"Have you run a background check on her?" Cooper asked.

"In the works," he said. "Unfortunately, her closest relative and I don't agree that this isn't about some parking ticket." He paused. "Her cousin is Annabelle Foster."

Cooper's desk chair creaked. Finn had his partner's full attention now. Cooper said, "I knew Annabelle. Used to drop in at the diner now and then with my folks. She was always there helping out—not that her parents ever seemed to appreciate that. I'm surprised to hear about her objections. Annabelle never said boo to anyone."

"Well, she did with me." *There must be some mistake.* The moment when Finn had teased her about doughnuts hadn't lasted long. Too bad his heightened awareness of her did. The sunlight on her hair, the way she'd approved of his adopting Sarge, her concern for Sierra…he almost didn't hear what Cooper said.

"Wait a minute. Sierra Hartwell? If I remember right, she and Annabelle were close then. I only met Sierra once or twice, and she could be, well, difficult, but I never heard of her getting into any real trouble. Keep me informed, okay?"

"Sure," Finn said. "Something will turn up about her and with The Brothers."

As he ended the call, he missed his partner even more than he had before Cooper phoned. He shoved his cell back in his pocket. At least their less-than-conclusive talk had given him some feedback on Sierra Hartwell, if not taken his mind off Annabelle Foster.

He almost missed Chicago as long as he didn't let himself think about what had happened…

And the black depths of his own loss. Or Eduardo Sanchez.

FROM THE SECOND Finn's car rounded the last corner onto his street in a tree-lined Chicago neighborhood near the station, his *nerves had been shooting sparks through his arms and legs. Beside him, his wife Caroline kept glancing at him, as if she sensed his unease. "What, Finn?" she finally asked.*

"Nothing," he said. "Feeling jumpy, that's all."

"You've been like this since you and Cooper raided The Brothers' headquarters."

Finn didn't think the term brother *suited. It didn't sound nearly dangerous enough— as if they were actually harmless. Their low-slung, abandoned warehouse ten minutes from his home was nothing more than broken windows, doors hanging by their hinges and trash everywhere. The place smelled of rotting garbage, and shattered liquor bottles littered the dirt yard. Inside, a few sagging couches, a half dozen wooden straight chairs and a scarred table made up the decor. A single match would have torched the area quicker than the time it had taken him and Cooper to surround the building, bust in and wrestle four gang members into handcuffs. Another two had left in ambulances for the hospital. And The Brothers had vowed revenge.*

Finn wasn't sleeping well, even on his off-shift days.

"*You really think they mean to harm you?*" Caro asked.

Finn was sure of it. He couldn't ditch the feeling he was being watched. He'd taken to carrying an extra handgun plus his service pistol and the backup gun that, like most cops, he kept in an ankle holster. But he wasn't really worried about himself.

"*I wish you and Alex would do as I asked. Go to your mother's for a while. I'd rest easier,*" he said, though he wasn't sure of that and he'd miss her as if a part of him had broken away.

"*I can't stay with Mother,*" Caro said, flicking her dark red hair from her face with that uniquely feminine gesture that had drawn him to her the day they met. In the back, three-year-old Alex sat in his car seat, his eyes—the exact match of Caro's gray green—glued to his mother's cell phone screen and his latest favorite, a video game with farm animals that squawked and mooed until Finn's last nerve shredded. "*It's almost Christmas,*" Caro went on. "*Remember all that shopping we did today? Or were you not there, Finn?*"

"*I was there.*" And looking over his shoulder the whole time they picked out presents *for family members, friends and the kid whose name Alex had picked from a hat for his day care gift exchange. The back of his neck still prickling, he pulled into the driveway. "I'll get Alex for you then unload the packages."*

"That's my man," she said, then teasing, "you too, Finn. I love you—and I can't wait for you to see what Santa's bringing you."

"Love you too, babe." Laughing, thinking I don't need a gift. I have you, *he got out of the car, bent to clear the rear doorframe then reached in to unbuckle his son, taking a moment to ruffle his hair—the same dark color as his own—imagining the glee Alex would feel when he saw his loot piled high under the Christmas tree. The big day was less than a week away. Alex was going to love the fancy trike they'd bought him.*

Finn had everything he'd ever wanted in these two people and didn't need anything else—other than a promotion that would allow them to buy a bigger house, have more children and get out of the city while he was still alive.

He set Alex down then started for the hatch to retrieve the first bags. Caro had outdone herself this holiday season; they'd be paying off the credit cards all next year, but as long as the generous giving made her happy— Wheels screeched around the nearest corner, speeding down his street to stop in a squeal of brakes at the curb. He'd half expected this but...he couldn't move.

"Finn!" Caro yelled, already running toward Alex.

Whatever he might have said died unspoken in his throat. Two men in dark clothes jumped out of the other car, ski masks hiding their faces. One of them he recognized from his eyes. Eduardo Sanchez. Before Finn could shove Alex out of the way or reach for his guns, it was over.

His worst fears had come true...and he would never love like that again.

CHAPTER FOUR

AFTER THE NEXT morning's breakfast rush ended at the diner, Annabelle went to visit Sierra again, though "visit" was a loose term. Annabelle grew more and more worried about her, and about her own upcoming trip to Denver. In two more days she would fly to Colorado. But Sierra didn't seem to be making progress.

As much as she fretted about Emmie, she was also trying hard not to resent Sierra. Not an attractive quality, but Annabelle had essentially been forced to take over Sierra's life, her responsibility to Emmie, and, selfish or not, that hurt.

In the meantime, Emmie was still with her. When Annabelle's friend Olivia had come to take her to the park today, Emmie had thrown another tantrum worthy of the Incredible Hulk. *I won't*, she'd screamed, refusing to put on her sneakers. *I want sparkly sandals*. Legs thrashing, she didn't get off the floor until Olivia finally managed to calm her. Sierra's little girl was handling her mother's continued absence, and Annabelle's ineptitude, in the only way she knew.

For now the only thing Annabelle could do was try to be patient, to be present, to keep caring for Emmie and whenever she could to sit by Sierra's bed, to hold her hand and speak a few comforting words she hoped her cousin would hear. The last time she'd talked about Emmie's on-again, off-again relationship with Cheerios and the way she fell asleep with her thumb in her mouth and how she asked every day for her mama. Today, praying this subject might rouse Sierra, Annabelle touched on their shared girlhood.

She didn't mention the closet in her parents' living room, being shut inside with only Sierra to heed her panicked cries, listening to Sierra's whispers through the door. To hold her fear at bay, Annabelle had dreamed then, her eyes squeezed shut, of faraway places… a sandy shore, a big city with people everywhere so she wasn't alone, a peaceful lake surrounded by white-capped mountains.

With Sierra now, she stayed close in memory to the good times they'd had.

"Remember the day you and I rode our

bikes down to the creek?" She stroked the back of Sierra's hand. The monitors beeped and whirred, and the flowers she'd brought smelled too sweet in the stuffy room. "When we left, my mom was already looking for us. She wanted our help at the diner, peeling potatoes and dicing carrots for her veal stew." Annabelle gave a mock shudder. "Oh, we wanted to be anywhere else but there." She still did. "You hated that steamy kitchen, too. The humidity ruined your hair, you said." Annabelle brushed her other hand along Sierra's tangled blond curls. "I couldn't stand being there," she said, "knowing I couldn't leave until breakfast, lunch or dinner service was over. Remember, Sierra? I still feel that way. I felt so free playing hooky then." *And I'm going to again. Permanently this time.*

Their getaway had been Sierra's idea. "We shouldn't have gone, I guess. Remember the storms we'd had all summer, day after day until the creek came over its banks? The current was so dangerous. That lazy stream became a raging torrent. I can't believe how foolish we were to try to cross to the other side just because you said you'd seen a doe and her fawn there. We almost drowned."

No response. Or had she seen a tiny movement of Sierra's lips? A twitch of her eyelids, which Annabelle had glimpsed before?

A moment later, to her relief Sierra did open her eyes and squeezed Annabelle's hand, the movement so faint she wondered if she'd imagined that, too. "You heard me!" Annabelle's voice turned husky. "Hey there, you. Welcome back, Sierra. It's Belle, honey." *Sierra is awake!*

Her cousin licked her dry lips. "Water," she croaked. Sierra had been on a ventilator for the first few days. Her throat must be sore.

Annabelle rang for the nurse then filled a glass from the iced carafe on the bedside table. She lifted it to Sierra's lips and let her sip, water dribbling down her chin. With a tissue Annabelle dabbed the moisture away.

"I'm here, Sierra. You were always there for me," she said. "When my parents got angry with me for not setting the tables sooner or because I'd forgotten to pick up the fish for dinner at the market, you defended me." And when they'd pushed her into the punishment closet that day for playing hooky.

"I stuck up for you because…you didn't… for yourself."

The top of her bed was in its raised position, propping her body more upright than the last time Annabelle came, which she took as another good sign. Sierra's bruises had changed color from purple to yellow to, now, a ghastly green. She didn't look good but... "I've buzzed for the nurse. She'll want to see that you're awake and so will your doctors."

Sierra shook her head, obviously troubled. "Emmie," she murmured, tears brimming. "My baby? Where is she?"

"Oh, sweetie. She's fine." Of course Sierra's first thought would be of her small daughter. "She's at my house—or rather, with one of my friends right now. If you feel better, I'll ask if Emmie can come to see you tomorrow. I'm so sorry I told you not to visit when you called me, Sierra. I wish you hadn't hung up before—"

Sierra pulled her hand free. "Doesn't matter."

"Yes it does," Annabelle said. "You mentioned some 'loose ends' then. Did you mean with me? I don't blame you for being unhappy." She took a sharp breath. "And whatever happened in St. Louis—"

Sierra's brows drew together. "What are you talking about?"

Annabelle swallowed. "The sheriff says there's a warrant in Missouri for your arrest—" She stopped again, not wanting to say anything to worsen their already broken relationship.

"He's lying!" Sierra's weak voice strained with emotion. Her eyes met Annabelle's, a fierce look that made her heart trip all the more because it seemed to sap the last of her strength. "Worry about Emmie, not some warrant. Are you taking good care of her? Really?"

Annabelle's mouth set. The past few days of trying to manage a temperamental three-year-old hadn't been easy for her. "You didn't have to ask. Of course I am."

Sierra obviously didn't believe her, and maybe she shouldn't. Annabelle had rejected her when she phoned. In their teens, when her parents ended their friendship, she had blindly accepted their order not to bring up Sierra again—except that she had phoned her a few times when they weren't around. Now her attempts to help, even with Emmie, were being called into question. By the time Annabelle left the room, she felt drained.

She wished they'd refrained from fighting, especially when one of them had just been in a coma.

In the hallway, fretting about Sierra's re-action, she fidgeted for half an hour until Sawyer McCord, her friend Olivia's fiancé and Sierra's doctor, appeared to give her an update on Sierra's condition which was now guarded but more hopeful. Then, dis-appointed in herself, she headed out to the parking lot.

And that was when she remembered that she hadn't asked Sierra about Emmie's fa-ther.

FINN OPENED THE back hatch on his car and Sarge jumped out onto the pavement, tail wagging. In the distance Finn's apartment building, a modest two-story complex that backed up onto some woods with a little stream where Sarge liked to splash, was lit by the setting sun. Before the dog bounded off to do his business, he suddenly growled and Finn caught his collar. "Stay."

Sarge sat on his haunches. His ears had pricked and Finn saw why.

His cop instincts went on red alert. Tall, solidly built, and with a thatch of dark hair, wearing jeans and a hooded black sweat-shirt, Derek Moran strolled across the lawn between the parking lot and the building.

Most people, including Annabelle Foster, liked Finn's dog, but Sarge picked his friends wisely and Finn considered him to be a good judge of character. He had to agree with the dog.

Every time he and Moran met, Finn tried to suppress the surge of anger that washed through him. But the reminder was always there. Derek didn't belong to a gang like The Brothers in Chicago who had wreaked such havoc on Finn's life, but he had a habit of finding trouble, and a cocky attitude. Like Eduardo Sanchez.

"Moran," he called out, keeping a tight grip on Sarge's collar. He didn't need animal control coming after the dog for biting, not that he could fault him for snarling at Derek. The dog's potty break, though, would have to wait.

With a hard expression in his pale blue eyes, Derek stopped. "'Evening, Sheriff." He gestured at Sarge. "That your K-9 department?"

"All the help I need," Finn said. Sarge kept grumbling deep in his throat. "Thought you were working nights at the 7-Eleven these days." *What are you doing here?*

"After I helped myself to a few Cokes and a burrito, management and I didn't see eye to eye." Derek shrugged. "No big deal. I figure they owed me something more than the lousy few bucks an hour I was getting to stand behind the counter and card every kid who wanted to buy a six-pack. Noblesse oblige, I guess you could say."

"Fancy words," Finn said. The right word was *theft* and he figured Derek had sold to those minors, perhaps for an extra fee. "So you got fired." He stroked Sarge's head until the dog quieted. "You're unemployed again?"

Derek shook his head. "Don't jump to conclusions, *Sheriff.* Folks tend to do that with me but they're wrong and so are you." His chest puffed out. "Got me a new daytime job. Salary, full benefits, even a place to sleep."

The hackles rose on Finn's neck. "Where?" But he could guess.

"Wilson Cattle," Derek said, confirming Finn's suspicion.

His heart sank. "What's the job?"

"Ranch hand. Could become foreman one day—if I play my cards right. Dusty Malone isn't getting any younger. I plan to take his place."

Finn couldn't believe his friend Grey, who owned the cattle Derek stole, and with his recent marriage was Derek's new brother-in-law, had hired him. Maybe he'd done it to ease his conscience. Years ago, Grey was wrongly accused of killing Derek's older brother. According to local legend, that tragedy had ruined Derek's young life. Finn could understand that, but was Grey actually willing to risk the future of his ranch? What if Derek decided to steal more cattle from him? That case, which Finn had handled months ago, was still pending after numerous delays and a continuance from the judge, but Finn didn't believe for a minute that Derek would use this opportunity to make something of himself. By his age, Eduardo Sanchez already had a rap sheet a mile long, and at twenty-five Derek was running out of time to keep messing up.

"Let me give you some advice." He pointed a finger at Derek's chest, making Sarge growl again. "Keep your nose clean this time."

Derek snorted. "Whoa, I'm not afraid of you, *Finn*. I heard about you chasing the bad guys in Chicago until you almost lost your job. If you couldn't find the people who offed your wife and kid—"

Finn's hand loosened on Sarge's collar. How did Derek know that? Freed from constraint, the dog lunged at Derek then backed off short of reaching him, as if he knew he would get himself in trouble if he attacked, and Finn with him. Sarge returned to sit at Finn's feet, his throaty rumble breaking the silence. "Don't ever mention my family again," Finn said, his voice shaking.

"I don't have to. Think you can do a better job here in Barren?"

Finn refused to take the bait. Moran was likely angling for a fight that would only bring disciplinary action down on his own head. He turned away. "Good luck at Wilson Cattle." He took two steps toward the building then stopped. With his back to Derek, never a good choice, he said, "Tonight's your lucky night. I'm not even going to ask why you're on this property or what you're doing miles from that ranch."

"Last time I checked, I didn't need your permission. I've got a date," Derek said with a sudden grin in his voice, surprising Finn. There weren't many women in town who would go out with Derek, a ladies' man in his own mind. And certainly not many who'd bring him into their home.

Finn let that go. For now. He had no probable cause to detain him.

"I'll be watching," was all he said.

Derek's laughter followed him up the steps and into the building. The back of his neck hot, Finn climbed the steps to the second floor with Sarge. Finn would have to take him out again for that potty break, but he needed to collect himself first.

His worst memories walked with him to his door where he abruptly halted. Before he read the handwritten notice tacked to the frame, Finn knew what it would say. His landlord had warned him about Sarge's barking whenever Finn left him home, one reason he'd been taking the dog to the station most days. Finn was already in violation of his lease and the building's no-pets clause. He hadn't owned Sarge when he moved in, but apparently several tenants had complained of the noise.

Sarge isn't really a pet, Finn wanted to tell the man, *He's my roommate*. And although he'd try to change his landlord's mind, he doubted he'd succeed. They were being evicted.

CHAPTER FIVE

"FINN DONOVAN IS a go-by-the-book kind of guy. Everyone in town calls him Mr. Law-and-Order."

Keeping one eye on Emmie, Annabelle stiffened at her friend Olivia's comment. The playground rang with childish laughter. On this perfect October morning, the sun had burned off the chill from last night and cleared the dawn clouds away. The big sky overhead was now a brilliant blue, almost the exact color of Olivia Wilson's eyes. Wearing sweat pants and a T-shirt, her blond hair in a loose ponytail, she sat beside Annabelle on a bench, watching the kids play. Olivia had brought Emmie here before, but this was the first time Annabelle could join them.

Although Olivia and their other two friends had been right to suggest getting together, she didn't welcome this topic of conversation.

Seated on Annabelle's other side, Shadow

Wilson was married to Olivia's brother Grey and thus Olivia's new sister-in-law. Slim and dark haired, she chimed in about Finn, her brown eyes warm. "You mean, Mr. Hunky-Law-and-Order." She fanned her face.

"Please," Annabelle murmured.

"You disagree?"

"No, but I'd rather focus on the warrant he has for Sierra."

"Whatever the explanation," Olivia said, "it does seem Sierra was reaching out to you about those 'loose ends' when she headed for Barren. I'm glad she's finally conscious. Once she's able to talk more, everything will get sorted out."

Shadow nodded. "I don't doubt for a second that you'll help her."

"Because that's what you do, Belle," Olivia said, her engagement ring from Sawyer McCord sparkling in the sunlight.

Helping others was what Annabelle had always done, sometimes to avoid getting another reprimand from her mother or a slashing criticism from her father. A do-gooder, he'd sometimes called her, but the trait had served her well. Besides, that was her nature, and her friends', too.

"Our kids will watch out for your Emmie,"

they'd said before. *My Emmie*. Annabelle couldn't wrap her tired head around that and, besides, it was no truer than Finn's accusations must be about Sierra. Still, her friends' older children had already taken Emmie under their wing. After teaching her how to pump her legs on the swings, they were now showing her how to go down the slide. Emmie was poised at the top, giggling.

Her heart in her throat, Annabelle said, "Are you sure she's all right?"

"Trust me, kids bounce." Shadow's nine-year-old daughter Ava, who had her mother's dark hair, stood at the bottom of the slide waiting for Emmie, her arms spread wide. Beside her, Olivia's son Nick, who was seven, appeared ready to step in if anything went wrong.

"Bounce? I wish we could convince Blossom of that," Olivia said with a wry smile. Their other friend had crossed the park on the outskirts of Barren near the creek and was pushing her daughter in her elaborate carriage. Every time the baby let out a peep, Blossom instantly reacted.

"First-time mother," Shadow murmured.

Olivia leaned on Annabelle's shoulder. "I was just like her when Nick was small."

"You were Momzilla," Shadow said with a grin. "Remember, Belle? She never let Nick out of her sight. She wrapped him in a cocoon. She—"

Nick flew across the yard and barreled into them. "Mom! Emmie went down the slide all by herself!" He beamed at Annabelle. "Me and Ava taught her."

"Great job," Annabelle said, smoothing his blond hair from his sweaty forehead. Then she waved at Emmie who didn't wave back. She was climbing the slide again. "Do me a favor, though. Don't show her how to use the jungle gym."

The old, sprawling wooden structure had a crow's nest, a sagging cargo net, another long slide and a series of stairways that looked more treacherous than Annabelle had realized. She'd never thought that, like Olivia, she had a protective maternal bone in her body. For the moment, however, she was still in charge of Emmie. She'd been as taut as a wire for the past half hour, and watching Emmie dart from one dangerous-looking piece of equipment to another made her stomach tighten again.

She looked up to find Olivia and Shadow staring at her.

"What?"

"For a minute, you sounded like one of us." Shadow bumped her other shoulder. "A mom. You sure you don't want to make this playdate a weekly thing to go with our Girls' Night Out?" Their group had become a regular social event, though it was for adults only.

"Annabelle won't be around long enough," Olivia pointed out.

And she was right. Annabelle was very sure. She wouldn't be here much longer… or so she hoped. Sierra's condition troubled her. What if she didn't get out of the hospital in time and Annabelle couldn't leave for Denver? She should be home now beginning to pack, and the temporary situation of caring for Emmie only convinced her that her friends already had their lives in order. The prospect of being the group's lone wolf forever didn't appeal to Annabelle, but she knew they weren't as excited as she was about her trip to Colorado.

"I'll hate leaving you all, but my parents' house is the only house I've ever lived in, this town the only town, and Kansas the only state." She waved a hand to include the playground. "The rest of you have seen places I've only dreamed about."

Olivia frowned a little. "We know how your parents treated you, Annabelle. But they're gone now and, well—we're here for you."

Annabelle couldn't tell them that wasn't enough. They meant well.

"I love you guys but—"

Shadow pointed. "Look at Emmie. She's having the time of her life."

"As long as I'm nowhere near," Annabelle said. "I'm worn out from our morning wrangles over breakfast. Never mind mentioning her afternoon nap, which is hard to come by when I have to take her to work with me. And unless she's in my bed every night, no one gets any sleep."

"Par for the course," Olivia said. "I don't think I slept an hour straight until Nick turned four. I still have bags under my eyes to show for it."

"Where?" Shadow leaned around Annabelle to peer at Olivia. "You have perfect skin. You're gorgeous, and with that glow today…but I agree, sleep can be hard to come by for the first few years. It doesn't help to be overprotective, does it, Libby?"

"Guilty as charged." But Olivia's face did

indeed glow as if she'd had an expensive facial, and everyone noticed.

"What's this about, Mrs. Soon-to-be-McCord?" Shadow studied her again.

"Um. I, uh, Sawyer and I…" Olivia stopped stammering and grinned. "We're pregnant!"

Shadow and Annabelle shrieked, forming a group hug and making the children's heads turn toward them from the highest level of the jungle gym. Annabelle barely noticed that, despite her warning, Emmie had climbed with them. Even Blossom had stopped pushing her carriage, her coppery curls dancing as she trotted back toward them, a small frown on her face. Annabelle was glad her own first response was a happy scream not a frown. With Olivia's announcement she felt even more like an outlier. Alone, as she'd been all her life.

"We weren't going to tell anyone yet," Olivia said, "but you guys had to be observant."

A flurry of questions followed. How did Olivia feel? When was the baby due? Did this mean she and Sawyer would change their wedding plans?

Finally, she held up a hand. "I have an appointment with Doc Baxter this afternoon.

After that, we'll make decisions. I feel great. I'm about two months along."

The baby carriage rolled up to the bench. "What did I miss?" Blossom asked.

Olivia said, "You're not the only one who will have a newborn soon."

Blossom's brown eyes softened. "Eeekk!" Another round of delighted shouts ran through the group and Annabelle almost missed hearing Emmie's cry from the jungle gym or, rather, the ground beneath it. To Annabelle's horror she'd fallen from the top level!

Annabelle jumped up from the bench and raced across the playground. Their faces white with shock, the other kids were looking down at Emmie from above. She scooped the little girl from the dirt and held her tightly to her chest, feeling her heart beat fast and hard. To Annabelle's amazement Emmie buried her face in her shirt.

"You shouldn't move her, Belle." Her phone in hand, Shadow dropped to her knees beside them. "I'm calling 911."

"I hurt," Emmie whimpered.

Nick had gotten down from the jungle gym. He laid a hand on Annabelle's shoulder. "She'll be okay. I fell from the hayloft at the ranch once—and I'm fine now."

Olivia drew him away. "Annabelle told you not to show Emmie that jungle gym."

"But she wanted to play in the cargo net and she's fast." His eyes, a deep blue, brimmed with tears. "We didn't mean for her to get hurt, Mom."

"I know you didn't." Olivia sent him and Ava, who was standing there trembling, a comforting smile. "Nick, in our bag there are some juice boxes and granola bars. Sit with Ava on the bench with your snacks." She watched them head across the yard before she turned to Annabelle. "How is she?"

Emmie clung to Annabelle, and Shadow raised an eyebrow as if to say *And you don't think you're a mother?*

Annabelle stroked Emmie's damp hair, absorbing her tears in the cotton of her shirt. "She's calming down. I think she'll be okay." She heard a siren in the distance, moving closer, and mouthed a quick prayer of thanks while Olivia, Shadow and Blossom looked on. She laid a hand next to Emmie's head and felt her own heart, which was pumping way too fast. "My, that was a scare. I'd rather handle a kitchen fire at the diner."

Emmie raised her eyes to meet Annabelle's. And she smiled.

"I like the diner."

Annabelle couldn't agree, but Emmie seemed to find comfort there, far more than at Annabelle's house, and the staff tended to spoil her. At the moment she didn't care. As long as Emmie was breathing, talking, able to move her arms and legs, Annabelle was good, too. Her tears were happy ones—if only for the moment. In spite of her friends' support, she wouldn't stay. Sierra would leave the hospital and Emmie would return to her mother. Then Annabelle would be on her way to Denver and a new career—and she could leave her memories, the diner and her hopeless crush on Finn behind her.

FINN'S CRUISER PULLED UP in front of the barn at Wilson Cattle. Earlier this morning, after making sure Emmie Hartwell was okay following her playground mishap, he was paying a visit to Grey. It couldn't hurt to caution him about Derek.

Grey must have heard the car approach because he suddenly appeared in the open doorway, his trademark black Stetson pushed back on his head, hands stuck in the rear pockets of his well-worn jeans.

"You heard," he said, his blue-green eyes serious.

"I heard. Are you crazy?" There was no sign of Derek, and Finn was glad. He hoped to talk to Grey without being overheard.

Grey ran a hand through his light brown hair, one shoulder propped against the door-frame. "Look, I know what you think of Derek. Maybe that's natural. Being sheriff makes you suspicious. But I've told you before that you're wrong about him."

"Maybe. But that doesn't mean you should hire Derek and give him a place to live."

Grey's mouth hardened. "Yeah, Derek stole a bunch of cattle. They've been returned. End of that story—assuming the court finally agrees. I'm hoping the judge will, one reason Derek has a job with me as long as he does the work."

"Meaning that will look good to the court? I never knew he was a skilled cowboy." He did know Grey had refused to press charges against Derek, which had made the case more problematic. But Finn wouldn't see anyone get away with…anything that was against the law.

Grey cracked a smile. "He's my apprentice. I'll shape him up."

"I wish I had your faith. I wouldn't trust him any further than the front gates of Wilson Cattle—with him going the other way." Which Finn would definitely prefer.

He had strong opinions about right and wrong. It was the same with Emmie Hartwell. He could have taken care of her the night of Sierra's accident, but he'd preferred to see Emmie stay with Annabelle. After all, they were related.

But Annabelle was selling her diner. She seemed to think Sierra could heal faster than she would. That Emmie wouldn't stay with her much longer.

He brought his mind back to the present. "I've got a bad feeling about Derek that won't quit," he said. "Since you don't seem open to hearing that, it's all I'm going to say," but in Derek's case Finn couldn't stop himself. "How does Shadow feel about this?"

"He's her *brother*. How do you expect her to feel? Bottom line, he's family."

"If you don't watch the henhouse, Grey, you might lose more than a few eggs—and of course, more cattle."

Grey straightened from the doorframe.

"Come on in the barn. I want to show you something before we end up throwing punches at each other."

He didn't wait for Finn to finish wrestling with his concerns about Derek—and with today's brief view of Annabelle at the park, her face pinched with worry about Emmie. He was glad Emmie hadn't gotten hurt, but the sight of her in Annabelle's arms while the paramedics checked her scrapes had stayed with him. Not his business, he told himself. Annabelle meant to leave Barren, and Finn was hunkered down here just trying to survive. Still, the memory nagged at him like Sarge with a ball. He didn't think Annabelle was seeing things clearly.

Inside, the barn aisle looked dim except for some rays of sunlight that filtered through the windows in the hayloft to slant across the lower floor. Dust motes, even a piece or two of straw, floated in the air. Finn sneezed. He figured he was allergic to barns, just as he considered himself to be allergic to horses. Of course Grey led him right to a stall where a big brute of a dark-colored animal breathed through its nostrils like a dragon about to spew fire. A heavy hoof the size of a dinner plate pawed the bedding. The animal had a broad white blaze down its face and a pair of large brown eyes that gazed at Finn in apparent curiosity.

Grey gestured at the horse. "I know what you're gonna say. How *big* is he? Doesn't matter," Grey said. "He's a gentle giant. A hard worker and easy on the bones. Step closer and say hey." He pulled the horse's forelock. "Big Brown, meet Finn, our local sheriff. He doesn't know it yet but one of these days I'll turn him into a rider."

"Hey," Finn said dutifully, wishing he hadn't come by after all. He hadn't gotten anywhere with Grey about Derek, and now that he'd let Annabelle trip through his mind again—along with the image of little Emmie's sweet face—all he wanted was to head back into town. Tell himself he shouldn't care about either of them. "Thought your regular ride was named Big Red."

"They both fit. Why not?" Grey handed him a carrot from his rear pocket. "Make friends," he said then started off down the aisle, talking to each horse as he went.

Finn stood there. "What am I supposed to do?"

"He likes his face rubbed. That's one reason he's pawing the floor—not because he

wants to kill you like some bull. Tell him
your life story if you want. He's a good lis-
tener. If you don't want, then pat his neck.
But above all, give him that carrot before
he takes your hand off." Grey laughed and
kept going.

The horse stamped its feet again. For a
moment Finn felt tempted to turn around and
disappear. But he'd already had words with
Grey today and he didn't want to jeopardize
their friendship. Or drive back to the diner
to tell Annabelle something yet. So he held
out the carrot. The horse sucked it up then
stuck out his face, looking for more.

"Sorry, pal. You've got the wrong guy."
He backed up a step, swamped by another
memory. This one didn't hurt as much as last
night's or this morning's at the park. On one
hand, the sight of Emmie always made him
want to smile, on the other she reminded
him of Alex. He traced a line along Brown's
nose. "I hope you understand why you and I
are never going to be best friends."

Having heard everything, Grey wandered
across the aisle from another stall. "Big
Brown and I know what we're doing. Once
I get him fine-tuned, you and I will go riding again." He threw down a gauntlet. "Even

Ava could ride him. You should see her. My daughter is all over this ranch on her new horse. She's fearless."

Finn's shoulders slumped. "You trying to make me feel like a coward?" Maybe he was one. Certainly, he couldn't seem to put Chicago behind him—probably wouldn't until justice was served—and he was having just as hard a time trying not to get involved with Annabelle. Or worry about Emmie.

"No, I mean to turn you into a Kansas cowboy," Grey said. "You can't sheriff all the time." *Or wallow in your memories*, he might have said.

Grey insisted he say goodbye to Big Brown, which Finn did with reluctance. Then Grey walked Finn out into the sunlight. They stood by his cruiser, sharing the warmth of the day, knowing there wouldn't be many more like this before winter set in. "Kidding aside," Grey said, "I won't allow Derek to get in more trouble."

"I'll hold you to it."

"He's doing a good job, shows up on time and he's saving his pay to buy a new truck." Grey rapped a knuckle against the roof, as if a judge had gaveled the court to order. "One more thing—what's going on with Annabelle Foster?"

Finn's hand clamped around his open door. "Going on?"

"Shadow says Emmie Hartwell got hurt at the park earlier, and you came roaring in, light bar flashing..." He added, "She couldn't help but notice how fast you responded. The EMTs had everything under control—"

"And I'm sheriff here, as you reminded me. What was I supposed to do, ignore the call?" He couldn't meet Grey's eyes. When he'd heard the news, Finn couldn't get there quick enough. "Stay in my office and push papers around?"

Grey laughed. "No, but seems to me— and Shadow—there might be something else 'going on.'" He paused. "Annabelle's a fine person, Finn."

Finn got into the car, fired up the engine. "If I had a mind to...pursue someone who doesn't plan on sticking around." *If I wanted to care again.*

"That's one issue," Grey said, "but if a man were so inclined..."

"I'm not." Which provoked another memory he'd rather avoid. Not that long ago, before

Shadow was married, and thinking he might get out of his shell, Finn had asked her out to dinner. Grey hadn't liked that at all. Finn slipped the cruiser into gear but Grey hadn't finished about Annabelle.

He removed his hat, put it back on again. "Maybe not yet," he said, "but something to think about," then stepped away from the car as if to close the subject. "And just remember this: there's nothing better for the inside of a man than the outside of a horse. Old saying," Grey said with a half smile, "but true."

"You couldn't prove it by me," Finn replied.

CHAPTER SIX

COFFEEPOT IN HAND, Annabelle heard the bell jangle above the diner's door, and before she could prepare herself Finn walked in. From the look on his face she suspected he wasn't here to eat.

This couldn't be good news, and Annabelle didn't want to hear it.

"You have a minute?" Finn asked.

"Sure." *But do make it brief.* She led him through the diner into her office, a cramped space off the hallway that connected the restaurant to the kitchen and had once been a storage closet. It had room enough for a small desk, a hutch above with cubbyholes—Annabelle's bookkeeping system—and two chairs. She gestured for Finn to sit, but he stayed on his feet. Another bad sign.

At the park that morning he'd barely spoken to her, his attention focused instead on Emmie in her arms. What had happened since then?

Annabelle sank down on her desk chair.

Today Finn wore his usual pressed jeans with a yellow polo shirt that contrasted with his dark hair, his hazel eyes hidden behind a pair of aviator sunglasses that made him appear both tough and even more handsome. He smelled of fresh air and sunshine. She felt tempted, as Shadow had done, to fan her cheeks.

Finn glanced at her laptop. "Didn't mean to interrupt your workday," he said. "How's Emmie?"

"She took a rare nap, which should have alerted me that she wasn't feeling well, then woke up with a fever."

"Could be her body's reaction to that fall." He looked at the laptop again. "What's her temperature?"

"I couldn't tell. I don't own a current thermometer." Annabelle had rooted through the bathroom cabinets but all she'd found was an old glass version that contained dangerous mercury. What if Emmie broke it? Contaminated the room and herself? Another failure on Annabelle's part. Maybe Emmie had an infection from the scrapes she'd gotten at the playground and the germs had already spread through her system. "She's with Blossom right now. After we see Sawyer Mc-Cord, I'll stop at the pharmacy to buy one."

Her face had warmed. Finn looked at the computer a third time, and she turned the machine so he could see its screen. "You didn't interrupt my work. I'm a sweepstakes junkie. For years I've entered contests. This prize would be an all-expense-paid Caribbean cruise."

"I saw your travel posters at your house." Finn removed his sunglasses. "Ever win anything?"

"A fifties jukebox." Annabelle welcomed the safer topic. "For a while I had an unlimited supply of oldies but goodies to play." She had to smile. "Smaller items, too, over the years. A 'diamond' necklace I thought was so expensive I'd need to insure it." Her mother had said, *Didn't they have anyone else to give it to*? "But the necklace turned out to be paste. Oh, and I won a weekend at a spa in New Mexico—including nutritional advice and some sort of cleanse—" she shuddered "—but my parents were ill then so I couldn't go." *Leave a sick man to take care of himself*? her dad had asked. *What kind of daughter are you?*

"Sorry about the diamonds," he said.

"I don't need them." She took a breath. Better to let him know she wouldn't be here much longer than to let him see how she felt about him. "I'll be embarking on a new career very soon. I've signed up for a course in Denver."

His gaze sharpened. "What kind of course?"

"To become certified as an international tour director. I always envied Sierra her job, which as I told you, takes her to different places. At first I thought I'd like to do that, too, but I want even more travel. I want to meet new people, go to all the places I've never been." She went on, "Once the diner is sold, I'll need a new way to make a living, and this seems perfect." She paused. "I paid for it the very day Sierra phoned that she wanted to come visit."

"Sierra's still in the hospital, Annabelle. I haven't even tried to ask her about the warrant yet, and I'm sure you haven't been able to talk to her about Emmie's long-term care." He turned the computer around to her again.

Her heart sank. "Sierra's awake more now and even alert, but when I tried to bring up Missouri, she called you a liar, and accused me of not taking good care of Emmie. That was the end of that."

Finn's gaze hardened. "Well, it's not, and I don't care what she called me. In my business I have a thick skin. I realize you don't accept the fact that your cousin has been involved in illegal activity in Missouri, but I've talked to the police in St. Louis. Apparently Sierra did steal some money—"

Annabelle stood up. "Just because someone accused her doesn't mean—"

"—she's guilty, I know, but she has to answer the charges. And since she's here in my jurisdiction I'll have to serve that warrant—which I can't do until she's been medically cleared." Finn leaned over her desk. "Let the system work, Annabelle. If she's innocent, that will come out in the evidence and I'll apologize. I wish I could do more to help."

Annabelle flushed. Her gaze was level with Finn's yellow shirt, which covered his very masculine chest. "I wasn't asking for help."

She could tell he didn't know how to take that. Finn shifted his weight, his gun belt jangling with the motion, his expression opaque.

He put one hand on the butt of the pistol.

"Maybe you should think about your relationship with Sierra. From what you say, she wasn't exactly grateful to you for taking Emmie. Could be she's not the person you remember."

That thought had crossed Annabelle's mind but she wasn't ready to condemn her cousin, even when Sierra had all but accused her of neglecting Emmie. Sierra must be in pain. After what had been that near-fatal accident, and with drugs on board, she couldn't be held accountable for what she'd said. Besides, Sierra knew that Annabelle made an easy target. She had rarely fought back, the story of her life. *I stuck up for you…because you didn't for yourself.*

"Not the same person?" Annabelle echoed. "Maybe not, but for now I'm her protector—and Emmie's. Someone has to believe in Sierra."

Finn studied the floor. "I have to admire your loyalty."

"Which you consider to be misplaced."

He raised his gaze to Annabelle, looking as if he didn't want to say what came next. "That's your business. But have you asked yourself the serious questions? What if Sierra stays in that hospital? She's shown few signs of being able to go home so far. Even if she could, considering that warrant, she might end up in jail. And if you're gone, what would that mean for Emmie?"

"I haven't thought that through. The next time I talk to Sierra, I hope to ask her about Emmie's father. Maybe he could take her and I won't need to—"

"Maybe you will. Time is short and there's a three-year-old child to consider here. You can't just up and leave even if that's what you want most in this world."

"You're saying I'm selfish."

"I'm saying you need to think of Emmie's welfare." This from someone who didn't have children, but Finn made her feel guilty anyway.

"You sound like Sierra, but I'm doing the best I can," she said. "I'll do what's right for Emmie—and for me."

Finn put his sunglasses back on, started for the hallway then stopped. "And I'm sure Emmie trusts you to do just that. Sierra, too. Everyone in Barren does, Annabelle, and people rely on you too much. Doesn't leave you any protection for yourself." He glanced back over his shoulder, catching her with an astonished look on her face. "But don't let Emmie down."

She wasn't accustomed to validation from anyone—and not from a man who'd also implied she wasn't doing a very good job. That she didn't care enough about Emmie. Coming from Finn, rather than Sierra, that hurt even more.

She watched until he disappeared around the corner into the main room of the restaurant, heard him greet the mayor, Harry Barnes, and several ladies who were having a late lunch.

Finn's department motto was To Protect and Serve. He hadn't meant anything else. For Emmie. Or her.

"Remember Miss Clara's shop, Sierra?" Annabelle asked, having spent the past half hour at her cousin's bedside. She would have to leave soon to pick up Emmie, who was with Blossom, for her doctor's appointment. Annabelle's earlier talk with Finn, except for his parting words, had already ruined her day. "We laughed so hard we couldn't breathe."

Sierra waved a limp hand in the air, almost dislodging the IV line in her arm. "Your mother grounded us for the next week."

Annabelle caught her arm. Sierra had torn

out that line before, and half of Annabelle's
visits seemed to involve calling the nurse to
redo it. "That was the last time we went to
the store," Annabelle said, "but Miss Clara
did have the most interesting things for sale."

She didn't go on. All at once the memory
didn't seem funny. At the store, to her horror,
Sierra had slipped a cheap, flashy ring in her
pocket, and that night Annabelle's mother
had found it. Of course she'd blamed Annabelle, too—*Now my daughter is a thief?*—
and the next summer Sierra hadn't come
to stay. She'd never come again. Better not
to pursue this topic, which might bring another angry outburst from Sierra about Annabelle's parents.

For the first ten minutes today, Sierra had
ranted—resting between bouts—about them
and about Finn.

"Never mind Miss Clara," she said. "If
that sheriff walks into this room again—"

"You can't blame him for doing his job,"
Annabelle pointed out although she'd come
close to the same accusation. Never mind
how good he'd looked in those aviator sunglasses.

"Don't believe him, Annabelle." Sierra
waved her arm again. "He's nothing but a

small-town cop looking to make his name. Accusing me of something I didn't do should get him fired. Instead, you're actually buying into his lies."

Annabelle rubbed her forehead. "I'm on your side, you know that." All the more after Finn's visit to the diner. "It would help, though, if you'd tell me why the sheriff has that warrant." Her mouth turned down. "Maybe someone else has the same name as you or some clerk entered the wrong charges on the form."

Sierra struggled to sit straighter in the bed. "If you value our friendship—and for years it hasn't seemed like it—stop talking about this. By the time I'm released from this hospital, Finn Donovan will know how wrong he is."

Annabelle sank back in her chair. Sierra had a point. Annabelle hadn't been a very good friend, and because of her trip to Denver she'd discouraged Sierra from coming to Barren. No wonder Sierra had accused her of not caring properly for Emmie, which, as Finn had implied, could be partially true.

She reached out, brushing the blanket that covered Sierra's legs. "I'm still your friend.

I've told Finn you must be innocent. Please believe me."

"Why should I? You didn't even bring Emmie to see me like you promised."

Annabelle's mouth tightened. Why was Sierra being so difficult? "I wanted to, but the hospital's regulations wouldn't allow her to come," she said. "The age for child visitors in this facility is twelve years old."

"They need to make an exception. I'm her mother! I need to see her."

Annabelle tried to find patience. "You've talked on the phone." And Emmie had seemed upset afterward. "For now that will have to be enough." She gently pushed Sierra back against her pillows. "The sooner you get well, the quicker you can come home. You'll stay with me as long as you want. I promise, Sierra."

Sierra turned her face away. "All I've got left," she murmured as if Annabelle's vow, like her care of Emmie, wasn't enough.

"That can't be all," she said, trying to choose her words carefully. Was Sierra depressed? "If you don't believe me, you still have Emmie."

"Worried." Sierra's eyes brimmed. "If something happens to me…"

Her pulse leaped. Had Sierra lost hope that she'd survive? "The only thing that's going to happen is you'll walk out of this hospital soon and be with Emmie again."

"But if I don't…" She clutched Annabelle's hand. "*Please. Promise* me—you'll find Emmie's father."

"I would love to. I've wanted to ask about him. You're right, he should know about your accident and where you are, how you're doing now. He needs to know where Emmie is, too."

A bitter smile touched Sierra's lips. She'd said she had loose ends to settle in Barren. Before the accident had she been on her way to see Emmie's dad, not Annabelle after all? And what was their relationship to each other now?

Sierra's arm sliced through the air again and the IV popped out. Blood began to pool on the tile floor.

Annabelle reached for the call button. "Sierra. Tell me more about him." In the minute or two it took for a nurse to appear, she leaned closer to Sierra. "Give me his name. Tell me where I can reach him…"

But Sierra didn't answer that. "*Find* him, Annabelle. He's tall, not so dark, and dangerous," was all she murmured before she seemed to lose the last of her strength and didn't go on.

When the nurse swept into the room, Annabelle stepped back from the bed while the woman clucked her disapproval of the IV line that had come unhooked again. And, with a last glance at her cousin's still form and gray complexion, Annabelle slipped back into the hallway. Sierra's fading bruises were the only color in her face.

This visit hadn't gone well. Tomorrow she would press Sierra again about Emmie's father.

CHAPTER SEVEN

ANNABELLE FOLLOWED SAWYER MCCORD from the exam room into his office across the hall. They'd left Emmie in the reception area playing with the toys that had been there since Annabelle was born. A grape lollipop seemed to be soothing Emmie's sore throat, and she'd accepted the treat with as much enthusiasm as she might another doughnut. Sugar was apparently her favorite food, as it had been for her mother years ago.

Sawyer, who was engaged to Olivia, had recently joined Doc Baxter's practice. He gestured at the old-fashioned surroundings, a battered wooden desk, a bookcase stuffed with medical texts, a creaky desk chair. A faded Navajo rug covered the floor. "I thought it would be easy to share this space with Doc." Sawyer sent her a rueful smile, his deep blue eyes sparkling. "But he's not easing into retirement after all."

"We grew up seeing him for our aches

and pains, not to mention all those vaccinations." Annabelle settled into the other chair in front of his desk.

"Good times," he said. "I only wish more people would ask for me when they call for an appointment. It's harder than I expected to get traction here."

"Over time Doc will hand off more of his duties, I'm sure. Thanks for taking such good care of Sierra. And Emmie today."

"No problem," Sawyer said, glancing at her chart. "The scrapes she got at the playground look clean and are already beginning to heal."

"Her fever, though...does Emmie have strep?"

"No, it's likely viral. Not connected to her fall. Doc and I have seen quite a few kids this week with the same symptoms. Her throat hurts now but will mend on its own. Probably within the next five days or so. If not, bring her in again. Don't hesitate to call me, Belle. You have my number."

Five days? She'd be in Denver then. "It's good to hear it's nothing serious, but how is she doing otherwise? I'm concerned about her language development. I have nothing to go by except for being around Nick and

Ava now and then. They're older than her, but they've always been real chatterboxes. Does Emmie seem a bit behind?"

"Nothing to worry about that I can see. Kids vary—a lot—and I'm sure she'll be fine." Sawyer eyed her for a moment, arms crossed over his chest. "What about you? Holding up all right? Running your business, worrying about Sierra and having Emmie with you must take a toll. Olivia tells me you've put the diner up for sale."

She tried a smile. "If you know anyone who's looking for a white elephant, let me know. I'm open to negotiation."

Sawyer nodded. "That's a lot to have on your plate, but I've always thought your heart wasn't really in that diner. I can't blame you for wanting to do something else. Seeing the world's a great idea—for anyone—but we all have roots somewhere. Mine—and yours— are here. Maybe you're not looking for adventure as much as you need to simply get away for a while."

Sawyer should know about that. He'd left his family's ranch, the Circle H, to finish medical school then journeyed halfway around the world to establish his clinic in far-off Kedar. He'd only been back for a few months.

His gaze seemed to look through her. "Be aware, though. There'll be times when, away from home, you'll lie awake wondering at the choice you made. Wondering if you could fit in again where you once took it for granted that you belong."

Annabelle had never felt she belonged here. "Are you trying to discourage me?"

"No, only hoping you don't make the right choice for the wrong reasons."

He must mean her family. Certainly they'd factored into her decision to sell the diner and eventually the house, her strongest reminders of how they'd treated her. How to explain to Sawyer that her parents' restaurant made her feel trapped? That they'd named it after her when she was born seemed worse because their lifelong expectation was for her to stay here, preserving their legacy while keeping Annabelle from discovering herself.

"I have to do...what I have to do." She held his gaze. "Right now that means taking care of Emmie and, yes, worrying about Sierra. I know her condition has been upgraded... but she didn't seem good at all to me today. What's her prognosis?"

"She has a long way to go." Sawyer mentioned her broken bones, including a number of ribs, numerous contusions, internal organ damage. "Her kidney values still aren't normal. We're doing all we can but at this point a lot of her recovery is up to Sierra. I'm not happy about her mental outlook either. She doesn't seem to be really...trying."

Annabelle told him about Sierra's concern for Emmie, her plea to Annabelle to find her father. "I have no idea about Sierra's relationship with him but she never mentioned him until today. And she's also worried about Finn Donovan." Annabelle remembered her earlier conversation with him. "I'd be worried, too, if I knew the sheriff was waiting for me to get better so he could see me extradited to some other state, to jail."

Yes, she would find Emmie's father for Sierra.

Tonight she had to start getting ready for Denver.

"WHAT YOU DOING?"

Emmie's voice shot through Annabelle as if she'd been caught trying to steal from her own suitcase. Tossing a pile of underwear in on top, she turned to find Emmie standing in her bedroom doorway.

"Packing," she said. But after seeing Finn earlier that day, her visit with Sierra and then Emmie's appointment with Sawyer, she had come home with her spirits flagging. She studied Emmie's face. "Are you okay, sweetie?"

She nodded but, clearly, she wasn't well. Her cheeks had bright flags of color, and her temperature had been too high when Annabelle checked it with the new thermometer.

She'd hoped Sierra would be released from the hospital by now. Concerned about her own course in Denver, she'd been too optimistic. She'd hoped that while she was gone Emmie and Sierra could stay here at the house, where Annabelle could stock the refrigerator for them and arrange for an in-home caregiver, if need be. But it didn't seem like Sierra would improve enough in the next few days for that to happen.

Sawyer's words about Sierra's prognosis hadn't been encouraging. Sierra would probably still be in the hospital when Annabelle had to leave town. As she'd told Finn, she would find the right solution for Emmie— she wouldn't ask her busy friends to babysit for two weeks—so it looked now as if that meant taking Emmie with her. Annabelle could look for childcare in Denver, but would the school permit Emmie in the classroom even temporarily in the meantime?

Emmie's eyes looked dull. "Where you going?"

Annabelle hesitated. Any notion that her fragile security with Annabelle was at risk might set off another tantrum, especially when Emmie was sick.

"Denver." Annabelle doubted that would register with such a young child, and their conversations always seemed awkward, but to her surprise Emmie's look of curiosity suddenly morphed into recognition. Her blue eyes brightened.

"Big," she said.

"You mean the city? Yes it is," Annabelle agreed. Did Emmie know about Denver, or was she making that up?

Her brow furrowed. "Noisy cars. Buildings. Mama had…brown stuff. Me juice."

Annabelle blinked. "I thought you didn't like juice."

"Don't like orange. Apple."

Annabelle decided not to pursue that. At least she and Emmie were having an actual talk without any tears or temper. She slid the suitcase aside to finish packing later.

"Were you at the Brown Palace Hotel?" No answer, but then its name might not be familiar to her. "I'd like to go there, too."

The famed landmark served tea every afternoon in the elegant, high-ceilinged atrium lobby where cattle barons and millionaire miners had once held court during the gold rush.

"Who you going with?" Emmie asked.

"Myself," she said, trying to keep her explanation simple. This wasn't the right time to tell Emmie she had to go with her.

Emmie shook her head. "Me and Mommy go."

She had a point, and in that one way Annabelle hadn't looked forward to her first plane ride alone. Would she like leaving the ground, flying through the clouds, finding the sun and clear skies above them? She imagined gripping the armrests of her seat—or clutching the stranger next to her in a death grip?—as the jet barreled down the runway. Or, she hoped, that first takeoff would be exhilarating, and she'd soon become a frequent flyer.

"Do you travel—I mean, go lots of different places with your mom, Emmie?"

"Uh-huh."

Have you ever been to Missouri? Annabelle didn't ask that aloud. She was still thinking of Finn and the warrant, but she wasn't about to use a child to get information.

"A-bel?"

Annabelle's heart turned over at this new version of her name. The first night here she hadn't called Annabelle anything.

"Yes, sweetie?"

"Want juice now."

"I don't have any apple juice, Emmie." Annabelle made a mental note to buy some. So far, Emmie appeared to be in danger of starving, although Annabelle's friends had assured her that she would eat when she was hungry. Still, Annabelle had brought home baked goods from the diner each night to tempt Emmie, only to have most of them rejected too. It was as if Emmie was on strike, yet she needed food and certainly fluids to help her get well, Sawyer had told her.

Annabelle held out a hand. "Let's see what's for supper."

Emmie said, grinning, "Doughnut."

To Annabelle's relief, an hour later Emmie's forehead felt cooler.

Annabelle might not know exactly what she was doing, but she'd learned her instincts were often better than expected. After feeding Emmie a bowl of chicken noodle soup with crackers, she'd given her a tepid bath, hoping to bring her temperature down. After a brief mishap in the tub, they'd curled up on the sofa while Disney entertained them with another showing of *Mulan*.

"Princess," Emmie murmured, eyelids drooping. At any other time she would be dancing around the room, humming the melody to any tune that played on the screen. At least until she saw Annabelle watching her and stopped, one thumb thrust in her mouth.

"You're a princess, too," Annabelle said, stroking her hair. She rewrapped the fleece blanket from Emmie's bed around them like a cocoon, and Annabelle's weary bones seemed to melt. In the time—less than a week—Emmie had stayed with her, Annabelle had acquired quite a few things she wouldn't have any use for once Sierra was well and could take Emmie with her again to wherever they went. This blanket, a few toys, half a dozen outfits to replace the clothes that were lost in the accident and some books and DVDs now graced her temporary home. Annabelle had signed up for a new trial cable package that included several children's channels.

They were both half asleep when the doorbell rang.

Finn stood on the porch with a serious expression that made her heart skip a beat. Annabelle touched her throat then stepped back to let him in, willing her face not to heat until her skin felt as warm as Emmie's forehead. He carried the clean scents of night air, a hint of smoke from someone's chimney, the leather of his jacket and a subtle aftershave.

In the front hall Annabelle laid a finger across her lips. "Emmie's almost asleep." She hadn't said the words before Emmie wandered into the hall, the blanket trailing with her. Blinking in the light, she looked Finn up and down. He looked back, as if uncertain what to say to her. Then her face cleared and she walked up to him and leaned against him, a trusting look in her baby-blue eyes.

"You the man," she said, which made Finn laugh.

"Hey, Emmie." He reached down to brush

a hand against her tangled hair then quickly drew back. "I heard you aren't feeling well."

She spoke into his knee. "My froat hurts."

After another brief hesitation, Finn picked her up then patted Emmie's back, murmuring words Annabelle couldn't make out, and the very tone of his voice, low and deep, seemed to work. Emmie nestled her face into the crook of his neck. "She's just about out now," he said. "Want me to carry her up to bed?"

"Please." He'd done that once before, the night of the accident, then escaped as if he hadn't wanted to be here.

In the spare room Annabelle stayed back while Finn gently put Emmie on the bed. He half smiled, tucked the covers around until only her face showed and with a brightness in his eyes bent down to kiss her forehead. "Not much fever," he said, straightening then turning toward Annabelle.

He blinked a couple of times then walked back into the hall with her, leaving Emmie's door ajar. "In case she wakes again." Annabelle crossed her fingers that she wouldn't.

In the living room, taking a seat on the sofa, Finn laced his hands together between his knees, his gaze avoiding hers. He appeared lost in thought. Annabelle didn't relish another talk about Emmie's welfare. She'd had enough from him and Sierra today. What might his objections be if he found out she was thinking of taking Emmie to Denver with no real plan for her care there?

"You're good with her," she said to fill the silence.

Finn's mouth tightened. "She reminds me of…someone." He cleared his throat. "Annabelle, I didn't come here just to see how Emmie was doing—though I am glad she feels better—or to put you on the spot again about her, and, before you ask, I'm not here about the warrant." He looked toward the stairway, and Annabelle guessed this had to do with Emmie. "I won't have to serve it after all," he said.

She stiffened. What was he saying?

His gaze lifted to meet hers. "I got called to the hospital an hour ago. They said they tried to contact you—"

"My phone isn't working." She hadn't been able to check her voice mail. "While I was bathing Emmie, it fell into the toilet. I've put it in a bag of rice to dry out but—"

"I'm sorry, Annabelle," he said. "Sierra's gone. She didn't make it."

For a long moment, that didn't register with Annabelle. *I just saw her this afternoon.*

"She took a turn for the worse and crashed. The hospital staff tried everything to bring her around—Sawyer was there with her—but..." He shook his head.

The look of sympathy in Finn's eyes didn't penetrate either until she thought of Emmie, sleeping soundly in her bed in the house Annabelle meant to sell. Emmie, without her mother now and with a father Sierra had called, "tall, not so dark, and dangerous," but then said nothing more about him.

Sierra is dead.

Except for Annabelle, Emmie was now alone in the world.

CHAPTER EIGHT

FINN STAYED OVERNIGHT on the sofa. He didn't want to but remembered how it felt to be alone in Chicago after Caro and Alex died. He'd seen the exact moment when shock set in for Annabelle. She had no family here except Emmie, who had wakened, crying—as if she already sensed her mother was gone. Finn had suggested they not tell her until morning, and in the meantime he'd tried to be of help to Annabelle, phoning other people who would want to know about Sierra—Grey and Shadow, Blossom and her husband Logan, Sawyer and Olivia for starters—and trying to keep Annabelle from what appeared to be an imminent breakdown.

She knew as well as he did that her cousin's death changed everything, and Finn had plenty of experience in dealing with the aftermath of tragedy—as well as he knew how. Even over coffee now, which he'd brewed at five this morning, Finn tried not to make things worse for Annabelle.

"Sierra said nothing more about Emmie's dad?"

Annabelle rubbed her forehead. "No, but he needs to be notified, now more than ever. I wonder if Sierra made any arrangements for Emmie's care—if something *should* happen to her? I mean, other than asking me to find him."

Finn toyed with his coffee spoon. "Sierra's personal effects are still at the hospital. As next of kin, you can pick them up. Maybe there's something in them that will help. It's possible that, because of Emmie, she made a will but that also means finding the lawyer who drew it up."

"Who could be anywhere, too," she said, and Finn guessed she was about to cry again. "I don't even know where to start. At least your department still has her car. I know it was totaled, but there might be something— other than that warrant—in the glove compartment that we overlooked."

"Maybe." She didn't seem to realize she'd said *we*, as if she and Finn were a team, working together. "And there should have been an insurance card, which might help, but there wasn't." He shifted in his chair. "I'll have a deputy empty the glove compartment before the car gets towed away for scrap." Finn didn't want to care about anyone. Yet, at the moment, Annabelle and Emmie both needed him. He couldn't help but respond to that. For Emmie's sake, he'd have to put aside his awareness of Annabelle, the sleek fall of her hair, the changing brown to green of her eyes, even that ever-present apron she wore at the diner that always made him want to smile.

For now he'd avoid any discussion about Emmie's future. He needed to get past the events of the next few days...then return to his solitary routine. "I hate to bring this up, but you'll need to see the funeral director this morning—pick out a casket, decide on a service, prepare an obituary for the newspaper."

Annabelle's mouth quivered. "I don't have any idea what an obit should say."

She must have written ones for her parents, but Finn let that go. He didn't mention the funeral home transporting Sierra's body from the hospital either. He knew that would make the sad fact of her cousin's death seem all too real, but before he could offer to go with Annabelle—and risk bringing up his memories of Chicago—he heard footsteps on the stairs.

Her thumb in her mouth, Emmie padded into the kitchen. "Why you still here, Finn?"

He half smiled at the tone of her voice, curious yet pleased to see him again when he'd thought, from Annabelle's reports, that Emmie wasn't a morning person. In spite of his vow to avoid her, too, her calling him by his first name was charming, and when she climbed onto his lap Finn automatically drew her close at the same time he struggled not to push her away. He would never hold Alex like this again. He was here only to fulfill his official duties. Call it community outreach.

Annabelle rushed across the kitchen, as if she were trying to prevent the scene with Emmie that might come next. "We have oatmeal for breakfast," she said in a questioning voice, "or I can fix eggs. Which would you like, Emmie?"

Finn expected her to say *doughnut*, but instead she looked up at him then pressed her tiny hands to either side of his face. "What you want?"

"Eggs," he said. "They're good for you and they taste great."

She wrinkled her nose. Then, "Okay. I eat eggs too."

With one hand on the refrigerator door, Annabelle gaped at him. "How did you do that?" Her reddened eyes held his gaze.

"Emmie made her own decision."

With the kind of brisk efficiency she displayed at the diner, Annabelle put breakfast together. Bacon sizzled in one skillet, scrambled eggs in another and glasses of apple juice and a slice of cinnamon coffee cake waited at each place. "I brought this home, hoping Emmie might like it," she said, setting their plates on the table then going back for her own. "But I doubt she will."

As if to prove her wrong, Emmie devoured every bite, glancing now and then at Finn to see if he was eating too. When he asked for a second helping, so did she. Annabelle was still shaking her head when they finished—she had eaten hardly anything—and Finn knew they couldn't wait any longer to tell Emmie about her mom. Earth-shattering news. How to say this without traumatizing her any more than he knew they would?

When he'd lost Alex and Caro, at first Finn was the only one to absorb the blow.

He tilted his head toward Emmie who sat on his lap again, leaning against him. She felt warm, smelled sweet in his arms. "What do you think?" he said, dreading what had to be done. "Now?"

"We'd better. I expect Shadow, Blossom and Olivia to show up any moment. I have the best friends in the world and I know they'll want to help." She hesitated. "But I'm glad you're here, Finn. I couldn't do this without you."

"Yes you could, but maybe it's better this way. Strength in numbers." For sure, he never relished giving bad news, especially to someone who was alone. He turned Emmie in his embrace so she could see his face, and the memories shot through him with the speed of those bullets heading for their targets. *Caro and Alex.* The two people he'd loved most. The loss still seemed unbearable, and he was an adult who should cope better. What would this do to Emmie?

"Sweetie," Annabelle began, her hands folded on the table. "I wish we didn't have to tell you this—with all my heart, I do—but it's about your mom. She's been very, very sick..." Annabelle clamped her lips tight but didn't continue.

"Her froat sore, too?" Emmie asked. "The doctor make her better. Like me."

Finn winced. From the look on Annabelle's face, he knew it was his turn. Stalling, wishing he was anywhere else, he stroked Emmie's hair, his fingers gently untangling the long blond strands, but Emmie spoke before he could.

"She coming home now?" she asked, her eyes wide.

"I know you want that, baby." Finn pressed her head to his chest again. "But she can't... she isn't able to come home."

Emmie's head popped up, nearly hitting Finn's chin. "When?"

Annabelle managed, "I'm so sorry, Emmie, but..."

"She's with the angels now," Finn murmured, his voice tight. Could she understand even that? At three, the very concept of death must be foreign to her.

"Mama's not there!" Emmie cried out. "No a—a *angle*!" She lurched from Finn's embrace, tumbled to the floor then ran toward the stairs, her little legs pumping. Climbing at a rapid clip, slipping on one step, she yelled, "Mama!" as if Sierra were waiting for her upstairs. *"Mama!"*

Annabelle sat frozen at the table. "Oh, Finn," she said.

He fought the urge to go to her, to embrace Annabelle as he had Emmie. But all he could get out was, "Give her time."

IN HER ONE AND ONLY black dress, Annabelle stood in a short receiving line—just her, actually—at the only funeral home in Barren. Tasteful music played softly in the background, and the lights were dimmed. It was the night of Sierra's viewing, but thank goodness the walnut casket was closed. She could only term the past two days *horrid.* Emmie had alternated between bouts of crying and insisting her mother would be fine. She'd taken up a vigil near the front door, certain Sierra would walk in any minute.

Tonight, wearing the new dress Annabelle had bought her with a red-and-black-plaid taffeta skirt, she'd stayed beside Annabelle for only a moment before she wriggled free, and now with her patent leather Mary Jane shoes flying, made a beeline across the thick carpet to Finn.

A fresh wave of gratitude washed through

Annabelle. He'd just come in wearing a white shirt, dark blue suit and somber striped tie. She'd wondered if he would come tonight or if he'd feel he'd already done his part. As soon as Annabelle's friends had begun to stream into her house that first morning, Finn had made his excuses and left for work.

When Emmie bounded into his arms, Finn's gaze flickered. He looked as if he had no choice but to catch her, an expression she'd seen before, then carried her across the room to Annabelle. A few other early mourners were here too, and several interested glances took them in, as if she, Finn and Emmie had formed a little family.

Annabelle touched his sleeve. "Thank you for coming."

Finn didn't respond. She said the same words to everyone who stopped to offer their condolences. Within the first half hour most of her friends had showed up, the room was full, and Emmie had left Annabelle's side again to dart among the crowd, greeting people she knew. Shadow, who looked stunning in a well-cut black suit with killer heels, leaned close to Annabelle. "I know how hard this has to be." She looked toward Grey, who stood near the closed casket talking to Blossom's husband. "When my brother Jared died, my whole family fell apart. If there's anything I can do—" She broke off. "Of course there isn't, really, or not enough. What are *you* going to do, Belle?"

"I should have been on the plane today but of course I canceled my trip to Denver." Later, she'd have time to regret the missed opportunity. With the funeral and Emmie to worry about now, her studies had no longer seemed all-important. "But that's not what you mean, is it? All I know is, when this is over I have to find Emmie's father," which was never far from Annabelle's mind.

Blossom had joined them to kiss Annabelle on the cheek. "I'll keep Emmie for you tomorrow unless you're taking her to the service?"

Annabelle hesitated. "I think she's too young." She and Finn had discussed that, deciding Emmie would be okay here tonight; tomorrow would be a different story. "I wasn't sure about bringing her to the viewing either, but she seems to think this is a party." Annabelle glanced across the room at Emmie who was chattering away with one of the diner staff. "At least for the moment."

"Do you have plans following the interment?"

Annabelle shook her head. "But people are welcome to come to the house," she said. "I must have two dozen casseroles in my freezer already."

Blossom and Shadow beckoned to Olivia, who had just walked in with Sawyer.

Olivia folded Annabelle in her arms. "Sorry we're late. We dropped Nick at a friend's birthday sleepover and his mother wouldn't stop talking. I think she was afraid to be left with eight little boys."

"Who could blame her?" Shadow asked. "Ava is sulking in her room because she wasn't invited to the party. You know how she and Nick are—best friends forever. Grey's parents are with her at the ranch. They'll drop by here after we get home, Annabelle."

Olivia released her. "You don't have to do another thing. Focus on this—" she gestured at the room "—and on Emmie. We'll handle the rest tomorrow."

Annabelle's face crumpled. She'd expected them to show their support, but their generosity broke the last of her control. "Oh, no. I promised myself I wouldn't do this."

The women formed a group hug, whispering words of comfort and avoiding the other topic that troubled Annabelle. She could get through this viewing, through the service tomorrow and the limo ride to the cemetery to lay Sierra to rest. Then she would have to somehow decide what was best for Emmie.

For now it would be disloyal to her cousin's memory for Annabelle to even think about her own future.

THE RAIN STREAMED down in torrents. At noon the next day the sky stayed a dark, forbidding black with occasional flashes of cloud-to-ground lightning and, standing beside Annabelle, Finn wished he was anywhere but at this gravesite. Sierra Hartwell's casket would soon be lowered into the raw earth. Annabelle had made the right decision to leave Emmie today with Blossom at the Circle H, even in tears. She seemed to have finally grasped the concept, at least in part, that her mother was gone.

Finn had ridden with Annabelle in the limousine, but after the memorial service he'd retrieved his car at Annabelle's house for the drive to the cemetery. In spite of the abandoned expression in her eyes, Finn needed a personal escape hatch. Funerals were never a welcome event, and the reminders of Caro and Alex were now making him tremble inside.

Half listening to the minister intone a few words to end his graveside remarks, Finn felt Annabelle lean against his shoulder. A few people standing on the opposite side of the green canopy cast curious glances at them but Finn didn't care. For the first time since Sierra's accident, and for the past few difficult days, he and Annabelle weren't at odds about the outstanding warrant or her continued loyalty to a woman Finn believed was not innocent. And, of course, about Emmie. Finn had his opinion on that subject, and he meant to voice it. But not today.

He waited beside Annabelle while the others filed around the casket, each person laying a single red rose on top. Then it was his and Annabelle's turn. Finn wanted to step away, let her have this last moment with the memory of someone she'd loved, yet he couldn't seem to make himself move. Just as he hadn't delivered the sad news that night then climbed back in his cruiser—his official duty done—and gone straight home.

She needed his support, and Finn also felt sorry for Emmie.

When Annabelle swayed, he steadied her and fought another strong urge to run for his car. He didn't want the feelings she roused in him, or to see the soft sorrow in her eyes. The faint scent of lavender rising from her skin drew him like a bee to a flower. Though he didn't want to get any closer, he guided her to the casket, handed her a rose from the nearby standing vase and took one for himself. Rain dripped steadily through a hole in the canopy above.

And, not moving, Finn could no longer help but remember another day like this one except colder. In Chicago the gray December sky had looked ominous and thick with the threat of snow. He'd shivered in his dark suit from the chill—or the shock that had frozen him from the second he'd heard the first gunshot, seen Caro fall, then Alex. *Dear God.* He still saw their faces…the dying light in their eyes.

"Daddy," Alex had moaned. Caroline hadn't said a word.

There had been two caskets then, one of her favorite oak, the other white for their child's innocence. *My son.* Alex had been cut down before his life really began.

Finn looked toward the hillside. He needed to get a grip before he fell apart. After placing their roses, most of the other mourners, friends and acquaintances, including the town's mayor, had slipped away, walking toward their cars across the still-green grass. Water droplets hung from the red-and-orange-and-russet leaves of nearby trees, falling and soaking into the spongy ground.

A few people were still climbing the hill, but one man looked out of place. Dark hair spilled from his hooded sweatshirt and he stopped for a moment, gazing down at the place where Annabelle stood. His gaze seemed to single out Finn.

Finn tensed. Derek Moran. He'd always had a hunch that Eduardo Sanchez had come to his family's funerals, staying hidden from the crowd as he surveyed the devastation he'd wrought. But why was Derek here? A second later he was gone, striding the rest of the way up the rise, almost as if he hadn't been there at all.

His hand trembled on the rose as Annabelle said, "Finn?"

She was waiting for him to place his

flower. Then hers would be the last. And still he stood there, mute and frozen as he had in his driveway that other day, the car filled with Christmas presents. If he'd reacted in time... "Sheriff," the pastor prompted him.

His shoulder brushing Annabelle's, Finn reached out, blindly laid the rose across the walnut casket beaded with raindrops and said "Sorry" in a strangled voice.

Then he ran, leaving the minister to see Annabelle to the waiting limousine.

ANNABELLE WASN'T SURPRISED that by the time she got home, Shadow and Olivia had the dining room table set for a buffet that practically groaned with every sort of food. Sliced ham, beef and turkey. Potato salad, coleslaw and baked beans. All kinds of salads. Desserts including fruit pies and cobblers, cheesecakes, cookies and candies, none of which Annabelle had to prepare. Odd, that this was her first day off in years. Even yesterday she'd overseen breakfast at the diner.

Blossom arrived with more covered dishes and her husband Logan stepped inside the suddenly too-small house carrying Emmie.

Annabelle hoped Emmie would come to her as she had after her fall at the playground, but instead she looked around the room. "Where Finn?" She stuck her thumb in her mouth.

Annabelle couldn't answer that question. Finn had been like her Rock of Gibraltar until he'd gotten that odd look on his face at the cemetery then sprinted for his car. "I don't know, sweetie," she said. "Maybe he'll be here later."

But Finn never showed, and even though she tried to tell herself it didn't matter, and she was wrong to rely on him, his abrupt departure had bothered her. So did his absence.

"Want Finn," Emmie insisted.

Having overheard them, Shadow approached. "Let's get you something to eat, baby. Are you hungry? I'll fix you a plate."

Emmie shook her head. "I not a baby. I eat with Finn."

"Oh, dear," Shadow murmured at which point Grey crossed the room. He took Emmie's hand and asked if he would do for now, and Emmie gave in, going with him to the buffet table where Grey helped her select what she was willing to eat. "Am I a lucky woman, or what?" Shadow asked, then, "I wonder where Finn is."

"At the cemetery, after you left, he…" Annabelle trailed off. "He left too. I don't know where he went. Maybe he had to answer an emergency call."

"Strange, even so, that he'd disappear without an explanation."

Annabelle twisted her hands together. "He was so good with Emmie this week, but sometimes I get the feeling he'd rather not be spending time with her." *Or with me*.

She needed to remind herself of that.

Her feelings for Finn had always been hopeless, and they weren't important now.

Annabelle had bigger problems. She had to figure out what would be best for Emmie. Which meant finding her father.

CHAPTER NINE

FINN DROVE THROUGH the gates at Wilson Cattle to see Derek Moran. So far his day had been a bust.

On his way out of town, Finn had stopped to eat lunch at the café located at the other end of Main Street, the back of his neck prickling the whole time. In his usual rear booth at Annabelle's Diner, he wouldn't have that problem; he wouldn't be seated in the middle of the restaurant, fully exposed and half expecting Eduardo Sanchez to burst through the door and start shooting. But for several days, since Sierra Hartwell's interment, Finn had stayed away from the diner even though he preferred watching Annabelle serve coffee to her customers, chatting and laughing over the news of the day, and sometimes commiserating with them when that news was grim.

Not long ago the bad news had been hers about Sierra. And Finn had behaved badly.

What kind of jerk am I? Running out on Annabelle at the cemetery? Turning his back on her surprised expression? Her disappointment in him? He couldn't think how to make that up to her, or if he should try. She would be better off—*he* would be better off—if he stuck to himself, as he'd done ever since he'd fled Chicago. Or since Caro's and Alex's deaths months before that. His only confidant then had been his partner, but even Cooper had backed off. If Sanchez was still around, Cooper couldn't find him.

Wishing he'd handled Sierra's funeral better, Finn went up the dusty drive, passing the ranch house where Grey and Shadow lived with their daughter Ava. As he approached the barn, his muscles tightened. He didn't see Grey anywhere.

Just as well. His friend wouldn't approve of this visit. Grey's foreman stepped out into the sunlight, blinking and holding a bridle in one hand. A former rodeo rider, Dusty Malone had graying sandy hair and washed-out blue eyes. He wore a battered gray Stetson, a striped Western-style shirt with faded jeans and a huge prize belt buckle from some past event. He had the bowed legs of a longtime cowboy, and Finn wondered if he knew Derek meant to replace him.

"Hey, Finn," he said. "What brings you by?"

"Grey not here?"

"Went into town with Shadow. Important doings," the older man said, cracking a smile. "Miss Ava has outgrown her clothes again. So they went shopping. Grey does love to spend money on that girl."

"Tell him I said hey." Finn touched his gun belt. "I'm actually here to see Derek."

Dusty gestured with a thumb over his shoulder. "Mucking stalls inside. Don't expect to find him in a good frame of mind." Pause. "Is he in some trouble?" Finn didn't answer and Dusty looked toward the nearby pasture where a small herd of Grey's prized Black Angus cattle munched grass, their soft lowing sounds drifting on the afternoon air. Most were cows with calves at their sides. Finn inhaled the gamy aroma of hides and hooves and, of course, manure. Similar odors floated toward him from the barn, making Finn sneeze. He wiped his nose on his handkerchief.

Dusty ran a hand through his hair, which was getting sparse on top. "Would you believe? Rustling his own brother-in-law's cattle. Don't have to tell you, Grey and I see that differently. I heard about Derek's continuance. Nothing since then?"

"Just waiting on the judge. Without charges from Grey, the state may have to settle for less—even a dismissal."

"No trial?" Dusty obviously sided with Finn, not Grey.

"We'll see."

Dusty walked with him into the shadowy barn where the sound of a pitchfork clanging off metal set Finn's ears to ringing. The foreman waved him toward the far stalls. "Moran's in there. Fair warning. He can be mean as a rattler."

Finn passed by the stalls, some empty, some with horses that stared out through the bars as if they were in prison waiting for parole. Finn recognized most of them: the buckskin appropriately named Bucky. The horse called Nugget. Next came Cinders and then Grey's own horse, the huge sorrel he'd named Big Red. Finn passed the stall and skirted a wheelbarrow in the middle of the aisle, then stopped.

Derek stood in the adjoining stall, which was Big Brown's, pushing soiled bedding around with a pitchfork. Finn would bet he'd heard him come into the barn.

Derek looked around Brown to peer at him. "What can I do you for?"

Finn wanted to wipe that smirk off his face. Every time he saw him, he felt the same way and Derek obviously knew it. He liked to pull Finn's chain and Finn wasn't good at hiding his feelings where guys like Derek—and Sanchez—were concerned.

"A few days ago I thought I saw you at the cemetery."

Derek leaned on the pitchfork's handle.

"My brother's there," he said, his gaze narrowed. He recited the dates of Jared's birth and death then finished, "'Beloved son and brother.'" Derek straightened then, holding the pitchfork, ducked under Brown's muscular neck to step into the aisle. He shoved the pitchfork and it banged into the wall beside Finn, startling Brown. "I see Jared whenever I can. We talk," he said. "About whatever's on my mind, the weather, what's new in town, who's seeing someone…"

"So you were there to 'visit.'"

"Yessir. Why is that your business? A man grieves however he can."

Finn had to agree. He crossed his arms.

"Well, it seems that after the funeral someone toppled a bunch of headstones. You know anything about that?"

Derek couldn't hold back his smile. "Zero, nada. Whose funeral was it again?"

"Sierra Hartwell. Annabelle Foster's cousin."

Derek raised one eyebrow and shoved past him. He opened the door to a stall across the way then pushed the wheelbarrow over. He retrieved the pitchfork, coming close enough to Finn to make him step back or get hit with the handle.

"You got probable cause to hassle me?" Derek asked.

"No," Finn said. "Just asking questions."

"Then maybe you better climb in that cruiser and hightail it to the road. Before I file charges against *you* for police harassment."

WHEN THE LUNCH SHIFT had ended, Annabelle walked down the street to the sheriff's office. Finn wasn't there so she waited by the front reception desk until he finally came in. "Late lunch?" she asked. Obviously, he hadn't eaten at the diner.

Finn's gaze focused on the desk sergeant.

"Kind of a busy day, Annabelle." He started toward his office. "Come on in. I've got five minutes."

Annabelle followed him, though she didn't exactly feel welcome. Finn hadn't even looked at her except for a first, startled glance when he walked into the station. She should have told him she was coming. Was he avoiding her? Maybe that should be okay with Annabelle, but Emmie kept asking for him.

She dropped into the chair in front of his desk. Sarge lay in his usual position by the window that overlooked Main Street, one hind leg twitching in some doggie dream. His face wore what could only be described as a faint smile so it must be a good one.

Finn tracked her gaze. "He's staying here a lot of the time. Got kicked out of my apartment. His howling disturbed the neighbors. Apparently Sarge has separation anxiety. I need a bigger place anyway." He said, "My landlord says move by the end of the month or the rest of the town might learn I'm being evicted. Frankly, that would be embarrassing—as he pointed out."

"Because you're the sheriff."

Finn made air quotes. "And should be the

model of a law-abiding citizen." He paused. "I've been looking around—signed with a Realtor—but so far, no luck. There's a cottage for rent by the creek with a yard that backs up to the water. Haven't seen it yet. There's another house closer to my office. Ditto. An apartment above the hardware store might be available soon, but I don't know if there's enough room out back for Sarge to do his business."

"I wouldn't expect there to be much on the market here except—you wouldn't want to buy my house?"

He frowned. "I imagine you need your house. For Emmie." Without a pause, he said, "She doing all right now?"

Well, at least he'd asked about her. "Off and on." Finn seemed to be in a mood today. His manner didn't invite idle conversation, but his features had softened at the mention of Emmie. With one foot she nudged the bag she'd brought with her then glanced out the window. "She's with Olivia at her antiques shop. Nick's there today, home from school with the sore throat he caught from Emmie, so Olivia was happy to provide him some company. Unfortunately, while the kids were playing, Emmie broke a milk glass bud vase. It shattered like a bomb."

He flinched in sympathy.

"Olivia insisted the vase can easily be replaced and not to worry, but I left money for it anyway, left Emmie there a little longer so I could see you."

His gaze flickered. "What about?"

Annabelle reached for the bag at her feet. "I've gone through Sierra's belongings from the hospital. The clothes she wore the night of the accident, her purse—"

She drew out a thin sheaf of papers then held them out. "As I'd hoped these were with her clothes. They might be important."

Finn barely glanced at them. "You know the warrant in her glove compartment no longer matters. And I didn't find anything else in there. All you'll need to do is send the local DA in St. Louis a copy of the death certificate and, with Sierra's death, the charges will be dismissed." Finn propped his chin in one hand. "What else have you got?"

"This may take more than five minutes," Annabelle murmured.

He didn't quite smile. "You protect yourself better than I thought. Sorry, I didn't mean that to include from me." He set the papers aside. "A bunch of old bills?" He picked one up again. "This is dated five years ago. A credit card statement that's even older? And in arrears. She may have paid these off, but your cousin seems to have had quite the checkered past."

"You don't think these could be helpful? Why was Sierra carrying them with her? Most people don't lug their old financial statements everywhere."

"She was on the road. Why not?" He added, "Maybe—or even likely—she didn't intend to go back to wherever she'd come from with Emmie. So, sure, I can see her tossing these into her carry-on bag. Maybe she didn't want to leave any clues behind."

"I thought following leads was part of your job. Finn, each of these bills has an address for Sierra at some point in her life." Why was he being so dense? "Look at the bottom one. A pay stub from one of the events she managed. Maybe someone at that company would know about Emmie—and her father."

Finn sighed. "You'll really try to find him? Why? Seems like he hasn't been around since Emmie was born. Maybe he likes it that way and he doesn't want anything to do with a kid."

"What if he doesn't know about her? He might be thrilled to learn he's a father, to see Emmie…"

"And take responsibility for her." Finn shook his head. "Sounds like a simple solution—providing you *can* find him in the first place—"

"Simple for me, you mean."

"But what if he *doesn't* care? She's already with you, Annabelle. You're Emmie's only living relative, as far as we know—other than this guy who either doesn't know she exists or wouldn't give a hoot about her."

"Yes, I'm a relative. But that man is her father, her *closest* relative. He should be the one to raise Emmie. I'm not—"

"Qualified?" Finn held her gaze. "You've done okay so far. I think her best place is with you."

"Obviously that's your opinion. What happens, though, when the diner finally sells—and the house where I grew up? I'll be moving on, and I'll need a new means of making a living."

"Look. I realize you're disappointed that your plans for Denver got canceled. But you can do that another time—"

"That particular course—from one of the

best schools—is offered once a year. Yes, I could sign up for next year, even take Emmie with me if I had to. But after that how would we manage? I'd be traveling for my job without a home base for her. The certification is only the first step, and tour directors are on call twenty-four/seven. That wouldn't be fair to Emmie." *And I'm not cut out to be a parent. Not yet, maybe not ever.* Her own mother had always said that, and Annabelle wasn't about to ruin her cousin's child.

"You'd find a way," he said, his jaw set. "If you're determined to locate Emmie's father, I'll help you if I can but—"

"What, Finn? Why are you so determined that I should keep Emmie?"

He shifted. For a long moment he stared past her out the window. "Because of my son," he said at last.

Annabelle straightened. She'd thought he was an eligible bachelor, if something of a loner, and she'd tried to hide her own interest in him, but all this time… "I didn't know you had a family."

"I don't. Not anymore." He picked up a pen then put it down again. "When I worked in Chicago, my wife and our three-year-old son were murdered."

Annabelle pressed a hand to her chest. "Oh, Finn."

"I don't often talk about this. They were… gunned down in our driveway by members of a gang called The Brothers." He told her about the drug raid he and his partner had made and Eduardo Sanchez's vow of revenge. He toyed with the pen. "A few months later I quit the force. I left Chicago—left that gang still roaming the streets." His voice broke on the next word. "Hurting people."

Annabelle wondered if that was one reason he'd seemed so harsh about Sierra and the warrant and, according to rumor, about Shadow's brother Derek. Was that why he was called Mr. Law-and-Order? Emmie must also remind him of that tragedy, of the evil that exists in the world. "Finn, I don't know what to say."

He raised one hand to cover his eyes. "I'll spare you the details." In a hoarse tone he said, "My ex-partner in Chicago has been hunting The Brothers for me, but he's hit a wall and I can't seem to process that. I can't imagine a future in which no one pays for what happened. What Sanchez did." He admitted, "I almost lost my job there trying to track him down. It was Cooper—my partner—who told me about the election in Barren. Being sheriff here is still The Job, as cops call it," he said, "but far less dangerous than in Chicago."

"You're a good sheriff," Annabelle said.

"I hope so. It matters." He glanced up. "So does Emmie. I don't mean to come down hard on you about her. I hope her father turns up, if that's what you really want, but I still think she'd be happier with you."

"I understand. You're worried about her having to make another adjustment with a man who's likely a stranger to her. I worry about that, too."

Finn blinked. "And every time I see Emmie, I think of Alex—"

"Of course you do."

"—and it breaks my heart all over again. I had a child. I won't have another."

Or another woman you could love? But Annabelle didn't say that.

His gaze strayed from hers as he rose from his desk chair. "Obviously we're not going to settle any of this now."

Her heart sank. "I guess not."

"I hope you'll reconsider, though. About Emmie."

He took a few steps toward the door.

Annabelle gathered her bag, trying not

to notice his broad shoulders, his lean form and long legs, knowing now why he'd all but given her the brushoff at first—knowing why he was so adamant about Emmie staying with her. She might disagree with him—Emmie was her decision to make—but his quiet words had shut Annabelle from his life too. *She* wasn't his responsibility, and he didn't owe Annabelle anything.

Her fantasy of Finn lay shattered by his grief on the floor between them. She needed to focus on her new career, on Emmie. And leaving Barren.

He walked her down the hall and past the front door. He held it open until Annabelle stopped trying to catch his eye and stepped out onto the sidewalk. "I'll let you know if I come up with anything," she said, her back to him. "About Emmie's dad."

CHAPTER TEN

"NIGHT, NIGHT, SWEETIE," Annabelle whispered to Emmie, who lay in the center of Annabelle's bed, thumb in her mouth and eyes drifting shut.

Annabelle tried to focus on their nighttime ritual, not the scene she'd gone through earlier with Finn. Her heart ached for him, and what had happened to his family. No wonder he hadn't seemed eager to spend time with Emmie, or to think about a relationship. Maybe he was even right about Emmie's father—a man who might not want to love her. Annabelle hoped the father would want to be involved, and she meant to pursue the search. With or without Finn. Reading books to Emmie had made for a more peaceful evening than sparring with him and created a warmth inside that Annabelle had never known before.

Still, Emmie's silence about Sierra troubled her. Since her mother's funeral, Emmie had stopped mentioning her. She'd even stopped crying. Yet Annabelle sensed her underlying grief.

Emmie had flatly refused to sleep in her bed across the hall, which meant Annabelle wasn't getting much rest either. Emmie thrashed all night, and by morning she took up most of the bed.

"I not sleepy," she insisted now.

Perched on the edge of the mattress, Annabelle gazed down at her. What a sweet little girl she could be when she wasn't pitching a fit about getting dressed or going to see Sawyer for a follow-up visit—*don't want a shot*—or not seeing Nick and Ava because they had school and couldn't play—*I want school too*. And after her breakfast with Finn, Emmie had asked for scrambled eggs every day. Amazing.

"Not sleepy? I won't argue with that," Annabelle said. She wouldn't have to. She dropped a light kiss on Emmie's hair, but before she rose from the bed, Emmie's eyes closed again, and this time they didn't open.

Ha, she thought. Her brief experience caring for Emmie had taught it was better to pick her battles. She wasn't bad now, at least with mundane tasks like giving baths, bundling Emmie into her car seat, getting her to take her medicine. Today she'd gotten a clean bill of health from Sawyer—and no shot. Emmie's sore throat was gone.

Annabelle put the books they'd read tonight—including Ava's longtime favorite, *Janie Wants to Be a Cowgirl*, which she'd lent to Emmie—back on the shelf. She tucked the little girl's lamb close, rose from the bed and left the door a little ajar. Then she went downstairs to the living room where she opened her laptop and started her search.

She didn't need Finn's help, though he'd reluctantly offered, or his approval of her choice for Emmie. Google made finding anything—or anyone—easy, or at least she hoped it would. She was about to type Sierra's name into the search box when she remembered Emmie saying she and her mother had once gone to Denver. That had to be recent. Maybe it wouldn't be necessary to look in other places. If she got lucky…

Minutes later, she sat back and rubbed the aching tension line between her brows. She'd found no address, no listing for a Sierra Hartwell in the city or anywhere in the state of Colorado. Possibly, the trip Emmie mentioned had been only a visit with a brief hotel stay.

Maybe this wouldn't be as simple as she'd hoped. For the next hour she entered every town and state on Sierra's bills, most, as Finn had said, overdue. Did her cousin really move each time to avoid paying them? For the first time, Annabelle could imagine her running from the law, or at least from her responsibilities.

Annabelle had learned that wasn't always a breeze with Emmie, just a bit easier now than at the beginning. What if Annabelle's own mother had been wrong about her ability to care for a child?

When she reached the end of the stack of papers, she was no further along than when she'd started. Annabelle straightened. What about the state of Wyoming? The address on Sierra's last known driver's license. Annabelle would need Finn's help for that. Even a quick search on a white pages site had turned up nothing. It seemed as if Sierra had vanished until her car smashed into Ned Sutherland's pickup.

Where had Sierra been all this time? Not with family. Her parents had died long before Emmie was born, which meant there were no grandparents, no aunts or uncles because Annabelle's family was gone too. She was the only cousin.

And who had Sierra worked for when she started driving to Kansas? Perhaps from west to east? If only Emmie was a bit older, she might be able to tell.

Annabelle had already probed gently about her father, but Emmie didn't seem to know what she was talking about.

Her ears alert, Annabelle heard a sudden sound from upstairs. A soft moan, a feeble cry. Emmie often woke during the night. She'd give the little girl a chance to fall back to sleep. She closed her browser and sat there, listening. If Emmie began to cry in earnest, Annabelle would go to her.

But she heard nothing more, so she turned back to the computer then tapped a key to return to her home screen. An image of Las Ramblas, the pedestrian walk in Barcelona, appeared as part of her usual slide show, and a soft wave of yearning went through her. Tonight she had no more possible leads about Sierra, and at the moment Annabelle wasn't going anywhere.

Her course in Denver, as she'd told Finn, was only offered once a year. To say she couldn't go—and felt disappointed—didn't cover it and, because of Emmie, Annabelle couldn't simply pick another school. For now she brought up the website to enter the contest for the Caribbean cruise again, which she did once every day, as the contest rules allowed. Might as well dream.

But even that longtime hobby didn't ease her mind. How could she find Sierra's last known address or any place of business that might fit another piece into the puzzle that had been her cousin's life? That might eventually lead to Emmie's father?

THE NEXT NIGHT Finn wandered down the pet food aisle at the local market on Main Street. The store wasn't far from his office, and after work he'd stopped in for basic supplies, including more kibble for Sarge. The dog was waiting for him in the car and likely, as always, not only eager to get home but hungry. He ate as if he never expected another meal.

As Finn reached for the largest bag—stocked on the top shelf—something slammed into his knees. Finn dropped the bag back onto the shelf with a thud. He'd been a high school quarterback, but he didn't expect to be tackled in a store, and his legs buckled, almost sending him to the floor before he caught himself. Then he looked down and had to grin. The little girl gazing up at him was just too cute, no matter how he wanted to resist her.

"Hey, Emmie."

"I see you, Finn. I say hello." She rested her cheek against his leg. Then, like the strong woman she would become, taking him to task, she said with a scowl, "Come to A-bel's house?"

Finn put the dog food in his cart then scooped her up. How to explain to a three-year-old that he thought it better to stay in his apartment and concentrate on packing his things for his coming move? To stay away from Annabelle. Finn wished he hadn't told her about Caro and Alex. He should have kept that to himself, like his stubborn awareness of her. Annabelle couldn't wait to settle Emmie with her missing father then get the heck out of Dodge, or rather, Barren.

He hoisted Emmie higher in his arms. Her innocent blue eyes made his throat tighten as if someone had slipped a noose around it. Alex had always wrapped his heart up with just a smile too.

"I'm, uh, pretty busy."

"Doing you sheriff job?"

"Yep. How've you been, kiddo?"

"My froat okay now." Her frown deepened. "You buy me candy?"

Aha. His grin widened. Apparently, she'd had some disagreement with Annabelle. He looked around but didn't see her anywhere. Then he heard a familiar, frantic voice calling, "Emmie! Emmie, where are you?"

She ducked her head. "C'mon," he said, lifting Emmie onto his shoulders. "You shouldn't hide. Let's go find her."

He turned the first corner only to meet Annabelle rushing down the cereal aisle.

"Oh. It's you," she said. He guessed he couldn't blame her for that reaction. Her gaze homed in on Emmie who peeked around Finn. "Emmie. You mustn't run off like that. I didn't know where you were."

Emmie's mouth firmed. "I right here."

"Yes, I know that—now—but I've been looking all over this store. You frightened me. I was afraid you'd gone outside…" She trailed off, obviously not wanting to continue with a worst-case scenario that starred Emmie wandering into traffic.

Though she hadn't left the market, Finn

understood a parent's fears when a small child suddenly disappeared. His Alex had been like Houdini. If only he'd run off into the backyard that day, before the shooting started. If only Finn had been able to protect him. "She's all right, Annabelle. She spied me and decided to come visit. She's safe."

"She might not have been."

"Yes I am," Emmie insisted.

Finn swung her down and set her on the floor between them. "Maybe you could say sorry, Em. You don't want to worry your A-bel."

"She not mine. Not my mama."

Great, Finn thought. He'd only been trying to help, but the shaken look on Annabelle's face told him he'd failed. Which he seemed to do with her every time they met. And Emmie's words must have hurt, as his probably had yesterday. He touched Annabelle's arm but she flinched.

"You ready to check out?" he asked. "I am, and I need to talk to you."

Annabelle didn't argue but she didn't look at him either. "I'll get my cart."

Outside, the night air was crisp and clear. Overhead, the stars were strung like crystal ornaments across the darkened sky. He buckled Emmie into her car seat then loaded the bags into Annabelle's trunk. After stowing his own in his car, he gave Sarge a treat then turned back to Annabelle.

"I need to talk to you, too," she said though the prospect didn't seem to please her. She started her car, put on a video for Emmie then leaned against the half-open door, her arms folded. "Well? You first."

Finn lowered his voice. "I suspected there were other outstanding warrants for Sierra and there are. In five other states," he said, "besides Missouri. Texas, Arkansas, Nevada, Wisconsin and Ohio."

Annabelle's features fell. "That many? What charges?"

"More of the same. Fraud, embezzlement, theft, grand larceny..."

She turned pale. "That...can't be. I don't... want it to be." She sounded on the verge of tears.

"I'm not making this up, Annabelle." In Finn's mind, Sierra Hartwell had been a swindler, a con artist, but he wasn't about to say that. "Along with the St. Louis warrant, you'll need to repeat the process with these, too, but that should clear everything for the courts. I hate to point this out again,

but you *didn't* really know Sierra anymore."
He said, "You really want to find the man
she was involved with? I was a...father myself, so I can understand that, but there's no
telling what he'd be like."

"Yes. I do need to find him. To know—
for Emmie's sake—I've done everything I
could."

"Even if he turns out to be a criminal?"
Because he knew people tended to hang out
with their own kind. Like Sierra. "That's a
possibility, you know."

"And in that case I'll know what to do. If
I don't try, there could also be legal ramifi-
cations."

"I realize that but—"

"I mean, what right would I have to keep
Emmie, as you think I should? I'm not her
closest relative," she reminded him.

"Close enough," Finn murmured even
though she had a point.

Annabelle tucked a lock of hair behind her
ear, and her breath frosted in the cold air. She
told Finn about her search the night before,
her frustration at not finding any solid lead
to Sierra's whereabouts or Emmie's father.

He hated to burst her bubble. She and Sierra had been like sisters growing up. It must

hurt big time to realize that, after defending her, Sierra was nothing but a crook. "She left no forwarding address anywhere, which doesn't surprise me. She must have skipped around a lot, worked her scam then moved on."

Annabelle glanced back into the car at Emmie whose gaze stayed glued to the video screen. "With no connections to Sierra, I may never locate Emmie's father. I suppose that would make you happy."

Finn agreed but not aloud. He understood Annabelle's desire to get away from her painful memories of Barren—just as Finn tried to escape his of Chicago. He knew she'd put those dreams on hold for Emmie and Sierra. What would happen to those dreams if she never did find Emmie's dad? What would happen to Emmie? Finn didn't want to think about Annabelle turning the little girl over to the State. Some foster care turned out well, but often it didn't. If Annabelle made that choice, he wanted to be able to understand why, but he'd hate to see Emmie damaged when she could be with Annabelle instead.

"Something has to turn up," he said at last to ease her mind. "In the meantime…"

She tried to smile. "I need to get Emmie

home. It's after her bedtime." Not realizing that she'd paired Emmie with home, she turned again to the car, giving Finn a nice view of her in her jeans. He looked away and at the same time saw Emmie. Her eyes were still on the video that was playing. Finn could hear its soundtrack, the music and laughter. Emmie wriggled one hand into the grocery bag beside her on the rear seat and Finn felt guilty. She fumbled around then pulled out a glazed doughnut and shoved it in her mouth, her face quickly smeared with sugar.

"Where did that come from?" Annabelle asked. "I didn't buy—"

"Me," he admitted. "I bought that box of Krispy Kremes and put them in one of your bags, but I didn't think she'd see them until you got home."

To his surprise, Annabelle's face cleared. She laughed.

And, to break the tension between them, so did Finn.

THE NEXT MORNING Annabelle moved through the diner to refill her customers' cups with fresh coffee, chatting as she went. The close air inside the restaurant smelled of eggs, hash browns and bacon. At the middle two-top Annabelle's former high school English teacher sat with the new principal, earnestly talking, from the little she could hear, about next semester's curriculum changes. Annabelle didn't interrupt them but kept going with a brief nod of acknowledgment. Seated at the rear table for six, across from Finn's usual booth, Mayor Harry Barnes was in a good mood today. The council had approved his budget for next year, and when he headed for the door with his entourage in tow, he was still smiling at his constituents.

When he came to Annabelle she said, "How's your family, Mr. Mayor?"

He straightened his tie then ran a hand over his already neat blond hair. "Couldn't be better. Elizabeth's about to enroll our youngest in day care, get a few hours to herself. How are you doing?"

Annabelle wondered if he'd ask about Emmie, too—she'd seen him at Sierra's funeral—but he didn't. His bland gaze shifted to someone behind her, and he called out a hearty greeting to another local resident.

"I'm fine," she murmured. Harry was an effective mayor, just as Finn was a good sheriff, but he seemed to always be campaigning, working the room, and his attention span could seem limited. Still, he'd left Annabelle a big tip.

Pocketing the money, she began to clear the mayor's table. She glanced at Finn's empty booth, which looked lonely without him. Or was it Annabelle who felt lonely? That was nothing new, like feeling unappreciated, but for a moment last night their shared laughter over Emmie's doughnut had lightened things between them. With Emmie's future to consider, she doubted that would last.

When the door opened, a blast of chill autumn air blew in—and Annabelle's pulse sped. Maybe Finn had finally come for breakfast, but instead her friend Nell Sutherland glided in wearing a sheepskin-lined jacket, well-worn jeans and scuffed cowboy boots. She was blowing on her obviously cold hands. "Brrr," she announced to the entire restaurant in her husky voice. "I can all but smell snow. Looks like an early winter."

She slipped into the nearest booth, which had just been vacated by the women's library auxiliary group. Lost in some discussion of a new novel, they'd formed a phalanx that nearly knocked Nell over when they rushed past.

Annabelle hurried over to wipe the table, put down a fresh cup then pour Nell's coffee. "'Morning," she said. "It's so good to see you," with a rueful glance toward the departing women.

"They're a force to be reckoned with." Nell took a first sip then reached for the sugar. "I do like your coffee, Belle, but I love the heat in this place even more, and I've already had at least six cups at home. I was up all night with a sick cow. On my way to talk with the vet when my stomach started to growl. Not sure whether I should order breakfast or lunch."

"We don't serve lunch until eleven." Which, of course, Nell knew. They were the same age and had been good friends all through school. There wasn't much they didn't know about each other, which was true of Shadow and Olivia as well. As she had with Sierra, Annabelle had always envied Nell her staunch independence. She probably never thought about feeling lonely or like an outsider, and no one would think of using Nell.

Though she wouldn't trade places. Unlike Annabelle, Nell seemed rooted to the area. She was running the Sutherland ranch virtually by herself, and seemed to love the job she'd taken over from her grandfather since Ned's accident with Sierra.

She told Nell about the menu special. "We do have an excellent frittata today."

With a blank look Nell settled deeper into the booth and pitched her battered Stetson onto the seat beside her. She shook out her hair, light brown to ash-blond and tumbling past her shoulders in a silky slide to the middle of her back. "Frittata? Whatever that is, it's too fancy for me," she finally said.

"It's really good. Try it. You'll get an extra dose of veggies."

At their long-standing joke Nell groaned. She was a meat-and-potatoes girl. "Make that three eggs sunny-side up with a rasher of bacon, an order of country-fried steak—heavy on the redeye gravy—you're on." Almost identical to Finn's preferred breakfast.

Annabelle didn't try to convince her the frittata would be far healthier. She put the order in, and by that time the morning rush had eased up so she had time for a short break. She slid into the booth, setting her mug of coffee on the table. "Nell, I have something to ask."

"If this is about your evening women's group—Belle, I don't have time and I'm not the type." She added, "I don't mean to put you or your friends down—"

"Your friends, too. I realize your responsibilities at the NLS have increased, but Blossom, Shadow, Olivia and I all think you need a little play time now and then. Come on," she said. For Annabelle, the group had been a lifesaver, though they hadn't met just for fun since Emmie had been with her. Which reminded Annabelle again of Finn and his opinion about Emmie's welfare.

She took a sip of coffee. "Some good food, plenty of conversation, a little wine… What's not to like?"

"Everyone else knowing my business," Nell said. "And I mean, look at you. You're the very definition of refined, and I smell of horses and cattle." She held up both hands. "Look at these scratches. Barbed wire. My hands are a mess but yours are as soft as butter. I'm country, you're town—"

"That's no excuse." Annabelle tried a smile.

"Come next time. If you want to sit there and never say a word, we'll cover the silence for you."

"Oh, I'm sure." She laughed. "I never did fit in with the likes of Olivia or Shadow."

"Then maybe you'll take quicker to Blossom Hunter."

Nell shook her head. She fiddled with her coffee spoon then dumped in another helping of sugar. She stirred and stirred. "No, and please stop asking me."

"You're hopeless," Annabelle murmured. She waited while the server put Nell's meal in front of her. She watched Nell pour ketchup all over her eggs. As she plowed into her breakfast, Annabelle asked the question that had been on her mind long before Nell walked in. "How's your grandfather?"

Nell's features softened. It was no secret in Barren or the whole of Stewart County that she adored Ned Sutherland and would do anything for him. "He's ornery but that's nothing new. Since he left the hospital, he thinks he knows better than I do what has to be done. Every. Single. Day. I try to cut him some slack. I nearly lost him when Sierra crossed that center line," Nell said.

Annabelle flinched. "At least the accident wasn't his fault." Another strike against Sierra, one that made Annabelle wonder even more about her. "I'm so sorry for what Sierra did but I'm glad Ned's okay. Stubborn can be a good thing." Except when it came to her own attraction to Finn.

Nell said with obvious pride, "I still do whatever I please, how I please, and last month the ranch did better money-wise than we have in months."

Annabelle pushed her mug away. "I admire you. At least you're happy there doing what you love."

She grinned. "You know me. I'm a born cowgirl, the terror of every man on that ranch, including PawPaw's foreman. He's six foot two and outweighs me by fifty pounds—but I'm still the new boss. I make sure he knows it."

When Annabelle said nothing, Nell tilted her head until she was nearly ducking under Annabelle's chin to catch her eye. Her fork poised above her steak, she said, "Sorry. I know you've been meaning to leave this place."

"Not just yet, it turns out."

Nell made a sympathetic face. "I should

have said how sorry I am about Sierra. And I heard about your trip. About Emmie Hartwell. When will you be able to go?"

She forced a small laugh. "I still intend to get out of this town but I guess it will have to be…later." She paused. "Emmie's with Shadow today—everyone's been so helpful—but I'm still searching for anything that might lead to Emmie's father. So far I've had no luck."

"That's a heavy load to carry." Nell frowned. "And God knows you deserve a life of your own. Sierra and I always talked about the way your parents treated you. I could never comprehend that."

Annabelle kept quiet. She understood Nell better than she realized—she didn't want people prying into her life either. She certainly wouldn't mention Finn, but their laughter last night still played through her mind like one of Emmie's favorite videos. She didn't want to admit it, but she'd missed seeing him today, a topic not open for discussion.

Nell smiled. "I bet you still have all those posters on your bedroom wall."

"I moon over them every chance I get."

"Keep dreaming, Belle." Nell polished off

the last of her bacon and eggs. "I'll be waiting for the day I get a postcard from Paris or London."

With Emmie to think of, and the guilt that inspired, Annabelle was waiting too.

CHAPTER ELEVEN

FINN HAD THE night shift and made his usual rounds through town. He stopped at the hardware store to make sure the alarm was on and working as it should, drove by a house on the far side of town to check for a car that, because of a restraining order on its driver, shouldn't be there. He checked the café, the stores along Main Street and the lock on Annabelle's diner. And for no reason at all, he rolled by her house.

Her lights were on but he didn't get out of his car. Parked on the opposite side of the street, he could see shadows through the filmy curtains at her front window. Remembering their talk in his office, he wondered— *Had* he been too hard on her? He envisioned her with Emmie on the sofa, reading a book, their heads bent low together, and his heart turned over.

Just call him the Lone Ranger. He'd made that clear to Annabelle, but on so many nights like this he'd watched Caro with Alex, the boy's hair damp from his bath as he snuggled with Caro. What was he doing here now? *Spying?* Or taking a mental snapshot of a home with warmth and light and love? Annabelle might not be able to see that, but he could. The kind of love he'd known once. Why would she let that go?

He was about to put the cruiser in gear when his cell phone rang.

"Hey," Cooper said, then blew past any pleasantries. "Remember when I told you I didn't have any informants left?"

From his parking spot Finn saw shadows move behind the curtains. Annabelle lifting Emmie into her arms and starting toward the stairs? "Yeah. I remember." His pulse began to beat a rapid tattoo.

"Go figure, but Sanchez's ex-girlfriend just called me. She has a story to tell."

Finn didn't think that sounded on the level. "As long as you're willing to do what for her?"

"There might be a payment involved, but I'll negotiate that—before we talk."

"No clue as to what her story might be?"

The excitement grew in Cooper's voice. "Apparently she was there, Finn. The night

Caroline and Alex were shot. Front-row seat."

"She was with Sanchez?"

"Sitting beside him. That's all she would say until we meet."

Finn didn't recall seeing a woman in the car, but then things had happened too fast. "This could be big, Cooper. Thanks."

"Don't thank me. Who knows if she's even Sanchez's ex. Or if she was in on everything and he's planning to make me his next target."

"I don't want you to put yourself in danger—"

"Day in, day out, that's part of the job."

Cooper's words sounded full of bravado. In Finn's case, that was no longer true. Checking out local businesses at night was as dangerous as it got. Well, except for shamelessly spying on Annabelle because he felt lousy about their conflict over Emmie and hoped to make himself feel better by stopping to see if she was all right. In Chicago, his job had become his family's fate, their doom, and The Brothers had broken him. Yet Finn was still alive and he wanted Cooper to stay that way too.

"Maybe I'd better take a leave of absence and come up there."

"Not a good idea, partner."

"I can be there tomorrow."

Cooper made a scoffing sound. "And leave your department without its sheriff? Or do you think I can't handle this on my own?"

"I know you can. I'd like to be there, though."

"Finn, that's not going to help you. You know that. Stay where you are."

Finn tried to argue with him further but Cooper refused to budge. "After my first meeting with Eduardo Sanchez's ex, I'll get back to you. Promise. We can go from there." Then he changed the subject to ask about Finn's eviction.

"I'm still looking for a new place," Finn admitted. "I went with my Realtor to see a cabin by the creek, then another house in town, but neither one suited me or Sarge's needs."

"You ought to buy something. Make a new start."

"Yeah, yeah. You keep telling me that."

He could imagine Cooper's smile. "I keep hoping you'll follow my advice."

But Finn couldn't do that, not before he

found justice for Caro and Alex. Maybe not even then. "Not going to happen, partner." Finn hesitated, his throat feeling tight. "Miss you anyway," he said. "Good luck with Sanchez's girlfriend. Thanks again, Cooper."

"No need to thank me yet. Miss you too. I'll be in touch."

For a long moment after they hung up, he sat in his cruiser—safe and sound in Stewart County, Kansas—half yearning again for his more exciting job in Illinois even if that would mean revisiting memories. Then he shook off the thought, and slipped the car into gear.

Was it really about safety here, trying to make a different, if lonely, life for himself—or was he simply hiding out, letting Cooper do the job?

Before he drove away, he glimpsed another shadow inside the house. Annabelle coming to the bottom of the stairs, alone? He wondered if, without Emmie, she would feel as isolated as he did without Alex and Caro. Or was she still as eager to leave Barren as he thought? There was nothing he could do to stop her, or to keep her from giving up Emmie if that was what Annabelle decided.

For a second he resented her for wanting

to find Emmie's dad and escape her family. All Finn wanted was for life to be the way it had been before those shots rang out. Nothing would, or could, bring back the wife he'd loved, the kid he'd adored. His world had crumbled then, and he couldn't see buying a new place, as Cooper had suggested, putting the pieces together again.

His grip tightened on the steering wheel, and he turned the cruiser toward the next place of business on his security checklist for the night.

He should keep his mind on finding him and Sarge a new place to live.

Keep his mind on the simple stuff. Block out the rest.

Including Annabelle and Emmie.

Girls' Night Out would usually have been held at Annabelle's Diner, but tonight they'd decided to gather at the Circle H. On the drive from town, Emmie had chattered away in her rear car seat, excited to be going to Nick's house.

"He has horses," Emmie kept saying in a tone of wonder. "I ride 'em."

"Maybe not today," Annabelle said. Unlike many of her friends in this ranching community, she'd been raised, as Nell pointed out, in town and wasn't familiar with horses.

"Nick's horse name He-wo."

"That's Hero, sweetie."

"He lets me ride now."

Annabelle considered trying to dissuade her but didn't want to turn a small disagreement into a full-blown tantrum. A three-year-old was a highly volatile creature, Annabelle had learned, and as they reached the ranch house the sun was setting behind the barn. Soon it would be dark. No one would be riding then. If Annabelle needed backup, she had her friends. How would she feel when she finally left them behind, along with Barren? How would she feel about finally letting go of her crush on Finn?

"Hey, Belle." Blossom met them at the door. "Who's that you have?" she asked, pretending not to know. "Oh, Emmie!" She drew the little girl in for a warm hug.

Emmie giggled. "Where you baby? In you tummy?"

Blossom patted her now-flat stomach. "She's asleep upstairs. She goes to bed early. She's not a big girl like you."

"Oh, thanks," Annabelle said. "Now she'll want to stay up all evening."

Blossom set Emmie down then took the bottle of wine Annabelle had brought. "I made white bean chili tonight. Sound good?"

"Don't like chili," Emmie said then wandered off toward the family room, looking for Nick. Olivia was dropping him off here at the Circle H to stay with her ex, Logan Hunter, who was Nick's dad and Blossom's new husband. So, in effect, Nick had two homes.

"That's a knee-jerk reaction." Annabelle lowered her voice. "I doubt she's ever had chili."

"But it makes such an easy topic to protest."

"You know her well," Annabelle said with a smile.

She filled Blossom in about their nightly bath routine, and the new cell phone she'd had to buy because hers never did dry out, the books they read and videos they shared, the foods Annabelle had introduced with some success. She even told the doughnut-face story from the night Finn had sneaked a box into her bag. Then a car horn tooted from the yard, and Shadow was there, followed by Olivia and Nick, which delighted Emmie. Olivia's stepmother Liza soon joined them. Liza was thirty-six, closer to their age than her husband's, and got along with the friends' group well.

Only seconds after they'd settled in the dining room with bowls of chili and hunks of homemade bread, someone asked about Nell Sutherland. The kids were in the family room with their dinner, eating on the coffee table.

"I invited Nell—again—but she said no," Annabelle reported.

Olivia tucked a stray hair into her ponytail. "I'll talk to her."

Shadow added, "I've mentioned our meetings half a dozen times. Nell always has some excuse."

Annabelle said, "She thinks she doesn't fit in with us."

There were several squawks of outrage. "We'll see about that."

They didn't get to say more before Emmie and Nick ran in to announce they were going to the barn. Blossom started to rise from the table.

But Olivia objected first. "No, you are not, young man. Finish your dinner. Afterward I'll put on a movie for you to watch with Emmie."

"Emmie's small, Nick," Blossom put in. "You know the barn can be dangerous, and your dad's not here to watch you. He and Uncle Grey went to have dinner in town."

Nick's mouth set. "We just want to see Hero."

The women all exchanged looks. Then Olivia sighed. "Do you promise to keep out of the stalls? Hero's included?" she asked, holding her son's gaze.

Blossom used her best stepmother voice. "And if you take carrots with you—" which, of course, they would "—remember to show Emmie how to keep her hand flat."

The kids ran off, shouting promises back over their shoulders, the bag of carrots bumping against Nick's leg. The women looked at each other again and burst out laughing.

"You really think they'll be all right?" Annabelle asked, which set off another round of laughter at her expense.

"You're behaving just like a concerned mother again," Shadow joked.

"I'm not," she insisted. "I mean, I do care and I'm worried about Emmie getting into trouble around all those big animals…"

"We're teasing, Belle." Olivia sobered. "Any luck yet finding her dad?"

Annabelle updated the group about her online search and Finn telling her about Sierra's other warrants.

"Wow," Blossom murmured. "Sounds as if your cousin was leading a very different life from the one you thought."

"I'm afraid so…" She paused. "I wish I could think of some way, any way, to get some insight on the life she led. There has to be someone, somewhere…"

"From what you tell us, Sierra must have been pretty good at evading her responsibilities—except for Emmie, I assume—but there must be some kind of track record. It's weird you've come up empty."

"I know, and I've racked my brain trying to remember anything specific. The last time I spoke to her, before the accident, Sierra did mention a new assignment."

"She organized events, right?"

"That's what she told me." She rubbed her forehead as if to find the answer there. If Sierra had lied to her about one thing, she might have lied about everything. Then she remembered. "Wait. The company that hired her for one event may have had an animal name, a bird or something…"

"What about location?"

"Sierra didn't mention that. Which," Annabelle added with a sigh, "seems to have been her modus operandi. The less said, the better, the harder it would be for someone to trail her."

"If only Emmie could help…" Blossom said.

Olivia put in, "There's no telling what Emmie's life with her mom was like either."

"I have no reason to believe Sierra *wasn't* a good mother," Annabelle said.

Liza, who'd been silent until now, said, "Keep looking, hon. Or maybe Finn will find a connection."

"Speaking of the sheriff…" Shadow said with a look at Annabelle.

"Let's not," she said and turned back to her meal. She didn't want to talk further about Sierra or Finn. "Let's eat our chili before it gets cold."

Like every lead she'd followed so far.

Dead ends for Emmie, and dead ends for Annabelle's fantasy of a relationship with Finn.

CHAPTER TWELVE

"TURKEY TODAY?" Emmie asked from her place at the table.

"Not yet." Annabelle grabbed a knife from the wooden block and sliced the meatloaf that Emmie probably wouldn't eat.

Two weeks after the meeting of her Girls' Night Out group, Annabelle had begun to think about Thanksgiving. As usual she'd already ordered extra supplies and food for the diner. Most years she worked late that Wednesday, baking pumpkin, mince and apple pies for her customers to pick up on Thursday morning for their family celebrations. Then, exhausted by all the last-minute requests for her baked ham or special cranberry sauce, Annabelle would crawl home and collapse. Her own Thanksgiving was spent sleeping and trying to recover from the preholiday onslaught.

Olivia and Shadow had invited her and Emmie to their first joint Thanksgiving this year at Wilson Cattle, but Annabelle couldn't make up her mind. Being the lone wolf at Girls' Night was one thing; being the extra person at the table on a family occasion was another. Annabelle would feel even more alone than she often did.

From Nick and Ava, Emmie had heard about their feast with all the trimmings, which made Annabelle wonder if Emmie had ever enjoyed a holiday dinner with Sierra—or where.

"I hungry," Emmie said, banging her spoon on the table.

"One more minute, sweetie." Annabelle laid smaller pieces of the fragrant meatloaf on a plate then added green beans and what Emmie called smashed potatoes with a just so "puddle" of gravy that she insisted on.

"We eat with Nick and Ava?" Emmie asked.

"We'll see," she said, one of her own mother's favorite answers that usually meant no.

Knowing that sounded like Nell Sutherland, too, making excuses, she set the plate in front of Emmie who pushed it away. "Don't like this."

"You haven't tried it. Take a bite. If you still don't like it, I'll...fix you something else." She shouldn't have said that. When they read together Emmie was an angel, but she could be unpredictable and Annabelle braced for a howl of protest.

Instead, Emmie brandished her fork. "Finn like this?"

Annabelle was no fool. "I'm sure he does."

Without another word Emmie dug into her meatloaf. She chewed then swallowed and a big smile spread across her face. "Good," she pronounced.

Annabelle grinned. "Yes, when I was your age, my mother made this."

Emmie looked around. "Where she go?"

"She, um, she isn't here anymore."

Emmie studied her plate. "She an an-gle?"

"That's angel, sweetie. Yes, exactly."

"My mama too," she said.

Annabelle put down her fork. This was the first time since Sierra's funeral that Emmie had mentioned her, and maybe she was ready to come to terms with the loss. On the subject of her own mother, Annabelle wasn't. *Can't you do anything right?* she'd asked so many times until Annabelle became afraid to do anything at all. Certainly, as she'd done in the closet under the stairs, she'd drawn into a protective shell. "My mother had a long life," was all she said.

"My mama's pretty."

"Yes she…was. You look like her."

Emmie glanced down at herself. "Why she go away?"

Annabelle crouched beside her. "Baby, she didn't mean to leave you. Is that what you thought?" When Emmie nodded, Annabelle hugged her, feeling her narrow shoulders shake. "Tomorrow, why don't we buy a nice picture frame? We'll look at some photos I have from when she and I were little like you—and try to find some as you remember her. Okay?" Emmie said nothing but she'd stopped trembling. "We'll make a collage…a group of all the pictures, then put it in your room. You can see her whenever you want." *Your room*, she'd said as if Emmie would always be here.

When she pulled back, Emmie looked dubious but then nodded.

"I help you, A-bel."

Annabelle brushed a damp lock of hair from Emmie's face. She wiped the tears from her cheeks. "Thank you. We'll do it together." For another moment, Emmie sat there mulling over their plan or reaching some silent point of acceptance about Sierra. "Whenever you feel sad," Annabelle said, a lump in her throat, "tell me. Okay?"

As Annabelle had never dared to do with her parents about her feelings. Enjoying this brief moment, she gave Emmie another hug then sat across from her.

"I stay with you?" Emmie asked, her blue eyes wide. "All the time?"

Annabelle didn't know how to answer. Despite what Finn thought, it wasn't in Emmie's best interest for her to stay, for Annabelle to try to raise her, probably do a bad job of it and end up in Barren forever. If she couldn't take another course or travel, eventually she would resent Emmie. She *had* to find Emmie's father.

Remembering the conversation with her friends, she cleared her throat. "Emmie, can you tell me where you used to live?" She might not know the exact address but…

With a fierce expression, Emmie swirled gravy through her smashed potatoes. "We always go in a car," she said.

"I know, but you told me you went to Denver once. That big city with all the noise? Where did you stay then? A hotel?"

"We don't stay."

"You mean you drove on to somewhere else?"

Emmie's mouth turned down. She probably didn't have a concept of time. One day might seem the same to her as a month. "Mama had lots of works…"

"She worked for different companies."

Emmie blinked. "What's a comp'ny?"

Annabelle sighed. Pumping a three-year-old for information wasn't something to be proud of, yet this might be the only way to find Emmie's dad. If she remembered anything more about their travels, Annabelle would have something to go on. "It's the place where your mom might have had her job."

Emmie dipped a piece of meatloaf into the gravy-potato mix. "Don't know." She glanced around the kitchen, her gaze on the stove, the counter then the table between them. "But no house."

Unwilling to press the issue, which seemed to upset Emmie, Annabelle didn't respond. She was clearing the table when Emmie hopped down from her chair and skipped into the living room, her attention already on something else. "I get books," she called.

Then she ran back, her blue eyes sparkling. "My mama work for a lion."

FINN HAD LEFT his office ten minutes ago and now, holding his breath, he turned off the road onto a rutted driveway. He'd been here before. This was the Moran farm, five fallow acres, its fences broken down and the house…from here it looked no better than it ever had. His Realtor had made this appointment, but she was showing another property so he'd come alone.

He doubted the place would suit him. The gravel path skimmed close to the abandoned henhouse where earlier this year Grey and Shadow had found a long-missing gun underneath the chickens' modest home, buried in a hollow where no one, even law enforcement, had thought to look ten years ago. That weapon had cleared Grey of any wrongdoing in Jared Moran's death. The path continued on past an old falling-down barn with its doors hanging by the hinges.

Wanda Moran, Shadow's mother, and Jack Hancock, the chef at the café down the street from Annabelle's diner, were waiting for him on the porch. Jack, who liked to pretend he was French, was tall and thin while Wanda, dark-haired like her children, Shadow and Derek, stood no more than five feet tall. They were what the locals called a romantic *item*.

Finn got out of his car. Wanda wasn't smiling and it was Jack who greeted him.

"Thanks for coming out, Sheriff."

"No problem, but I was surprised the farm is for rent." And the question he asked next had been in Finn's mind since his Realtor's call. "I thought the county was taking this property for unpaid back taxes?" Yet Finn frowned. He couldn't remember ever serving the eviction notice.

Wanda's face turned color. "Well, there may have been some rethinking."

Finn tried to gauge her expression. "Let me guess. Grey Wilson paid the taxes."

She lifted a shoulder. "He and Shadow did—one good thing about their marriage. I'm trying to overlook his part in Jared's death, but I'm still not his biggest fan." The accidental shooting of Wanda's eldest son had taken place at Wilson Cattle. Jared, Derek and Grey had all been there, involved in the tragedy. "I didn't want to be obligated to the Wilsons. I could accept help from my daughter, though."

"Then you didn't lose the farm after all."

Wanda looked away. "This place is the only real thing I own. For the money involved in back taxes, I couldn't let it go to the county and get sold at auction even when that meant taking from Grey."

Finn eyed the dirt yard, the one-car garage at the side of the house. If he ignored the fact that Derek had once lived here, he could imagine its potential. For an instant he could almost see Emmie running across the yard, Annabelle calling her to dinner from the front porch… Was he crazy? Unless— until—he found justice for Caro and Alex, some peace for himself, he couldn't even think of a future. Not that Annabelle would be around then anyway.

"I'd have a short commute from here to the station," he said at last. "Sarge would have his room to run." *But just being here reminds me of Derek…and Eduardo Sanchez.* "Let's take a look," Finn said though he didn't have high hopes. As they walked the property, Jack fell into step beside him. Wanda went ahead, pointing out this and that, like a tour guide—which only made Finn think again of Annabelle.

Inside the house, Finn walked through

the rooms, from the shabby living area and kitchen—it was one space and likely a first of the open concept idea that was so popular now—down the short hall to the one bath then back toward the front of the house. One of the bedrooms had been Derek's. Finn knew his father had been a hard man and not always an honest one. Could that explain Derek's behavior? Finn had never considered that before.

They found Wanda in the kitchen staring out the window. With a resigned look in her eyes she turned. She didn't seem to like Finn. "I'd rent furnished," she said, "if I rent at all."

Jack smiled. "Second thoughts, *mon petit choux*?" he said. "Let's not be delusional." He waved a hand at the old recliner whose sagging seat nearly reached the floor. "Your furniture is not worth a single franc, or should I say euro?"

Wanda bristled. "That chair belonged to my dead husband. It has sentimental value. So does the rest."

"I can appreciate that," Finn put in, starting to reconsider the old cabin by the creek instead.

She glared at him. "Not sure I want the

sheriff who *intended* to give me some eviction notice living in my home, not to mention that *sheriff* has something against my Derek."

"Wanda." Jack stepped forward, putting an arm around her shoulders. "Calm down. We talked about this. You don't need the house any longer. Derek finally moved out too—more or less," he said, "and even your chickens are happier at my place. Why cling to something that belongs to yesterday?"

To Finn's surprise, her eyes filled. "It's the only home I ever knew."

"Until you moved in with me. Be reasonable."

Finn held up a hand. "I know how painful this—even renting—can be. When I sold my home in Chicago, the memories—good and bad—rose up to choke me." He'd been eager to never see the house he'd shared with Caro and Alex again, to get away from the everlasting vision of them lying in the driveway, the sound of gunshots echoing down the narrow space between his and his neighbor's house. Yet... "It was like letting go, forgetting everything that happened there, everything that was a part of me." He still hadn't left it behind. Because of Jared's shooting death, Wanda must feel the same way.

She gazed at him for a too-long moment. In the months she'd lived with Jack, Wanda had begun a new chapter in her life and found the love that had long been denied her with Derek's father. But if she wasn't ready...

She shrugged out from under Jack's touch then leveled a hard look at Finn. "All right. You can have it. For the rental price I set." She marched through the living room, not even glancing at her husband's old recliner. "You want me to turn over a new leaf, Jack, I will." Then she turned again to Finn. "But if you want the roof or the fence repaired, Sheriff, that's on you. That's the deal. I'm done."

Finn followed her and Jack out onto the falling-down porch. He wasn't sure he'd gotten that good a bargain, and the rent was more than he wanted to pay, but it seemed he and Sarge had a new place to live.

The first thing he'd do—remembering Derek—would be to change the locks.

ANNABELLE WAS LATE for work, which almost never happened, or hadn't until she'd become

Emmie's temporary guardian. She'd phoned
earlier to tell her prep cook she needed to
drop Emmie at Shadow's house for the day,
but getting Emmie dressed and in the car
had taken far longer than she'd scheduled.
Until she found Emmie's father, Annabelle
needed a better solution for her care.

She was still puffing like a steam engine
when she rushed into the diner and found
Finn waiting for her. For a second, she froze,
then went on into her office to hang up her
coat.

She hadn't seen him since the doughnut
episode a few weeks ago, but she supposed
he hadn't changed his mind about what was
best for Emmie—meaning Annabelle.

Finn had followed her. He stood in her
doorway, and Annabelle wanted to tell him
to go away. Their laughter over Emmie's
doughnut hadn't eased her memory of being
dismissed before at his office or what he'd
said about Emmie staying with her.

Two could play that game. She turned, but
she never managed to block out the sight of
him, broad shoulders, dark hair, aviator sunglasses. "Yes, what is it? I got a late start this
morning—"

"I won't keep you." He leaned against the

doorframe, the motion pulling his shirt taut over his shoulders and biceps. He reached into his pocket for a folded sheet of paper. "I've spoken to the rest of those DAs who brought charges against Sierra. These are their contact numbers. All you need to do, like with the first warrant, is to send them—"

"The death certificate." She took the paper without glancing up and scanned it. Why should she care that after their brief laughter at Emmie's face smeared with doughnut glaze, she hadn't seen him again? That Finn was obviously eating his meals elsewhere? The problem was hers. "Thank you. I'll take care of it. Looks like I'll need more copies."

He came into the office then shut the door. "Annabelle," he said again. "You know I wish all this hadn't happened—Sierra's death, those warrants, Emmie being orphaned—and I wish the fallout hadn't landed on you."

"I didn't know," she admitted.

Finn stared down at his boots. "Anyway, I've followed Sierra's trail to the corporations that filed the charges. In every case she was suspect, all right. I wish that wasn't true either but it is. She had a bad habit of skimming money, padding expense accounts—

and by the time they found out she'd already moved on. No one, sad to say, spoke kindly of her. They just want their money back. Not that they have a chance of getting it."

"Which only proves your point about her," Annabelle said.

She immediately regretted the words. It didn't do her any good to give Finn the cold shoulder.

"What if you called those same people again," she said. "Ask about Sierra's contacts within each company? Maybe they'd be willing to point us to a friend, some confidante of hers. Sierra might have mentioned Emmie's father."

"I'll try," he said. "No one seemed interested in talking to me about anything except that missing money."

Annabelle glanced at her computer screen as an image of Prague rolled past in her slide show. And remembered Emmie's comments last night. *Mama had lots of works* and *my mama work for a lion.*

She told Finn, who said, "That's interesting. Could be the last job Sierra left in a hurry before she headed for Barren to see you—or whoever else she wanted to tie up those loose ends with." Finn's eyes, rimmed by thick lashes, darkened almost to brown. "Annabelle. Wait. Since Sierra was in the events business, what better place than Las Vegas? Caro and I went there for a long weekend before Alex was born. It's like Disney World for grown-ups. Have you been there?"

"No."

"Vegas is all about big conventions, which would suit Sierra perfectly. This may be a long shot, but she might even have worked for the MGM Grand. The resort's not one of those that charged her, but Emmie may have been onto something." He cracked a smile. "Their corporate trademark is a roaring lion. In Vegas, they actually have big cats on display."

Annabelle knew about the logo from movies, but she'd never been to Nevada or anywhere near a casino. She envied Finn his trip.

"Real lions?"

"Yeah, and they would have made quite the impression on a child. You can walk around underneath them in the glass enclosure—like in one of the newer aquariums. Mostly, they're sleeping so Emmie might not feel afraid but they're really something to see."

Annabelle said, "I'll put them on my bucket list."

"And I'll put in a call to the resort. Maybe HR will talk to me. It would be just the spot for a woman who worked the convention circuit. In fact, she might see that as the epitome of success to have gotten a job there."

"Thank you, Finn." This time she meant it. "If that leads to finding Emmie's father, I'm all for it. I haven't gotten anywhere since I last saw you." Annabelle ignored the twinge of regret that flowed through her. Locating Emmie's dad meant honoring what amounted to a deathbed promise to Sierra, hoping he'd be eager to take responsibility for Emmie, and that she would be well provided for. Only a few months later than she'd planned, Annabelle would be free to leave town.

So why did she suddenly feel that when Emmie left, Annabelle's heart would break?

In the brief silence Finn opened the door. "Sorry about the doughnuts. Did Emmie eat the rest of them?"

"Oh yeah," she said. "She didn't seem to feel guilty that I didn't get even one."

They exchanged smiles. For a moment, like that other night, they were joined in their shared affection and concern for a little girl who had lost her mother. It didn't mean Annabelle and Finn could have anything more. It didn't mean she wanted to stay—or that Finn had changed his mind about letting anyone into his life.

"Tell Emmie I'll bring her more doughnuts."

The sparkle in his eyes told her he'd been kidding. "Don't you dare," she said with a laugh, and at his gaze warmth spread through her straight to her soon-to-be-broken heart. Until Finn stepped out into the hall then said over his shoulder, like a challenge, "See you at the ranch on Thanksgiving."

CHAPTER THIRTEEN

WHEN HE COULD eat no more, Finn pushed back from the table in the dining room at Wilson Cattle. And glanced at Annabelle. She wore a pretty autumn-hued dress that brought out her eyes and matched the holiday pattern of Emmie's skirt. Frankly, he'd been amazed to find them here. When he'd mentioned Thanksgiving, Annabelle's face had closed as if she'd slammed a door.

In fact, he was half surprised at himself to be sharing the holiday with his newfound friends, a first celebration of any kind for Finn since tragedy had struck in Chicago. Yet, having accepted the invitation, he felt less…alone, less isolated.

"I'm finished," he said, smiling at the people around the table. Among them were Blossom, her husband, Logan, their baby and Sam Hunter, Logan's grandfather, who'd come from the Circle H next door. Two of their ranch hands were seated beside each other. Olivia and Sawyer, who was Logan's twin, plus her son Nick, were here along with Grey who was Olivia's brother. His wife, Shadow, their daughter Ava, Grey's father and stepmother, and of course Annabelle and Emmie completed the group. Finn had trouble keeping everyone straight.

Derek was notably missing. Finn had heard he'd joined his mother and Jack for Thanksgiving pheasant.

The huge table at Wilson Cattle was laden with food when Finn arrived: golden turkey, platters of roast beef from Grey's Black Angus herd, Virginia ham with a honey-mustard glaze and plump gulf shrimp. Side dishes—candied sweet yams, creamy "smashed" potatoes, which would please Emmie, roasted root vegetables, Annabelle's cranberry relish and different dressings, one with oysters—adorned the long buffet and side tables. The warm air smelled of the yeasty dinner rolls Blossom had brought.

Now most dishes stood empty, though that didn't mean the food was gone. The ranch kitchen held even more.

"I'm taking orders for dessert," Shadow said, a notepad in hand. She was co-hostess with Olivia for the first time since Shadow's marriage to Grey. His stepmother Liza had demurred, saying she was still a part-time resident, although her Dallas condo had recently sold and she and Grey's father would move to the ranch after the closing. "We have pumpkin, apple, pecan and mince. Vanilla ice cream, whipped cream…" Shadow trailed off as more satisfied groans sounded and Grey's dad, looking distinguished as always, patted his stomach.

"I'm ready for round two," Everett Wilson said, touching Shadow's arm. Apparently the longstanding feud between the Wilsons and Morans over Jared's death had been mostly resolved, except for Wanda. "Put me down for pecan, Shadow. Heavy on the whipped cream."

"Everett," Liza said in a softly chiding tone.

"I'll watch my waistline tomorrow," he said, "when the leftovers are gone."

"Next week," Grey put in, sharing a private look with his daughter Ava beside him. As Shadow passed by, he hooked an arm around her waist. "Sit down. I'll get the desserts."

But Shadow sent him a teasing glance. "Follow me."

When Ava offered to go with them, they quickly said "No, thanks," then disappeared into the kitchen. With her nose wrinkled, Ava said "Eeeww, kissing," and the whole group laughed. Finn did too, but a fresh wave of sorrow washed over him. He'd always loved Thanksgiving with Caro and Alex. There wouldn't be another.

"The honeymoon continues," Everett said. "Liza and I announce ourselves whenever we enter a room."

She swatted his shoulder. "That is not true. Ava, don't listen to your grandfather."

Looking curious, Emmie climbed onto Finn's lap. She framed his face in her sticky hands. "What's a honeymoon?" Which produced more laughter.

"Grown-up stuff," he said. Even with his arms around Emmie, Finn was already wondering when he could make his excuses and go—as he'd abandoned Annabelle at Sierra's funeral. He'd enjoyed the meal more than he expected, but there was nothing like a raucous family gathering to make him miss Caro and Alex even more. He glanced at Annabelle and noticed she looked the same way. Was she wishing Sierra could be here, too?

Finn rose from the table and put Emmie

in his chair. "Think I'll step outside before dessert. Annabelle, could I have a word?"

Curious gazes followed them as Finn shut the door then inhaled a quick lungful of cold air. "Going to snow soon," he said, "but nothing like Chicago in the winter."

Annabelle, he remembered, had a poster of the skyline on her bedroom wall. She stayed in the shelter provided near the door, and Finn turned to face her from the railing. He crossed his arms to ward off the chill inside and out and tried not to notice the glint of light on her hair, the warmth in her eyes that seemed to heat the colder air around them, or at least inside him.

"Lake Michigan," he said. "The wind blows hard enough to stop you in your tracks. You have to duck into a store every hundred feet or so to get warm enough to go on."

"You must miss your family today," she said, but then she didn't mention Sierra. "My parents didn't celebrate Thanksgiving like this," she said, gesturing toward the house. "They always kept the diner open." *We have no time for holidays. Get to work, Annabelle,* she could hear her mother say. "They made turkey and all the trimmings for anyone who stopped by, and a number of people did. So I helped." She looked past him at the nearby field. "I suggested they serve free of charge, but even Thanksgiving was an occasion to make money, especially from people who had nowhere else to go."

Finn crossed his legs at the ankles. Annabelle was too easy to talk to. "On Thanksgiving my dad usually found something to complain about. He wanted to be on the job, and by the time we sat down to eat no one was talking. It was better when my uncle was there—he was on the force too and knew how to handle my father—but Pat never married, had no kids and after a quick drop-in to get his to-go bag of my mom's turkey, he worked a double shift so other cops could be with their families."

"He sounds like a kind man," Annabelle said.

"Uncle Pat got me through my teens." When his father's neglect had made Finn think about a life of crime to send his dad's blood pressure through the ceiling, Pat had stepped in to cool things off. "He taught me to fish, took me to baseball games and my first rock concert, watched me play football, talked me down whenever my temper got out of hand…"

"And you followed in his footsteps, too. When did you become a cop?"

"Right out of college. Majored in criminal justice." He'd never expected murder to strike at home, though, to see crime scene tape stretched around his yard. His throat closed. "What about you, Annabelle?"

"I didn't go to college. My parents needed me at the diner, and the older they got, the more they relied on me. Then my dad's heart began to fail. After he died, my mother's health declined pretty quickly too, and before I knew it they were both gone. They passed away before you came to Barren."

"Leaving you the diner you don't want."

She studied the herd of grazing Angus, picking through the last sparse sprigs of green grass. "Would you believe it? My Realtor hasn't shown it even once. I keep hoping but…small town, few possible takers." She paused. "Today is all the more difficult because I feel guilty. I closed the diner as my parents wouldn't have, and I keep wondering what those people who always count on it for their holiday meal must be thinking." She looked back at him. "I donated meals to the local shelter, but I just couldn't work again—and I wanted Emmie to have something special today." Her only Thanksgiving here with Annabelle? At least she had that.

Finn gazed into the middle distance. "My son loved Thanksgiving. His first year he ate pureed turkey—baby food. The next he was old enough to have us cut his meat, enjoy 'smashed' potatoes like Emmie and screw up his face at cranberry sauce, which he termed *no*. Then not long after his third Thanksgiving, he was…" Gone. Why was he telling her this? He didn't want to ruin what was a touchy holiday for Annabelle, too. Why did he keep opening up to her?

"I'm so sorry about your family, Finn. Were you there when it happened?"

He took a breath, felt the knot in his throat tighten like a noose.

The nightmare he lived with now threatened to overwhelm him again, but all at once the words poured from him. "We'd just gotten out of the car. I took Alex from his seat, set him down and stepped back to get the big bag we carried everywhere with his stuff in it—when another car drew up at the curb. Two guys got out with guns. There was no time to react. I mean, I think I yelled at Caroline to get down but she was already moving toward Alex." He swallowed. "She must have sensed before I did what was happening, and her first thought was of our little boy. She was a great mother."

Annabelle's gaze filled with empathy.

Lost in the memory, he said, "It was over before I moved. A few quick double taps—and they were lying there on the gravel." Bleeding out. Finn swept one hand across his eyes. "I'll never forget that sight. I see it all the time. Driving home, on my way to work, pulling into a parking space…in my nightmares. Over and over…" He took another quick gulp of air that didn't seem to fill his lungs. "I keep replaying the whole scene, slowing it down, speeding it up, but there's never anything I can do—in time—to help them."

"You shouldn't blame yourself."

"But in a way it *was* my fault—and in that moment my training failed me. Days before, my partner and I had made a raid on The Brothers. But he—Cooper's not married and doesn't live near his mother—didn't make the same target I did. They retaliated against me instead through Caro and Alex."

"Because they knew that was the worst way to hurt you. With your family."

Why was he telling her all this? He couldn't take it back.

"It should have been me instead," he murmured then turned away. "Go inside, Annabelle. Please."

But no, she came toward him, letting the cold hit her like a slap and penetrate the pretty dress she'd worn for Thanksgiving, raising goose bumps on her bare arms and…before the thought could make itself known he'd turned to her, before he could keep from letting her see the devastation that must show on his face, before he could step away from her embrace. And then her arms were around him and she was weeping softly too. Finn tried to brush the tears from her cheeks but they kept coming like his, down his face and into the collar of his shirt, and he stopped wondering when she would leave Barren and the diner and Emmie behind, and all he could think of was being here with her on the freezing-cold porch with the oh-so-welcome heat of her against him. The last person he'd held like this had been Caro. He should pull away.

"Annabelle," he began, but she raised her

face to his, looked into his eyes for what seemed to be a long moment. Then her lips met his and they were kissing and Finn couldn't think of a single reason why they shouldn't.

For the first time, he wished Annabelle would change her mind about leaving Barren, would decide to give up the search for Emmie's father and keep her, raise her right here among the friends who were her family now, and he could feel what it would be like to really care about someone again. If he dared.

ON MONDAY MORNING Annabelle wheeled into the parking lot behind Barren's one-and-only day care center. Shadow, who'd recommended it, had assured her during Thanksgiving dinner that the facility had a good reputation. Because many local residents preferred to keep their little ones home on the ranch until kindergarten, it wasn't that crowded. Emmie should get lots of attention, which Annabelle couldn't give her during the day.

A few days after she'd kissed Finn on the porch at Wilson Cattle, Annabelle was still reeling. Had that been simply mutual comfort for their painful pasts? Did he have an interest in her after all?

Finn had an even sadder history than hers, one he might never overcome. And Annabelle had kissed him first. She couldn't let a kiss he probably didn't welcome complicate things.

The instant Emmie laid eyes on Mary Whitman, the director, an energetic twenty-something who'd taken over the center from her mother, Emmie burst into tears.

"You'll be fine," Annabelle tried to tell her. Although her friends always stepped in to help, they had their own children and businesses to consider. Before they burned out trying to juggle Emmie, too, Annabelle wanted to place her in a stable situation while she was at work. Here, in this inviting space, Emmie could play and learn while Annabelle saw to the diner—until it sold.

She surveyed the large room filled with toys, books and games. Low tables dotted the space, and child-sized beanbag chairs. She saw a dress-up area with racks of gowns, dozens of glittery tiaras on shelves, colorful boas that trailed feathers everywhere, pirate and soldier and firefighter outfits.

Emmie shrank against Annabelle's side.

Elizabeth Barnes, the mayor's wife, stood nearby talking to her little boy, obviously giving him a pep talk. Annabelle knew her but only by sight. The other woman glanced up and met Annabelle's gaze. "He doesn't want to stay," Elizabeth murmured.

Annabelle tilted her head toward Emmie. "Any suggestions?"

"I told Harry this would be easy." She stroked one hand over the boy's hair, fair like his father's. Elizabeth wore her dark hair in a sleek bob. "I didn't count on Seth balking, but I should have expected this. I never know how he'll react."

As if they were both mothers, Annabelle sent her an understanding look. Emmie had seemed eager to go to "school" like Nick and Ava, but now she had second thoughts about being separated from the familiar. What to do?

Emmie kept casting shy looks at Seth whose lower lip jutted out. He tugged at Elizabeth's hand.

When the director turned from another child who'd been having trouble getting out of his little jacket, relief flashed over Elizabeth's face and her green eyes brightened.

Holding the boy's jacket, Mary approached

then bent down to the children's level. She pointed at the dress-up corner. "Seth, would you like to try on that police officer's uniform?"

He glanced over at Emmie as if to ask her permission.

Annabelle relaxed a bit. She'd quickly learned the art of distraction when dealing with a child. Silently, she thanked Mary. "Look, Emmie, there's a kitchen, too. Like my diner. Could you bake some muffins, sweetie? I won't be gone long. We can share them when I get back."

Mary nodded her approval, but tears streamed down Emmie's face. "No." Her gaze homed in on the police officer's uniform and she swiped at her cheeks. "Finn can play with me?"

"Let me try," Mary said, then to Emmie, "Maybe your friend Finn will be here later. Regression is normal," she told Annabelle and Elizabeth, her voice low.

Annabelle tidied Emmie's hair, pulling the soft blond strands through her fingers, wondering if she was doing the right thing. But worrying about Emmie at the diner instead of here, concerned she might rush out the door into the street or burn herself on the huge industrial stove, had never worked. She couldn't keep taking Emmie with her or using her friends to babysit.

"Maybe I shouldn't leave her today," Annabelle said anyway. "She's already been through so much…"

"I'm sorry about her mother, Annabelle. But, please, don't change your mind." Mary looked at both of them. "You either, Elizabeth. Seth and Emmie will have a great time with us and make new friends. The hardest part for both of you will be walking out that door."

She was right about that. Would Annabelle harm Emmie more by leaving her here? A three-year-old seemed to be a confusing mixture of angel and demon, sometimes all in the same minute. Annabelle chose to remember the cherubic part.

"I'll keep them with me," Mary said, "until they're ready to approach the other children. Curiosity is a great leveler at this age." She turned to the children. "Would you two like to play?"

Emmie resisted for a moment then took Mary's hand. And so did Seth.

Talking softly, Mary led Emmie and Seth across the room. Midway to the dress-up corner, both children pulled away and Annabelle's heart rate leaped. This wasn't going to work. But instead of running back to her and Elizabeth, the kids sank down together onto a beanbag chair, talking, and when Mary lifted her gaze with a faint nod toward the door, Annabelle took the cue. She and Elizabeth stepped outside.

Annabelle breathed a sigh of relief. "We did it."

Elizabeth gave a shaky laugh. "We did," she agreed. "I hope."

The door hadn't shut behind them when Annabelle heard Emmie shriek. Her steps faltered. *Keep going,* a little voice said inside, *or she'll never adjust. I'm not really being cruel.* But her heart thundered all the way to her car, and she imagined Elizabeth's did too as they waved goodbye to each other.

As she tried to start the engine Annabelle's hand shook so hard she couldn't get the key in the ignition. What if Mary Whitman had been wrong? But in Annabelle's view, if not Sawyer's, Emmie's language skills were lagging. The center, Mary had told her, might improve Emmie's skills. But what if she ran away in panic from here instead of from the diner?

With a toot of her horn Elizabeth drove past, and Annabelle forced herself to stop obsessing about potential disaster. So far, she had managed, and she would keep on managing until she found Emmie's father. She had to, no matter what Finn's opinion was— she wouldn't think of putting Emmie into foster care—or her grand plan to travel the world would become another unread chapter in her life. Unless she wanted to drag Emmie around, and perhaps risk her social development, she would have to remain in Barren.

As she drove off she could all but hear Finn saying she was the best person for Emmie, but Annabelle imagined she could still hear Emmie crying. Hurt and furious that Annabelle had abandoned her.

Like Sierra.

CHAPTER FOURTEEN

CHANGING THE LOCKS for his new home obviously hadn't done the trick.

Finn had just pulled in the driveway with another bunch of boxes to unload when he'd spied the Chevy Nova parked beside the house. There could be no doubt as to its owner, and by the time Finn jerked open the front door he was fuming. He should have expected this. Derek Moran wasn't known to respect other people's property, including Grey's cattle. Did he think he could trample someone else's privacy?

For a second he wished he'd brought Sarge with him. "How did you get in?"

Hearing Finn approach, Derek spun around in the center of the living room, his hands full of the framed pictures that had been on the mantel of the fireplace that didn't work.

"Usual way." His drawl riled Finn even more. "I jiggled the doorknob—and I'm in.

Mama always scolded me for not taking my key."

Finn should have bought a new dead bolt. The locksmith had warned him he couldn't truly secure the entry as it was. The old door was too fragile, and the keys hadn't kept Derek out. "In my job we call that breaking and entering," Finn said. "Since you're already 'in,' take your family mementoes—if that's why you're here—and get out. If there's anything more you want, call me and I'll be home when you come for them."

"I'll take them now," Derek said.

Finn's attention stayed razor-sharp on Derek. He'd learned his lesson with Sanchez and wouldn't let another *criminal* get the upper hand.

At least this distraction would keep him from thinking about the kiss Annabelle had laid on him Thanksgiving night and Finn's all-too-willing response. Not to mention his inability to keep his worst memories to himself. He could have drawn back, prevented that kiss, but he hadn't.

Now he didn't feel as though he'd been disloyal to Caro; he felt as if he'd betrayed her with another woman. Hauling his mind back to the present, he dogged Derek's footsteps.

Finn had walked the property last night with Sarge at his side, and he had to admit he liked the notion of having these five acres to himself. He could see having roots here. Maybe that was what he'd wanted rather than isolation. "The lease I signed gives me one thing, Derek—the right to use this space. You've violated my privacy."

Derek sneered. "Privacy? My daddy claimed he could come into any room in this house whenever he wanted, welcome or not."

"Your father's not here."

"Neither is my brother," Derek pointed out. "You should be glad I came to pick up the rest of my stuff and a few things Mama left. Then we'll be out of your way."

Finn doubted that. Like a bad penny— like Eduardo Sanchez—Derek always turned up. He ambled through the house into his old bedroom, which Finn planned to use as a home office. Finn stood in the doorway, watching Derek pick up a police manual Finn had left on the dresser. Derek passed it from hand to hand before he set the book down to choose a tarnished brass trophy of some high school track meet. His or Jared's?

"Mine," he said. "Stop glaring at me. I don't like you and you don't like me. That's okay but I done nothing wrong—at that apartment building, the cemetery, here… Grey trusts me. Why can't you?"

"Because I know what you're capable of even if he doesn't." Derek was one more of the same—like Sanchez. Rustling cattle was no petty theft, and in Finn's experience one crime often led to another worse one. Like The Brothers cutting down Caro and Alex in front of him.

I'm so sorry about your family, Finn, Annabelle had said. Finn shifted his weight.

"If Grey wants to believe in you, I can't stop him."

Carrying the pictures and the trophy, Derek strolled into the hall, casting a look back over his shoulder, probably making sure Finn wouldn't come at him from behind.

His gut in knots, Finn stayed on his heels until Derek breezed through the other rooms, taking a quilt off his mother's bed and wrapping it around his treasures. At the next door he paused to study the faded posters on the walls of hot rods, rodeo stars and a few other celebrities. Jared Moran's idols. The room reminded Finn of Annabelle's with all the travel posters, and for an instant Finn thought he saw tears in Derek's eyes. He juggled his belongings then ripped a poster off the wall. Except for his attitude, Finn might feel sorry for him.

He cleared his throat. "Your brother meant a lot to you."

Derek stayed silent for another moment. "The way our daddy was, I guess Jared became my role model."

Finn followed Derek to the front door. Had that glimpse of his pain been authentic? Like his mother, Derek was leaving the only home he'd ever known, his memories of his brother and Wanda's son. Or was this another act?

From the doorway he tracked Derek to his car then down the rutted lane to the main road. The engine was blowing smoke, and he remembered Grey saying he was saving up to buy that new truck. Finn rapped his knuckles against the doorframe, dislodging a few splinters. The whole frame needed to be replaced, the door, too, and he would have that dead bolt installed.

Number one on his list would be to keep Derek out, but as he'd trailed him through the house Finn had changed his mind about something else.

The rental was to be for one year, but the expanse of land aside, the house needed more than new locks and a door. The roof and fencing had to be replaced, and the kitchen was an outdated disaster. On his first visit after signing the lease, the refrigerator had died a noisy, rattling death. And the one-car garage was falling down.

Finn mentally reviewed his finances. He'd lost money in the move from Chicago—had, in fact, practically given his house there away, as he suspected Annabelle would gladly do with hers—and Stewart County didn't pay him nearly as much for being sheriff as Cook County had paid him as a cop. Still…

He shut the rickety door then locked it behind him. The job would be much bigger than he'd thought—and, as Wanda had said, at his expense. If he made those improvements alone, he'd be into the house for too much money only to move again. Finn had a better idea—number two—and went back inside to call her.

The third item on his list involved Annabelle

Foster. After that kiss, and his betrayal of Caro, he needed to tell her where things stood.

WITH HER PHONE safely out of reach in the humid bathroom, Annabelle wiped beads of perspiration from her forehead. Leaning over the tub, she rinsed Emmie's hair, trying to ignore the howls of protest that had made up their day for one reason or another. In midafternoon she'd had a call from the day care center that Emmie had not only wet her pants but most of her other clothes. It was suggested that Annabelle leave a spare outfit or two for her there tomorrow morning and she'd apologized for not having the foresight to do so. Then, all the way home, Emmie had cried, seeming to lecture Annabelle without words for leaving her in a strange place. At dinner she'd refused to eat a bite of the one-pot goulash Annabelle had served.

She'd managed to overlook Emmie's full dinner plate and taken the silent lashing, but when the doorbell rang now, she felt tempted to swear, something she never did. She'd hoped to get Emmie to bed before Annabelle collapsed. She didn't want a visitor.

Tempted to ignore the bell, she bundled Emmie into a towel and carried her downstairs. She opened the front door to find Finn, jingling the keys in his pocket, and she flushed to the roots of her hair. Would she never stop reacting to him like this? After that Thanksgiving kiss her crush on him seemed worse. Her own fault.

Without warning, wet towel and all, Emmie launched herself at him. Finn caught her but barely in time, and Annabelle saw him flinch. The damp package of little girl fresh from her bath, hair dripping, made Finn step back as Annabelle had thought he would on the porch Thanksgiving night.

Emmie didn't notice. "Finn, I go school!"

"You did?"

"My school." She chattered on about the blocks and books, what appeared to be her new friendship with Seth Barnes, the dress-up area with feather boas, "and I had a crown. They got a kitchen, too!"

Finn smiled. "Sounds about perfect."

"Come in," Annabelle said, waving him inside. This was the most she'd ever heard Emmie say at once. "She's in day care now."

Finn gave up trying to protect his shirt, which was soaked and clinging to his chest. "I'd say that deserves a special prize."

"What?" Emmie wanted to know, all but dancing in Finn's arms.

In the living room he chose the sofa where he'd sat the night Sierra died then sank down with Emmie in his embrace. "Check my shirt pocket." Puzzled, Annabelle wondered why he was here now. Thanksgiving was still on her mind, the awful tragedy his family had suffered, and of course that kiss. Was he also sorry he'd confided in her about his wife and son?

"Look, A-bel!" Emmie held out a ring of brightly colored plastic keys. The toy struck Annabelle as more for a young toddler, one more sign that Emmie's development was lagging, but Finn knew more than she did about children. Hopping off Finn's lap, Emmie ran to the nearest door, which happened to be the living room closet under the stairs—the site of Annabelle's worst memories.

To her horror, Emmie tried to fit a key into the lock and Annabelle cried out sharply, "No!"

Her mouth set, Emmie tried again. "I open it."

Shaking, Annabelle couldn't take her eyes

from the closet. "I said *no*. We don't go in there. Come away, Emmie."

She felt Finn's gaze on her before it went to the closet then back to Emmie, her blue eyes wide, lips puckered. "I saw these at the store when I had new keys made for my place. Thought Emmie might like them." He paused. "Alex played with his until…"

Finn went silent. Keeping her eyes on Emmie, Annabelle filled the awkwardness by asking, "You found a rental house?"

"I just bought the old Moran farm." Finn told her he'd talked to Wanda earlier, and with his Realtor's help, they'd agreed on a price he could afford. "I've moved in—I'll rent until the closing—and unpacked a few boxes, started throwing out stuff Wanda and Derek didn't want. You wouldn't need some old furniture, would you?"

She chuckled. "I could offer you the same."

He frowned a little. "I still have a storage unit in Chicago. I should empty it, decide what to keep and what to get rid of, but I'm not ready."

The locker must contain his wife's and son's belongings, maybe furniture from the house they had shared. Unwanted memories, like this closet. Annabelle didn't want to know what was in there. "That won't be easy, but I was glad to see the last of my family's personal things go to a better home."

Emmie looked at Annabelle then jabbed the plastic key at the door lock again. When it didn't fit, she marched across the room then flung the set at Annabelle, the ring bouncing off her chest. "Hey," Finn said. "We don't throw things at people."

Those words had burst from Finn without his having to think, and she supposed he'd said the same to his little boy under similar circumstances. Then he seemed to realize what he'd said and drew Emmie toward him. "Sorry, not my job to scold you."

That didn't seem to faze Emmie. "I come to your house?" she asked, turning her back on Annabelle. "You got a doggie?"

"His name is Sarge," Finn said, looking as if he wanted to squirm.

"Do he bite?"

"No, he likes kids."

Emmie wrapped her arms around Finn's neck. "I like that doggie."

"I'm sure you would," he said but didn't issue an invitation. Emmie yawned, and Finn rose to his feet with her in his arms.

He looked as if he welcomed an end to the discussion about his new home. "How about I tuck you in bed?"

Annabelle handed her the keys and Emmie dropped her head onto Finn's broad shoulder and let him carry her upstairs. By the time he and Annabelle nestled her in the covers, the ring still in her hand, Emmie was fast asleep, curled around the lamb Finn had given her the night of Sierra's accident. She naturally gravitated to him, probably because she associated him with safety the night of Sierra's crash. Annabelle feared it was becoming a habit, one she would have to break if Finn didn't.

On their way downstairs, he laid a hand on her shoulder. "What was that about? She couldn't have unlocked that closet."

Annabelle couldn't answer. He might think she was crazy.

"She's a good kid," Finn said.

"Yes she is." Annabelle reached the bottom of the steps. "But just when I think Emmie and I are on the right track, something happens—like day care today—and I realize how little I know about caring for her." Annabelle's mother would be only too glad to remind her of that. She added, "I couldn't believe my ears when she told you she'd had a great time at day care. That's not what I heard."

"Parental punishment," Finn murmured. "Obviously, she wanted you to pay for sticking her in a new situation."

Annabelle felt tempted to remind him she wasn't a mother, but the words wouldn't come. "You've been there."

"I have—and I'd give everything to be there again with Alex," he said then seemed to shake himself from the memory. "Giving Emmie those keys wasn't the only reason I came by tonight. I finally got through to the MGM Grand resort where the HR person was happy to give me a report on Sierra. Apparently she did plan one event for them. When someone said she was skimming—and security at the Vegas casinos is tight, to put it mildly—they didn't find any proof but they still fired her maybe as a precaution."

"Did HR have a forwarding address for her?"

Finn shook his head. "No, and it seems she didn't make many friends there." His dark-lashed eyes brightened. "Except one, a dealer in their casino who also left the Grand at the same time to take another job at the Bellagio across the Strip."

"Do you have her name?"

"His," Finn said. "The HR person claimed Sierra and this guy had a brief fling. After suspicion fell on her, it fell on him, too, and when Sierra abruptly left town, their affair ended."

Annabelle's heart drummed. "He's the connection I need. What did he say?"

"I haven't reached him. They gave me a landline number and his cell but he didn't answer either one. I left a voice mail, but he hasn't called me back. No one wants to hear from a sheriff. But the affair happened about four years ago, give or take."

"Then this man could be Emmie's father!"

"Don't get your hopes up. We haven't found him yet."

"Finn, he could be the key—"

"Or like the ones I gave Emmie—one that doesn't fit."

Annabelle refused to be derailed. "This is the first real lead we've had. If he's wary of speaking to someone in law enforcement, then let me call."

He mulled that over. "All right. But try not to spook him."

"I wouldn't think of it, *Sheriff.*"

His gaze holding hers, Finn smiled. Then, just as quickly, it faded. "Annabelle, the other reason I came is about—"

"Thanksgiving," she said for him, certain she knew what came next. "I apologize. I was saddened to hear more about your family and the only comfort I could provide was to…hold you."

"You don't need to apologize," he said. "I mean, you *did* kiss me first but…"

Finn didn't go on. There seemed to be more he wanted to say, but without looking at her, he murmured a quick goodbye then bolted for the door.

He was gone before Annabelle could move, but she hadn't missed the panicky look in his eyes.

She could guess what it was he hadn't said.

CHAPTER FIFTEEN

ANNABELLE KISSED EMMIE'S forehead then closed the book they'd read. In the dimness of the room, by the glow of Emmie's night-light shaped like Belle from *Beauty and the Beast*, she lay already asleep, her lashes swept across her closed lids like a delicate fan, one arm around the lamb Finn had given her. With her guard down, Emmie looked sweet and innocent, which she was most of the time, and the warm rush of feeling for her nearly buckled Annabelle's knees.

When Emmie left to be with her dad, who-ever he was, and Annabelle was once again alone in this house until it sold, she would more than miss her. Her heart already ached. In roughly six weeks they'd formed a bond. Who knew Annabelle would be able to cope this long? *Hey, Mom, look at me.*

She went into the hall and down the stairs. If she got an answer from either number Finn had given her last night, Annabelle might solve the mystery of Emmie's dad.

The first, a landline, belonged to a woman who had no idea who Annabelle was looking for; the person had obviously moved and she now had his former number. When no one picked up at the other, Annabelle left a brief message on the cell. "Hi," she began then identified herself. "I need to talk to you. It's very important. Please call me back." She recited her number and sat back in her chair, wondering what to do next—until the phone she was holding suddenly rang.

The only people who called her were usually unwanted marketing ploys, so she barely checked the caller ID. She'd tell the person she wasn't interested in a home security system, a timeshare or a medical alert bracelet then hang up. "Hello?" She expected to hear a long pause typical of such cold calls, but to her surprise a deep male voice spoke.

"You called me just now? Who are you? What's this about?"

Annabelle told him her name again then took a breath and mentioned Sierra. "I'm really hoping you can help me. I understand you knew my cousin in Las Vegas and the only contact from there I have is yours."

"Sierra Hartwell?" he echoed as if he'd never heard the name.

Annabelle's spirits sank. The landline had been a Las Vegas area code and she'd been so excited. But the cell's code was different, one Annabelle didn't recognize. Maybe this was another dead end after all, but she had to see it through. She tried to refresh his memory. "I'm told she worked for the Grand around the same time you did."

"Until she got me fired. That was a long time ago. I'm not in Vegas now."

Fearing he was about to hang up, Annabelle rushed on. "Please, hear me out." Another dead end would put her right back where she'd started. "Someone there said you were, uh, more than friends…and when Sierra passed away—"

"She's *dead*?" He hesitated. "Wait, is this why some sheriff tried to reach me?"

Annabelle's hands were shaking. This man did know her cousin. "Yes, I'm sorry I didn't tell you that first." Trying to choose her words, she gave him a halting recap of events, ending with "Sierra didn't leave a will, as far as I can tell, or make any arrangements for her child if something happened to her which is why the county sheriff here in Kansas and I have been trying to reach you. Sierra's daughter is staying with me—"

"No will? That sounds like Sierra." His voice had turned wary. "She had a kid?"

Annabelle assumed his question was rhetorical. "Yes, but I can't keep her permanently. If I can find Emmie's father, she should be with him. Is there a possibility—"

"Hold on," he said. "You think *I'm* the guy?"

Her palms damp, Annabelle reeled off the dates Finn had given her for Las Vegas. "I understand you had a relationship."

He snorted. "That what you call it? Sierra and I had, maybe, one weekend together before she messed up everything. She *stole* from the resort and because of what they termed 'our relationship,' I was in trouble right along with her—like some accomplice. No way," he said. "It was me who turned her in, anonymously of course. Sierra Hartwell was a looker, but she was also a liar, a cheat and a thief. Didn't take me, or anyone else, long to figure that out. Don't try to pin her kid on me."

Annabelle stiffened. Her heart was pounding. Was he lying, as Sierra obviously had? This newest accusation against her cousin wasn't any easier to absorb than Finn's opinion of Sierra. But what if this man *was* Emmie's dad? The timing was right…even when she didn't like how this was going, and she had to press him further. "A weekend would be more than enough time to father her little girl," she said, casting a glance up to the second floor where Emmie was sleeping.

His tone had a sharper edge. "We took precautions, okay? I'm not about to get saddled with a mistake like that."

Annabelle bit her tongue to keep from giving him a piece of her mind and saying something she'd regret. Now she hoped he wasn't Emmie's biological father. She settled for telling him, "Precautions sometimes fail and I wouldn't call Emmie a mistake."

Had Finn been right? Even if this man agreed, she wouldn't turn an innocent child over to someone who didn't want her, someone who might spend his nights in a gambling casino rather than at home. Who would care for Emmie then? And what if he bounced around from place to place as Sierra had? *No house*, Emmie had told her. Surely, when Sierra extracted Annabelle's promise, she didn't want to see her daughter with this man. He couldn't be Emmie's dad.

She didn't want him to be now. This wasn't what she'd hoped for at all.

"I'm sorry you feel that way. In fact," Annabelle said, her voice brittle, "it makes me wonder why I phoned you in the first place."

"Couldn't agree more," he said. "Good luck, lady. Hope you find the right sucker."

Her mouth set, Annabelle struggled to contain her disappointment. Where could her search go next? She'd held such hope those two numbers, one of them in Vegas, would lead her straight to Emmie's dad.

Trying to settle her nerves, she turned to her laptop, intending to enter another sweepstakes, but nothing appealed. She hadn't won the Caribbean cruise—and what if she had? Emmie might have loved to take the trip with her, so that wouldn't be a problem, but it wasn't the long-term solution Annabelle was looking for either.

Yet something else could be. A Google search for all the schools in the US that offered training for tour guides and directors brought up several she hadn't considered before. Annabelle sat up straighter. The highly regarded institute in Denver didn't offer the course she wanted for a full year, but the newer International Tour College in Phoenix did—early next spring! Enough time to get Emmie settled.

With growing excitement, Annabelle keyed in the necessary information. She had enough money left from her parents' estate to at least pay the registration fee, though, again, she felt a bit guilty. They would expect her to use what they'd left for the diner. Annabelle completed the process anyway then pushed back from her laptop with a happy sigh that seemed magnified in the silent house.

Surely before spring she would have found Emmie's real father.

In spite of tonight's disappointment about the man she'd called regarding Vegas, she had something to look forward to. In the meantime, she had to tell Finn about the phone call.

STRAIGHTENING FROM A PILE of rusty barbed wire, Finn heard the sound of an approaching car. He put one leather-gloved hand to his aching back. The last thing he needed was another visit from Sawyer McCord, who'd come by before to discourage him from fixing up the Moran farm. *You sure you're up to this*? he'd said with a gesture at the falling-down fence.

In Chicago I could mow my whole yard in fifteen minutes, Finn had admitted. Now the farm was his to do with as he pleased and there was no one else around.

Going to take a lot more time than that here, Sawyer said. *More work.* Then he'd smiled. *Now that you're a landowner, Grey says he has a nice, easy gelding for you.* Sawyer had clapped a hand on his shoulder as they walked toward the house. *You up-to-date on your tetanus shot?*

But instead of Sawyer's truck now, Annabelle's car rolled up the driveway, stopping in a cloud of dust by the bare spot that had once been the henhouse. Finn had leveled it earlier, all the while wondering if she'd managed to reach the guy in Vegas. He felt his whole face light up as she got out of the car.

It wasn't only her shiny brown hair or clear, sometimes green eyes that made him want to dive in for another kiss when that would be the wrong thing to do. Still, in the past weeks she'd become a good surrogate mother for Emmie, whether or not Annabelle believed that, and just seeing them together could make Finn smile. If she wasn't determined to leave Barren…but what if she did stay? No, he was still determined to keep to himself, to never love again. He wouldn't forget Caro or his vow to get the justice she and Alex deserved.

Well, now was his chance to tell Annabelle exactly that. He'd chickened out the last time he saw her.

"Hey," Finn said, pulling off his leather gloves. "Where's the munchkin?"

"Day care." Annabelle was carrying a package wrapped in paper with a pattern of cowboys on bucking horses and tied with a big blue bow. "I'm struggling with that, and so is she, even though she seems to have made a friend of Harry Barnes's son."

"More tantrums?" He couldn't help a smile. "You have to give Emmie high marks for spirit."

Annabelle rolled her eyes. "I'll give her an A-plus when she moves out of this phase. Age four *has* to be better." As if she intended to keep Emmie.

"She writes her own rules." He paused. "My boy did too."

Seeing or talking about Emmie often led to memories of Alex, one reason he had to set Annabelle straight. He should have done so before. Instead he'd let her kiss him.

She handed him the box. "What's this for?" he asked.

"A housewarming present, but you don't have to open it now."

Feeling off-balance, Finn tucked the box under one arm. Why had she bought him a gift? He didn't want to encourage a closeness he couldn't handle. That wouldn't be fair to Annabelle. "Come on up to the house. I'm ready for a cold drink and we need to talk."

Her gaze faltered. "I can't stay. I only stopped to give you the present and tell you I talked to the man about Las Vegas. To say he wasn't interested in Emmie would be putting it mildly." She told him what he'd said and Finn's shoulders tensed.

"Nice guy," he said, wanting to throw a punch. "Good thing he talked to you, not me, or he'd be sporting a black eye by long distance."

"I was so disappointed by his reaction," she went on. "The only good part is, with his attitude I wouldn't have left Emmie with him anyway—even to honor Sierra's last request or if he felt obligated to take responsibility.

Which, as you warned me might happen, he didn't."

Finn caught her gaze. He almost welcomed this conversation to delay telling her he couldn't take their relationship any further. "I have news, too. I've talked to people at the other companies where Sierra worked. Nothing there, not even a name or a number."

"No one remembered her?"

"Oh, they remember all right. Nothing good." He slapped one glove against his thigh, raising a small cloud from his dirty jeans. "But one HR person did remember also meeting Emmie. Said she's a cute kid but they felt sorry for her, having a mother like that. Apparently Sierra left Emmie alone in their hotel room while she worked and Emmie screamed the place down. There was talk of bringing in Child Protective Services, one more thing for Sierra to run from." He added, "Sorry, I don't mean to pile on the bad stuff, but that's what comes out of people when I mention Sierra."

Her lips flattened. Arms crossed, she leaned against the side of her car. "Poor Emmie. She never says a bad word about Sierra. Maybe she thinks their life together was normal, but I guess I have to accept the fact that my cousin was not a good person."

Finn thought that was an understatement. "So what's next?"

She flushed. "I appreciate your help, but this is really my problem. I need to keep looking for her father. She needs the stability I can't give her."

"Yes you can. You already have." Finn studied his scuffed boots. "You have to consider the possibility that you'll never know the details about Sierra's life or Emmie's father. People who want to lie low find a way to do so even today when there's no real privacy. That guy you talked to could be Emmie's father—or not—but I can't make him take a DNA test. You have to ask what happens if you *never* find her real father? Or, as I said, if you do but he doesn't want her either?"

Finn couldn't understand why any man would reject his child, though. From the moment of Alex's birth, his first concern had been for his son. Alex and Caro had gotten all the love he had in him. Emmie's dad had never even given her a chance.

"I know that's how you feel." Annabelle dug at the dirt between them with the toe of her sneaker. "But I *have* to pray he does want her and that he simply doesn't know about her because…" She trailed off, biting her lip.

Finn took a deep breath. The gift-wrapped box seemed to burn through the sleeve of his shirt. "Emmie's used to being with you, Annabelle. Your house is home to her. Why do you think she throws temper tantrums with such abandon?"

Annabelle arched a brow. "Because she gets away with them. I'm a pushover. I'm afraid to discipline her very often. And Emmie is behind in her development in some ways—her speech—"

"No," he said. "She throws herself on the floor, kicks and screams because she trusts you. She knows you won't harm her. She feels safe, even acting out when she shouldn't. Alex—" there it was again, the mention of his son "—was the same way, but maybe for the first time in her life, Emmie does have some sense of security. The stability we know now that Sierra *didn't* provide. You'd take that away from her?"

"I haven't gone anywhere. I won't until…" Her face looked pale. "You really think she trusts me?"

"I do—and you'd better think before you destroy that trust."

For a moment he'd thought he might care for someone again, but he couldn't take the chance. This was the time to tell Annabelle that their kiss before, for both of them, had been a mistake. Despite her worry about Emmie, Annabelle still intended to leave Barren as soon as possible, and as far as he knew she didn't mean to come back. Yet Finn didn't say a word.

Her shoulders squared, she started toward her car then turned again to eye the gift she'd brought. "Thank you, Finn, for all you've done. I'll take it from here. Have a nice day, Sheriff."

Finn watched her get in the car, then turned to the broken fence. That cold drink he'd been thinking about forgotten, he pulled on his gloves and, as Annabelle drove off, went back to work. He'd gone too far again about Emmie, and again he hadn't told Annabelle a relationship for them wasn't in the cards.

Now, he supposed, he wouldn't have to.

To EVERYONE'S SURPRISE Nell Sutherland showed up that evening for the Girls' Night

Out meeting. Annabelle wondered if Olivia or Shadow had spoken to her, somehow convinced her to join them after all. Tonight everyone else had come too, and the diner, with its closed sign flipped around at eight o'clock, assured them of a real opportunity to enjoy the gathering without interruption.

"Nell! Welcome!" Annabelle rushed to meet her.

Nell pulled off her beige Stetson and shook out her hair. "Does anyone else here think it'll snow before we drive home?" She didn't seem worried. "Should have put the snow tires on my truck. Could be an adventure getting to the ranch."

"Nell, you thrive on adventure," Olivia reminded her.

"The bigger the challenge, the better," Shadow put in before they both said at once, "We're glad you're here."

Annabelle was too, plus it was a nice distraction to concentrate on her friends instead of thinking about Finn. "Who wants wine?" she asked.

"Everyone but Olivia and me." Blossom, who was nursing these days, stretched out her legs at the large table in the center of the restaurant. "I'm drinking juice." Like

Nell, she was wearing obviously new jeans, dark washed and pressed, that being Barren's standard of formal dress. "I'm ready for some girlfriend talk," she said. "Logan's babysitting."

Liza Wilson, Olivia's stepmother, glanced around. "Annabelle, where's your adorable Emmie tonight?"

"With Mary Whitman who runs the day care center. She does some babysitting, too."

Annabelle poured chardonnay from a freshly opened bottle, taking her time because her thoughts kept running back to Finn anyway. She'd started the day intending to tell him about her phone call to Emmie's possible father and give Finn his housewarming gift. Now she scarcely cared whether he opencd it. His pointed questions about Emmie had cut deep and ruined *her* day. She was glad she hadn't told him about the new course she'd signed up for.

Olivia turned to Nell. "Tell us what's been happening with you lately, my friend. No one ever sees you."

"I'm rarely in town," Nell agreed. "If I wasn't ready to strangle PawPaw, I would have stayed home tonight, so don't think this is setting some kind of precedent."

No one pursued the matter. They all knew she loved her grandfather, who could certainly be difficult, and his accident with Sierra had scared the daylights out of Nell.

Annabelle tipped the last of the wine into Nell's glass. "How's that sick cow you mentioned the last time I saw you?"

"Better. Pregnant," Nell announced, as if she were the one having a baby. Then she too changed the subject. "Speaking of ranches, anyone know why Finn Donovan bought the Moran farm? There must be half a dozen ranches—real ones—he could buy instead."

"He didn't need that much space," Shadow said, "but Grey says there's enough room there to run a horse or two."

"Ever the cowboy. My brother thinks everyone needs a horse," Olivia muttered. Then she turned to Annabelle. "You have more contact here at the diner with Finn than anyone else in town. We all wonder what makes that man tick except, I mean, for that everready citation book of his."

"I couldn't say." Or rather, she wouldn't. "He and I had a difference of opinion earlier today." She told them about the latest dead end in her search for Emmie's father and the gauntlet Finn had thrown down about Emmie's future.

"Finn had a point. That Vegas guy sounds like someone I used to date," Nell mused, taking a sip of her wine. "I've sworn off men. I'd rather wrestle a mad steer than try to handle another romance."

Annabelle swept a practiced gaze around the table. Everyone had finished the before-dinner drinks and, wanting to avoid any further talk about Finn or Emmie, she hurried into the kitchen where a pot of her award-winning beef ragout simmered on the stove. Later, she'd serve molten-lava chocolate cake with vanilla bean ice cream for dessert. No one was counting calories tonight. Annabelle stacked plates and bowls, but her thoughts of Finn hovered over the table as if he was sitting there, waiting for her to make the right decision about Emmie. There was no decision to make about *them*. They didn't have a romance, weren't a couple and never would be.

"…tragic about his family," Shadow was saying when Annabelle entered the room and she froze, a batch of silverware rolled in cloth napkins precariously balanced on the crockery. Finn had implied few people knew about the murders of his wife and son.

"Who talked?" she couldn't keep from asking.

"Finn can be pretty closemouthed, but there are people who know, you among them, obviously, Derek for another, who Grey says heard from someone in Farrier. If half of what he said is true," Olivia said, "I can't blame Finn for not wanting to talk about it."

"Let's not gossip," Annabelle said. "Finn has a right to his privacy." She went back to the kitchen for the ragout, which she brought out in a large ceramic tureen that had been her mother's. Any of her friends would cherish such a family heirloom, as Finn did the best memories of his family, but Annabelle planned to sell the diner fully equipped. She wouldn't take anything with her. When she returned, she heard only silence, as if her faint reprimand had stifled conversation.

Maybe they were shocked that she'd spoken out.

Finally, as if reluctant to speak herself, Nell pushed her empty glass around on the table. "I wouldn't believe a word Derek says." All eyes turned to her. "I see no one remembers that he and I dated a while back—so briefly it can't be measured. I'm ashamed to admit, I had a crush first on his older brother until Jared got shot—pardon me, Shadow, for mentioning that—then later on I liked Derek." She added, "I chalk it up to the usual 'bad boys are exciting' phase of a girl's life. Now I'd cross the street to avoid him."

Again, no one pressed Nell, though Annabelle certainly had questions. They dug into their food, and Annabelle heard the usual praise for her cooking. She wished she could really believe it when people said positive things to her, not just remember her mother's negativity.

Yet as she ate her attention lingered on the Moran farm, Finn and his challenge about Emmie. Annabelle couldn't shake the feeling he'd wanted to bring up something else but in the end he hadn't. Not for the first time.

After their Thanksgiving kiss, Annabelle could guess what that was about.

CHAPTER SIXTEEN

"DON'T LOOK A gift horse in the mouth," Grey said.

Finn stared at him in shock. Behind them, parked at the top of the driveway in front of Finn's still falling-down barn stood a trailer with a bay inside—Big Brown, he saw—and a smaller, spotted pony Grey claimed was the horse's stablemate.

"What am I supposed to do with them?" Finn gestured toward the new fence, which wasn't finished, then propped both hands on his hips. "I'm putting everything I have into the barn and the house. Now I'm supposed to pay to feed two horses I don't know how to ride? And don't want to," he muttered.

Grey grinned. "One horse. You can't ride the pony. I should have asked before I drove over, but I knew you'd say no. You own a ranch—you need horses."

Finn thought of the gift from Annabelle. "So they're a housewarming present?"

"Couldn't think of a better one. Shadow didn't agree—said I should have made sure you wanted them first—but I thought these two would give you a start."

"You thought wrong, Grey. I'm not ungrateful but—"

"The bay's a sweetheart."

Finn tried to ignore the hopeful look in Grey's eyes. His friend meant well, but he would never turn Finn into a cowboy. "You can take the man out of the city," he said, "but you can't take the city out of the man." Especially when so much of his heart still lived in Chicago.

Grey only laughed. "Come on, you know you're weakening."

"Where would I put them? You'd have to leave them in the trailer. Even walking into that old barn means risking my life."

"Don't worry about it." Grey started back to the trailer. Before Finn could stop him, he'd unlocked the gate and lowered the ramp. Inside, large hooves stamped the floor and smaller ones danced in place. "I've already put a crew together. We'll be here tomorrow morning. Done by nightfall."

"To do what?"

"Build you a new barn." He added, "That's what neighbors—friends—do."

"Grey."

He was talking to thin air. Grey had gone through the small door at the front of the trailer and was backing the pony out. He handed Finn the lead rope. "I checked your barn before. It's not going to fall down by to-morrow. After I unload, we'll turn these two out in that small paddock—" he gestured at the side of the barn "—then put up the rest of your fence. I brought stall bedding and some feed."

"Grey," he tried again, but Finn was al-ready holding the rope, looking down into the soft eyes of the brown-and-white-spotted pony. It promptly stepped on his foot.

Minutes later, the bay joined the pony in the box stall closest to the main barn doors, and the two, which seemed like the odd cou-ple to Finn, had poked their faces out the side window to watch Grey and Finn wrestle the last sections of fence into place. He had to admit, Grey could handle a posthole digger like nobody's business.

As they worked, Grey chatted about his sis-ter Olivia and Sawyer's plans to marry after their baby was born, then about Shadow's growing health care agency. Finally, he leaned against a fence post, his black Stetson shoved back on his head. "So. What's the real issue? You're not just mad at me for bringing over the horses."

He frowned. "Sawyer thought I was in over my head here. Now I'm responsible for that bay and the pony? Even if you throw in feed temporarily, there'll be vet bills. And I'm no horseman."

"Well, *I* thought you could use a...diversion."

"Meaning?"

"You're a good sheriff, Finn. A good man. But there are things that could destroy you if you don't take care. When I was caught up in that mess with Jared Moran, never knowing if I'd be found innocent, later when my cattle were being rustled, and I learned Ava was my little girl, the one thing that could clear my mind was getting on the back of a horse. Just riding out somewhere, anywhere, and letting go. I was hoping it would work for you, too," he said, resetting his hat.

Finn sighed. "Thanks for thinking of me, even when I'm pretty sure I'm not ever getting on that horse."

"Change your mind, change your life," Grey said. And still, he wasn't done. "I'll teach you, or if you'd rather, I'll send Olivia over. She's doing a fantastic job of training that black colt Sawyer gave her and she's certainly got the touch. She'd have you in synch with the bay before you could say *cowboy*."

Finn had to smile. "You're relentless. I got on a horse at your place *once*. If I ever get the urge to climb on one again, I'll let you know."

"In the meantime I bet Emmie would love to get on that pony."

His heart stalled. "Oh, no you don't," Finn said. "I can tell you right now, I've seen the last of her and Annabelle Foster." Grey raised one eyebrow, and Finn probably shouldn't have said a word but then he did. "She was here the other day, told me her latest attempt to find Emmie's dad hadn't worked out. I was afraid it wouldn't—and the guy didn't want anything to do with Emmie."

"What happens next?"

"I wish I knew. All I do know is, I said the wrong things to Annabelle, including what if she kept Emmie with her?"

Grey's eyebrow rose higher. "I guess that's up to Annabelle."

"Yeah, well, she said *I'll take it from here* so I doubt I'll be in on any decision she makes—not that I should be." He hesitated. It wasn't in Finn's nature to come so near his deeper feelings, but he couldn't seem to stop himself. "Then there's the fact that I lost my head on Thanksgiving and let her kiss me on your porch. I sure didn't resist."

"So that's what was going on when you two left the house." Grey eyed Finn then grinned. "Duh. You're hung up on her, aren't you? As bad as a bull rider with his hand caught in his rope."

Finn could feel the back of his neck heat, then the tips of his ears. His mind filled with the image of her, that lush brown of her hair, the changeable brown of her eyes and the forlorn look on her face when she'd said, *Have a nice day, Sheriff.*

"I like Annabelle—and she's stronger than she thinks she is—but she deserves someone long-term who can commit. That lets me out." He said, "I'm in no shape to be 'hung up' on anybody."

Grey pulled away from the fence post, settled his hat all over again, then went back to work. "You are a sad case, Desperado," was all he said.

EMMIE HELD ANNABELLE'S HAND, her grip tightening as they neared the door to the day care center. "You come back?"

"By five o'clock," Annabelle assured her, although Emmie definitely had little concept of time. She was wavering again, torn between playing with her new friends and fearing she'd be left here as Sierra had left her alone in strange hotel rooms—another reason why traveling with Emmie wasn't the best option.

Their new routine had become second nature to Annabelle. Each morning, as soon as the day care center opened, she joined the flow of parents' cars into the parking lot then led Emmie inside and helped her out of her coat. Annabelle had bought her a new navy blue one with white frog closings, but Emmie couldn't work them yet. Once she was settled in the dress-up area or playing with trucks with some kids her age, including Seth Barnes, Annabelle slipped away.

She worked until four-thirty then left her head cook in charge of her waitstaff, returning with Emmie from day care for a few more hours until closing. So much juggling of time and obligations could be exhausting, but Annabelle was managing this new, if temporary, position pretty well by now.

"There's no parenting manual," Olivia had told her. "Well, there is, but we all learn by doing. So will you."

At the time Annabelle hadn't believed her, but here she was, leaning down to kiss Emmie goodbye for the day, savoring the sweet smell of her at the same time she tensed inside, dreading another meltdown. When the tantrum didn't come, she breathed a sigh of relief at the same time she knew everything might change soon. If an appointment later worked out…this would be a really big day. "Have a good time, sweetie. How does breakfast for dinner sound tonight?"

"Eggs," Emmie said. *Finn's favorite.* To Annabelle's surprise, the little girl stood on tiptoe to frame her face in both hands and kiss Annabelle's cheek. Her heart melted as Emmie ran off across the room, calling out, "I coming! Yellow truck mine!"

Annabelle was smiling through blurred vision when she stepped outside and met up with Elizabeth Barnes. They exchanged greetings as Seth raced past them into the center yelling for Emmie. "No more tears?" Elizabeth asked, looking much calmer than the first day Annabelle had seen her here.

"She's doing better. Seth, too?"

"He can't wait to see Emmie every morning. She's such a cutie."

"Emmie is a dear when she wants to be."

After they made plans for the children to get together for a playdate at the park, Annabelle headed for her car, but she'd no sooner said goodbye to Elizabeth than her steps faltered. Finn's cruiser had pulled in to a nearby parking space. She wasn't eager to see him. He had every right to his opinion, but he'd made her feel guilty that she couldn't keep Emmie, wouldn't give up her plan to see the world beyond Barren and the diner. And Finn didn't know about her upcoming course. Last night after Emmie went to sleep, Annabelle had searched online for plane tickets to Phoenix. She wondered if other people might think she was being selfish, but surely there was more to life than living out her days, as her parents expected, tied to a diner she despised? And when it finally sold, her livelihood here would go with it.

For a moment Finn stood beside his car, and with another start she realized he was wearing his full uniform, complete with a gold star on his chest. She'd never seen him in anything but jeans and a polo shirt or, once, the dark suit he'd worn for Sierra's funeral. His official presence, although more than appealing, reeked of authority and caught her off guard.

He strolled toward her. "Morning. You're out early."

"I'm always out early," she said, "to bring Emmie to day care."

His gaze didn't meet hers. "I'm here to give my 'a cop is your friend' talk."

"Emmie will be thrilled to see you." More than that, she thought. Emmie asked every night *When Finn coming to our house?* The question always made Annabelle feel guiltier than she already did. Her parents' home wouldn't be Emmie's forever.

"I'm speaking to the 'older' kids today," Finn said. "That means the four- and almost-five-year-olds. Emmie's group will get my talk next year."

If she's still here, Annabelle imagined him thinking, but he didn't say that.

A silence fell between them. Finn shifted his weight, and Annabelle said, hoping to break the awkward quiet, "How's your new place?"

"Coming along," he murmured. "I've already decided it will be a never-ending story." He cleared his throat. "Thanks for the bath towels. They're nice and thick."

Annabelle looked down at his hands, and a fresh wave of awareness washed through her. Finn had strong hands with sturdy wrists. "You're welcome. I wanted to get you something practical." And not too personal, although now she could imagine him using the towels after his shower and had to will the image from her mind. "Well, enjoy the farm and your speech to the children. I need to get to work."

She took one step toward her car before Finn caught the crook of her arm, his grasp light and warm. "Annabelle, the other day I was way off base. It's none of my business what you decide for Emmie. I know you'll keep her best interests in mind and in…your heart. I admit I'm a little touchy about kids. When I first came to

Barren, I was determined not to even notice them. Every little boy reminded me of Alex."

Her tone softened. "Of course they did. So did Emmie."

"I tried not to get attached to her, but who could keep from that?" They both smiled. In her better moods Emmie was a charmer. "At the same time I wanted to turn away, I couldn't stop myself from just…taking her in. I'm still not sure that's a good idea. For her either."

Annabelle could understand that. "Neither am I. But she liked you on sight, probably in part because she never knew her dad." That threatened to bring up the subject of Annabelle's search for him. She wasn't going there again. She eased her arm from his hand. "Apology accepted." She decided to share the news that had been bubbling up inside, even when Finn probably wouldn't like it. "The diner has been on the market for a while, but this afternoon— finally!—a possible buyer has an appointment with my Realtor to see the restaurant." Beforehand, she had to make sure the diner looked in tip-top shape. When she shut and locked the door for the last time, she would walk away from all the pots and pans, every piece of equipment for good. She'd also be walking away from Emmie.

"If that's what you want, I hope you get an offer." Finn looked toward the day care center. "I'll try to stop in and say hello to the threes while I'm here." He walked beside Annabelle to her car. There must be something else on his mind, as she'd thought twice before. "About Thanksgiving…" he began, proving her right.

Her lips firmed. "Yes, I kissed you first. That didn't mean—"

"No, I meant to say that wasn't just you. I did kiss you back." His voice was low and husky, his hazel eyes darker. "Another thing I need to apologize for. Annabelle, I'm carrying a whole lot of baggage, and I don't want to…lead you on."

She stiffened. Humiliating enough that he'd warned her off, but she wouldn't stand here and take it. "That assumes I'm interested." She hoped her face didn't flush.

"True," he said. Did he sound disappointed? "All I can cope with is to do my job here, try to make a home for myself on that farm—" he raised an eyebrow "—and keep fighting Grey's notion that, because he gave me a horse, I should become a rider."

"You own a horse?"

"And a pony. All I can say is, they got me up this morning better than an alarm clock or my watch. Sure makes the place seem like a real farm."

Annabelle couldn't resist teasing him. "Next you'll be getting some chickens."

"Not likely. First thing I tore down was that old henhouse." He paused. "I do have a new barn, courtesy of Grey and a bunch of other people..." He took a breath. "You're not tempted to clean my clock? After I all but told you to go away?"

"You don't want another relationship," she said around a tight lump in her throat. "I never expected one." Forget her daydreams about him. He'd all but said he regretted that one kiss.

If only her awareness of Finn would leave her. To reassure him that she was, indeed, about to disappear from his life, as he obviously wanted, she felt tempted to tell him about her course, too. But she would make arrangements for Emmie first.

Finn held her door open then lingered after she shut it and he leaned over at her half-open window. The relief she saw in his dark-lashed eyes made his apology hurt even more, but she had the impression he wanted to smooth things over.

He looked away. "If you have time some day, bring Emmie to the farm. She might like to meet the new pony."

ON HIS WAY back into town several hours later, wondering why he'd voiced the half-hearted invitation, Finn spied Derek near the café and pulled him over. *At last*, he thought.

"Aw, man," Derek said with a groan.

"That's *Sheriff* to you—official business." Finn stood by Derek's drive-side window. He'd gotten the call soon after he left Annabelle. "*Sir* would be even better."

Derek was in his new truck. Shiny and with a bright speed-yellow paint job, it made quite the show around Barren, and every time Finn saw Derek racing along Main Street behind the wheel, country music blaring from the speakers through a closed window, Finn's teeth ground together.

"I wasn't speeding," Derek said. "Why'd you stop me?"

"I need to question you. You can follow me back to the station. Don't decide to run for it instead and make me chase you."

"That sounds like fun." Leaning one shoulder against the steering wheel, Derek gave an exaggerated sigh. "What's the charge?"

"None yet but Earl's Hardware got hit last night."

"What's that got to do with me? The alarm went off again? That old thing nearly made me deaf at least once a week when I lived there. Me and Calvin got waked up in the apartment above the store all the time."

"In this case the alarm was valid. Guess whose prints were all over the main entrance?"

"That's all you have?" Derek laughed. "Yeah, I was there. We went out drinking on my paycheck last night from Wilson Cattle, and when we come home, I meant to stay the night. No drinking and driving, *Sheriff*, but Calvin had locked himself out. Only way we could get in was through the store up the back stairs."

"So you jimmied the door." Which, Finn remembered, was Derek's usual method.

"Yes, *sir*," Derek drawled.

"All right, let's go." Finn didn't finish before Derek gunned his engine and took off going zero to fifty in seconds.

Finn cursed aloud. Pursuing him down Main Street with shoppers walking to and from stores on either side wasn't his idea of good police work—innocent people could get hurt during a chase—but Finn hit the lights and siren and floored the gas pedal anyway. He was too mad to fall back.

At high speed Derek's new truck raced over the pavement, veering close to a parked car near the feed store then crossing the centerline toward the Baby Things shop on the other side. Adrenaline surged through Finn. If Derek leaped the curb, he'd plow right into the woman with a stroller—was that Blossom?—and an older couple who were shuffling along the sidewalk toward Shadow's agency. Derek managed to stay on the north side of the street, but by then he'd almost reached the local elementary school.

The buses were rolling in to pick up students, the morning-session kindergartners going home. A bunch of younger kids had gathered near the entrance with a teacher, but one boy darted closer to the road and Finn eased off the gas. An image of Emmie flashed through his mind. She wasn't there, but Finn couldn't risk anyone getting hurt, or worse.

Heart in his throat, Finn killed the siren

then slammed one hand against the steering wheel in frustration.

Ahead of him, Derek had swung onto Hemlock Street past Annabelle's Diner and was probably tearing toward the highway entrance that led to Farrier in one direction and Kansas City in the other. Finn shook his head.

Unless Derek left the county or the state, Finn knew where to find him.

CHAPTER SEVENTEEN

COFFEEPOT IN HAND, Annabelle froze. A yellow pickup truck blew past the diner with Finn's patrol car right behind, lights flashing, siren screaming down Main Street. Everyone in the restaurant stopped eating to look out the front windows, and Annabelle raised one hand to her throat. "Goodness, I wonder what that's all about."

With a scowl Harry Barnes was already on his feet, heading for the door, cell phone squashed against his ear. "Put lunch on my tab," he said, motioning his aides to follow, which they did like ducks in a row.

Several women who occupied the last booth that belonged to Finn in Annabelle's mind craned their necks, as if hoping to see the action. But by then, the two vehicles had disappeared. "They were almost at the school," Annabelle said, fearing for the students and grateful that Emmie's day care was at the other end of town. "I hope no one gets hurt."

Nell Sutherland set her napkin aside. "That was Derek Moran's truck."

"Are you sure?"

"He bought it a few days ago. He's been showing off all over town."

"He doesn't get along with the sheriff," one of the women said. "That boy has been in one scrape after another since he was ten years old—in part, thanks to that brother of his. Wanda certainly had her hands full with those two."

More unasked-for opinions followed but Annabelle had learned long ago to shut her ears to local gossip. "More coffee, Mrs. Whittaker? And how does the Italian crème cake look to you today?" She included the other three women in the booth. "Dessert, everyone?"

With their orders in and no more sirens shrieking through the normally peaceful air outside, the talk died down. Annabelle returned to Nell's table. The lunch crowd was thinning out hours before the dinner customers would arrive, and she'd have to clear tables, straighten things up for the Realtor's first showing, then help with the prep work for tonight before she picked up Emmie, but Nell had come in several times since the Girls' Night Out meeting and today she was still fretting about her grandfather.

"Thanks to him, I gave up on Derek pretty fast," she told Annabelle, "but I'm telling you, Belle, if PawPaw takes off for Montana, as he keeps threatening to do, I'll never speak to him again."

Annabelle smiled. "I thought you were fine on your own. Maybe spending time with his brother would perk him up and he'd come home able to work beside you."

"*If* he came back," Nell said, staring into her cup.

Annabelle frowned. "Ned loves the NLS like my parents loved this diner," she said.

She wanted to tell Nell about her upcoming course, but the news would spread all over town and reach Finn. He might not care, except about Emmie, but every time she saw him she feared he'd see the truth about Annabelle's hopeless crush in her eyes when she knew his view about relationships, and after their last talk she certainly knew his view about Emmie.

When Nell asked about her a minute later,

Annabelle said, "She hasn't let me alone since she learned Finn has a pony."

Nell grinned. "Let her start early. We can use more cowgirls around here."

"You would say that." Annabelle took a step away from the table. She wasn't about to take Emmie to the farm, or to open her own heart again to Finn. Maybe she shouldn't care what he might think about her course. "From my standpoint, I'm better off staying clear of the farm—and him." Nell's gaze sharpened, but before she could say anything, Annabelle said, "I have to wonder why he was chasing Derek."

"Could be any number of things. Derek has a bad streak and Finn's such a straight arrow." Nell rose from her seat then dug into her jeans pocket for some bills, which she handed to Annabelle. "I'm more than grateful Derek was a bad actor with me—and in PawPaw's mind—because my grandfather steered me to someone else. That didn't work out either, and Derek went on to sow his wild oats elsewhere, but at least I had a better—if limited—relationship after that."

"Someone serious?" Annabelle had never heard of a real romance for Nell, who kept to herself, like Finn. Rarely talkative about personal matters, she didn't respond.

"Oh, before you go, you *are* coming to our next meeting?" Annabelle asked.

"Not if it means talking about my private life." As Nell reached the front door, she turned back. "About those wild oats…you should know this much. Derek Moran tossed me aside like that old Chevy Nova of his for Sierra Hartwell."

WHEN SARGE STARTED BARKING, Finn glanced up from painting his new barn doors an eye-catching brick red. For the past several hours, he'd been stewing about Derek, and now Annabelle was coming up the drive again, her car bouncing over the ruts he hadn't filled, as if the hounds of hell were after her. The sedan slid to a stop mere feet from the bucket of paint he'd just opened.

Annabelle flung her door wide. "You won't believe what I just heard."

Sarge's welcoming yips and the demanding shouts from the rear child seat of Annabelle's car all but drowned out what she'd said. Emmie waved her hands in the air, beseeching someone to free her, yelling, "Want to see pony!"

"Hold on, Annabelle." Finn unbuckled Emmie's straps then lifted her out. "Hey, short stuff. You must be eating well. You're almost too big to carry."

"I eat doughnuts—and eggs." Emmie cupped his face in her hands, leaving a sticky residue. "See you too, Finn."

Glad to have her visit when he knew that wasn't wise, he affected a puzzled expression. "But what's this I hear about a pony? No horses here."

"You silly." Emmie peered over his shoulder at the barn.

Tail swishing, Sarge's entire body trembled with excitement. Sidestepping him, Finn faced Annabelle. He couldn't help but wonder what had brought her here. Had she taken him up on his invitation just for Emmie's sake? From what she'd said and her tense expression, he guessed this wasn't to be a social call. "What news?" Had she found Emmie's dad?

"Not for little ears," she said. "I'd hoped to tell you before Emmie got out."

Fortunately, Emmie didn't react to hearing her name. Her attention was focused on Sarge, and Finn set her down to play with the dog. He laid his brush on top of the red paint can then led the way into the barn. "Pretty spiffy, huh?"

"Beautiful," Annabelle said, but looked distracted by whatever she'd come to tell him. Finn wasn't sure he wanted to hear it. She followed him along the barn aisle to the large stall where his new bay gelding lived with his pony pal by his side. Emmie ran after them with Sarge at her heels.

When Finn reached the stall, two pairs of equine ears perked up. Brown snuffled his nose into Finn's palm, searching for treats. "Mind your manners. We have company." He produced a carrot from his rear jeans pocket and snapped off a piece. Emmie could give that to Big Brown, but the pony liked to nip. Finn fed it first. Olivia had come over yesterday to give him a beginner lesson, but he still felt leery around the pair.

Olivia had watched him on Brown with keen eyes. "You have a natural seat," she'd said.

"Is that good or bad?" Finn had no idea what that meant.

"Very good. You're nice and deep in the saddle." Then she'd let go of the lead rope and Finn was riding on his own like a kid with his first two-wheeled bike. He and

Brown had done all right, and a determined Olivia was coming back soon for another lesson. In the meantime he could lead Emmie around without worrying about her safety.

"I want to feed him!" she insisted.

Finn planned to caution her first, but her loud wail startled the horses. They danced in the stall, stepping on each other, ears laid back. "They don't like loud noises, Emmie—" she only yelled louder "—quiet down or we'll have to leave the barn. Then you won't get to feed carrots."

"Will, too!"

"Oh, brother," Annabelle murmured at his shoulder.

Emmie threw herself down in the aisle, rolled through the stray bits of straw and the dirt, kicking and screaming for all she was worth. Finn's mouth set. "No pony ride today then. You made your choice. Wow," he said to Annabelle. "I've seen tantrums but she's a pro."

Then he walked away from Emmie.

"Where you going?" she raged, heels drumming the dirt. "You stay!"

"Not while you're shouting at me. *No*," he said when she yelled again. "Annabelle and I will wait outside until you feel better."

"Finn! *Finn!*" Emmie's furious tone followed them into the yard.

"We just leave? I've never thought of that," Annabelle said, her eyes wide.

"Best way to deal with that kind of drama. She'll be okay, but Brown and the pony probably won't be able to hear for a week." He hoped they didn't hurt themselves.

Annabelle frowned. "What if Emmie opens the stall door?"

"It's locked. The bolt's up high where she can't reach it."

In the weak sunlight, they sat on folding lawn chairs by the doors. His ears quivering, Sarge plodded from the barn to slump down beside them. Emmie was adorable, like Alex, but she had a temper and Finn meant to wait her out. He inhaled the now-familiar scents of hay and leather, grain and manure.

A minute later the screaming stopped and Finn shot Annabelle a grin. "See? Whenever Alex did that, Caro and I left him to his tantrums. Without an audience they never last long. Now," he said, "what did you hear— other than Emmie?"

Annabelle fidgeted, hands twisting in her lap. Then, after taking a deep breath, she said, "Nell Sutherland told me a while back that she'd had a short relationship with Derek years ago but—that is, and wait for it, before he dumped her for my *cousin*! Finn, he and Sierra were *involved*."

Finn gaped at her. "Derek Moran and *Sierra*?"

"I know, seems like a stretch, but it happened. Nell and I are longtime friends but she keeps most things to herself. And Sierra never even told me about being in town then." Annabelle's mouth quivered. "I never imagined she was seeing him. Finn, if they had an affair, Derek might be the person she meant to 'tie up loose ends' with and—"

"Derek could be Emmie's father." Finn groaned aloud. "No wonder you couldn't believe what Nell told you."

Finn glanced at the driveway beside the house as if he might see Derek's new yellow truck there. "I chased that guy all over town today, which gave me reason to haul him in. Caught up with him finally at the Circle H acting as if the pursuit never happened. Right now he's in a holding cell, but he won't be there long. I'd bet my last dollar Grey's on his way to arrange bail for him."

"I saw you chase him past the diner. What did he do?"

"Breaking and entering—again—like he did here the day I moved in. Burglary. Engaging an officer of the law in dangerous pursuit. There's a shipment of chain saws missing from the hardware store, fancy toolboxes on wheels, and a few bags of dog food. Earl, the owner, isn't happy. And I'm still adding charges. Any cop could pile on half a dozen without having to think." Which didn't satisfy Finn. He was already waiting for the judge to throw the book at Derek for cattle rustling.

"Why would he steal a bunch of chain saws?"

"To resell probably, but he's not talking. And Grey will help him lawyer up."

Annabelle rubbed her forehead. "First, Sierra shows up and gets gravely injured in that wreck. Then, when she dies, Emmie's left alone—and now Derek is the only likely person I've found who might be her father."

"Can't quite see him as a daddy—except, perhaps, the biological one, and even that makes me shudder." Finn blew out a breath. "If the dates Sierra spent with him line up, we'll know more than we do now. I'll see if I can crack Derek before he gets sprung from jail."

"Be careful, though. Maybe you shouldn't tell him exactly why you're asking about those dates."

They rose from the lawn chairs at the instant Emmie emerged from the barn. Wiping her eyes, she gave a shuddering breath. She had dirt streaks on both cheeks, and Finn didn't know when he'd seen a more contrite-looking face. Even Alex hadn't been that good. Emmie wandered toward them and stopped in front of Finn. "I sorry."

"It's okay, kiddo." He paused. "We all get mad sometimes, but you need to handle it in a different way." Finn doubted she understood the fine points but wondered if he should take his own advice; the mere thought of Derek made him see red.

Emmie stared at him for a moment. Then, while Finn was congratulating himself for managing her tantrum so well, she strolled over to the paint can he'd left by the barn doors and knocked the brush off its top. Before he or Annabelle could intervene, she smiled like an evil child in some horror movie.

And kicked the can, spreading red paint over Finn's yard.

ANNABELLE WAS STILL laughing when she walked with Finn to the house. "Guess we know who won that one," she said. She was worried he was upset until he turned around and grinned.

"With that temper she might be Derek's kid. I didn't say my method *always* worked with Alex."

Exhausted after her tantrum, Emmie had fallen asleep on his shoulder. Finn put her on the sofa, covered her with an afghan then walked into the kitchen. Annabelle could see he'd been working there. Finn had bleached Wanda Moran's old sink, taken down the yellowed curtains and washed the window overlooking the rear yard. With brisk motions he filled his state-of-the-art coffee maker, telling Annabelle he meant to redo the whole place one project at a time.

"You wouldn't want to help me paint?"

Annabelle sat at the battered table Wanda had left behind. "I'll pass," she said. "That's beyond my pay grade." She'd only come to the farm to tell him about Derek. If Emmie hadn't needed a nap to recover from her drama, they'd be gone by now. "If I wanted to paint, I'd start with my parents' house. When they were alive every dollar went into the diner." She said, "I'll need to update a bit before I list the house."

When Finn turned back to the counter, Annabelle assumed he wasn't interested. Or didn't want to point out that her eventual move meant Emmie would leave that house too. "With so much going on with Emmie, I can't find time to paint."

She'd even had to leave the diner as it was today for the first showing when she left to see Finn. There'd been no time to make things neat. If an offer came in for the restaurant, Annabelle wouldn't haggle over price; like Finn with his house in Chicago, she just wanted to be rid of it.

"Your Realtor's right. Let me know if you change your mind," Finn finally said, and Annabelle wondered if he meant about painting or leaving town. "We could help each other."

Although tempted, Annabelle wondered why he was being so nice, as if he wanted to spend more time with her. That worried her. She didn't want to be more vulnerable to him yet the suggestion certainly appealed.

"I'll think about it." She stood. The less time she spent with Finn, probably the better. "I should be going."

He tilted his head toward the living room. "Emmie needs to sleep or you'll get another tantrum. By the time she wakes up, I could have dinner on the table. Why don't you stay?"

Annabelle took a breath. "Because you're giving me mixed messages, Finn."

He flinched. "Nothing wrong with having a meal together, is there?"

Like a glutton for punishment, Annabelle couldn't think of a good argument, except her unrequited feelings for him. She said yes, if a bit reluctantly, and helping Finn prepare their dinner turned out to be fun—as long as she avoided any mention of their last argument. They teased each other about Emmie's tantrum, talked about his plans for the farm and discussed Derek's possible paternity.

"You're a good cook," Annabelle told him, tasting the spaghetti sauce he offered her on a spoon.

"Necessity being the mother of invention. After I lost Caro, I either had to make my own meals, live on takeout or restaurant food—no offense against your diner—or go without. Hard to ruin spaghetti sauce," he said, looking into the other pot on the stove. "But I may have overdone this pasta."

"I won't complain. You can't imagine how sick I get of preparing food." She flushed. "I'd rather watch you."

When their meal was ready, Emmie wakened to announce, "Smells good."

To Annabelle's satisfaction, the little girl didn't find fault with Finn's sauce, the pasta or the garlic bread. In fact, she seemed genuinely sorry for the fuss she'd made earlier and ate all her salad without spitting out the bits of green pepper. Maybe Finn's method had worked after all to improve her behavior. Blotting her lips on her napkin, as Annabelle had taught her, Emmie grinned. "I like you food. Thankoo, Finn."

He and Annabelle exchanged smiles. "You're welcome, short stuff. If you're good, next time you can ride the pony. Nick's mom has promised to bring me a saddle she used when she was your age."

"I can?" Emmie bounded from her chair. "I a rider like Nick!" She ran into the living room then, already onto something else, came back with a video that had belonged to Wanda. "See this one now?"

Annabelle started to shake her head. She'd already stayed too long, but Finn was telling Emmie, "We'll watch with you."

Annabelle's arm quickly went numb with Emmie's head against it on the sofa, but she didn't want to move. Neither did Finn, apparently, who sat on Emmie's other side, his arm brushing Annabelle's shoulder now and then, his gaze joined with hers whenever Emmie laughed at the adventures of *Lady and the Tramp*. Emmie had wanted Sarge to watch with them, but he stayed outdoors, as if hoping to avoid another meltdown. Annabelle tried to ignore the rush that ran through her veins whenever she and Finn accidentally touched.

During the last twenty minutes of the film that had held Emmie riveted, she fell asleep again.

"I'm glad Wanda left that movie," Finn said, stretching. "Let me carry Emmie to your car. Want to take home some spaghetti? If you don't, I'll be eating it for a week."

"I wouldn't mind a care package, thanks." She knew Emmie would eat Finn's cooking without complaint.

As soon as the door opened onto the chilly night, they met the first real snowfall of the season. Huge flakes drifted from the sky to cover the ground—and the red paint Emmie had spilled—as well as Annabelle's car. Like the experienced father he'd once been, Finn buckled Emmie into her seat then began to clear the snow from the windshield. "You'll be okay to drive home?"

"I've lived here all my life," she said. "In Kansas I know snow."

Finn smiled. "Oh, yeah? I told you Chicago winters are the worst."

The banter reminded her of Thanksgiving and their kiss. "Tell me that when you're trying to get feed to your cattle next month."

"*My* cattle? Two horses are more than I bargained for."

Annabelle watched the snowflakes melt on Finn's dark hair. "Unless Grey is even more determined to turn you into a cowboy. Not a bad look, Sheriff."

His eyes darkened. His voice sounded husky. "You like cowboys?"

"What girl doesn't?"

Finn lowered the snow scraper to his side. Under the arc lights from the barn eaves, she could see his steady look that made her heart speed. "Then maybe I ought to consider those cattle. Buy myself a hat like Grey's black Stetson."

"Learn to line dance," she murmured,

knowing they weren't really talking about cowboys now. Why were they both flirting?

Finn moved closer in a determined way that should have made her step back yet didn't.

"Finn," she said weakly.

Before Annabelle could order herself to move, he'd slipped an arm around her shoulders to draw her closer. "I don't mean to give you mixed messages, Annabelle, but I liked having you and Emmie here. I haven't liked anything as much since I came to Barren. I don't know what to make of that either, but maybe I should stop trying and just try… this." His mouth angled to touch hers in a warm kiss that took away the falling snow, the cold night, and turned it into the heat of a summer day. "Notice I'm kissing first this time."

When Finn nudged her lips open, she didn't resist. She kissed him back. Again. She'd dreamed of being in his arms, of tasting his kiss, never thinking it could happen. But where could this lead? He'd made his position clear. He hadn't recovered from the tragedy in Chicago that had taken his wife and son, his job there and his belief in the future. In Barren he might care for Emmie, even care a little for Annabelle, but…her thoughts battled with the growing need inside for something more, something lasting and, if she were being honest, for Finn. Getting more deeply involved would only mean they'd all get hurt. Emmie, too. And he didn't know she had made plans to leave in the spring, the door that would open to a whole new career in different places with different people.

Of course she had Emmie's welfare to think of first, but…

"I'll be leaving here, Finn," Annabelle said against his lips.

"You sure about that?"

The word *yes* seemed to stick in her throat. She couldn't say it. She'd never imagined Finn would kiss her again like that, would even think of the brief closeness they'd just shared. She drew back and held his gaze with hers. "Why start something we can't finish?"

After that, there didn't seem to be anything left to say. Her gaze fell and Annabelle pulled away from him completely, already missing his embrace, then got into her car.

At home later she couldn't sleep. She replayed those kisses like another showing of *Mulan* or *Frozen* for Emmie, heard her own words over and over in her mind. After checking on Emmie, who was sound asleep with her lamb, which she'd named Finnie, she tiptoed downstairs and opened her laptop.

But the usual spam and half a dozen store ads for things she wouldn't buy didn't grab her attention. The email with the subject line "Important information about your course" most certainly did. "Oh, my," she murmured.

It was a message from The International Tour College!

Did she dare open it? Maybe they'd decided not to accept her after all and would refund her registration fee. But…no.

The class she'd signed up for was being cancelled due to low enrollment. That would have been not-so-good news—she'd have to wait even longer now—but instead the school was offering her the option of taking an earlier course.

It started soon. Very soon.

She reread the message, biting her lip, trying to decide what to do. This course was only for ten days rather than two weeks, and she could surely find someone to stay with

Emmie then. Maybe Shadow might be able to help, or Olivia. But that would only be the beginning. After that her new career would take her away more often, for longer periods of time, and she had to consider Emmie's well-being. Yet...

She glanced at the closet under the stairs. This was her chance to escape—maybe her one chance—to begin a better life. She couldn't pass up this opportunity.

"Yes!" she said aloud, punching the air.

She'd waited so long. Now her dream could come true—sooner than she'd hoped.

Annabelle took a deep breath then wrote her reply to the email.

They would manage. Somehow. Annabelle wasn't the same inexperienced person she'd been with Emmie the night of Sierra's accident. She could find a solution that worked for both of them. How hard could it be?

She hit Send then sank back in her seat, head spinning.

Annabelle was leaving Barren. She was going to Phoenix—to become a tour director.

CHAPTER EIGHTEEN

"LET ME MAKE this simple." Grey leaned over Finn's desk the next morning, his eyes as hard as tempered steel. "Derek did not take that stuff from Earl's store. Either Earl misplaced the shipment of chain saws—"

Finn fiddled with the pen he'd been using to finish his report on the incident. "One of which was in the bed of Derek's truck."

"Circumstantial evidence." Grey straightened. "In plain sight. Why would he do that? Derek tells me he bought the saw and I believe him."

"He has no receipt, Grey. Every time I ask the question he gives me a different answer—he never got one, he tossed it out, he doesn't remember where he put it—signs that he must be lying."

"Prove it." Grey pulled off his hat, tossed it on the desk and ran a hand through his hair. "Why would he let anyone see that saw if it was stolen? Come on, Finn."

"I don't know," he said. "Maybe because he doesn't play by the rules?"

"And of course you do."

"Yep." To Finn, it seemed Derek never did anything right, and for sure he didn't accept responsibility for what he did do. Finn had a niggling feeling after seeing Derek's emotional reaction in his brother's room at the house that maybe he wasn't being fair, but he could also envision Sanchez's face, superimposed on an image of Derek. Of course Grey disagreed.

"I admit Derek has a few character flaws—"

"You think?"

"But he's not a bad guy, only mixed-up. Shadow and I have talked this thing to death. I know he's her baby brother and that might influence me, but even you have to agree there are still doubts about Jared's death."

Finn threw down the pen. He hadn't been here ten years ago, but he'd read the file. "Three people struggling for control of a loaded weapon—Jared, Derek and you—someone was bound to get hurt. Or, in Jared's case, dead."

"I know Derek feels bad, too, about his possible part in that. He might have pulled the trigger, or Jared may in fact have shot himself, but the burglary at Earl's hardware is different."

"Maybe."

"Derek explained. I can't say I care for his friend Calvin Stern, but when he and Derek go partying neither one of them should be driving so you can't blame Derek for staying overnight at the apartment upstairs. Why wouldn't his prints be there? He used to live with Calvin Stern. He must have opened that door dozens of times. I doubt anybody's wiped the place clean since Derek moved out."

"He has a history," Finn insisted. "If a kid gets in trouble, which Derek did when he was younger, unless he's stopped he'll likely be in trouble as an adult."

Grey's voice dripped with sarcasm. "I see. You're trying to save him from himself."

"No, I don't know if he can be saved. That's up to him, not me. All I know is, a witness from the café saw him skulking around the hardware store that night. His truck parked in the rear by the loading zone—"

Grey swore. "Because that's where he and Calvin always park."

"—and I've seen Derek in too many situations where he doesn't belong."

Grey ticked them off on his fingers. "Your old apartment building. The cemetery—where, by the way, a bunch of preteen kids knocked over those headstones."

"I dealt with them," Finn pointed out. "Several of those stones marked your relatives' gravesites."

"So right away you decided Derek still has it in for me. You're wrong there, too."

"What about his breaking into my house on moving day?"

"Derek lived there his whole life until he moved in with Calvin then out to Wilson Cattle. He was only there to pick up his belongings."

"So you say. Call me jaded, but years ago my father and uncle dealt with people like Derek, and since then so have I. What are *you* trying to prove? Derek is who he is—"

"At twenty-five? He's not fixed in stone yet. I never knew you were such a cynic."

Finn shifted in his chair. "I know what I see."

"You see what you want to see. I told you. Derek's doing a good job. He even keeps his share of the bunkhouse clean…and he put most of his pay in that savings account so he could trade in his old Chevy for that new truck." Grey picked up his Stetson. "I understand about your wife and child. Their deaths were…horrendous. I've got a family of my own now, and I can't imagine what you went through. What you're still going through. You may be burned out, Finn. If so, you should quit law enforcement."

Yes, Grey had a family. Finn did not, and that was best for him, despite his coming on to Annabelle last night.

Grey obviously couldn't resist adding, "If you quit, you could turn that farm into a ranch full-time. In any event, you have no reason to tar and feather Shadow's brother for something he did not do."

"And in your view the judge was right to let him out on bail yesterday—which you paid, just as you've given him a job, a place to live, another chance he probably doesn't deserve. Which one of us is wrong?"

His face a blank mask, Grey resettled his Stetson. "I don't think that's the question. Why don't you ask yourself, Finn—what is this really about?"

"I UNDERSTAND HOW you feel about Derek," Annabelle told Finn. In spite of what she'd said the other night—*why start something we can't finish*—when Finn had called yesterday she hadn't said no, and tonight they were wielding paint rollers over the living room walls of her parents' house. She'd found the time after all. The first showing of the diner had gone okay, but so far there'd been no offer.

As long as they stuck to sprucing up their respective homes, she hoped they'd be okay for the rest of the time she was here. And Annabelle could store up these images of Finn, his dark hair mussed, a streak of paint across one cheek, his hazel eyes intent on the half-finished task. "Grey did have some good points," she said.

She wiped a hand across her brow, leaving a smear of taupe paint to match the one on Finn's cheek. As he wound up the story of his argument with Grey, she eyed the nearby closet door, remembering Emmie with the keys, the scene of her own childhood terror. "If I heard right, several of those stolen chain saws have turned up in Farrier. Some tool chests, too. That's what Olivia said, and she got it from Shadow."

"Hearsay," he said. "Derek must have sold them. Which I expected."

"How could he? He was in jail. And what

about the dog food also missing from the hardware store? I've heard that was Joey Foxworth." His mom sometimes worked for Annabelle at the diner.

"It was, and the thefts were not related."

She took a sideways step, realizing she'd inched nearer to the closet. She should trade places with Finn. She'd felt fine while they painted the opposite wall, but this close her heart was pounding in alarm. "Would you put that little boy in a detention home for trying to feed his dog the only way he knew how?"

"It's against the law, Annabelle. No, I didn't turn him over to detention, but I put his mother in touch with the local boys' club. He needs a male figure in his life and—"

"You paid for the dog food."

His face flushed. "Well, yeah. Again. He reminds me of myself at that age, making some wrong choices. His dad is gone, and I don't want him to wind up like Derek."

"Let me guess," Annabelle said, running her roller through the paint tray. "You're going to sponsor him at the club. Doesn't Derek remind you of yourself, too?"

"No, he reminds me of Eduardo Sanchez—a vicious killer."

"Derek's not a killer. Why not take a similar interest in him as in Joey?"

He forced a smile. "Derek's too old for the boys' club."

Annabelle sighed. "You know what I meant. I have to agree with Grey. You've been overly hard on Derek, and that's having an effect on your friendship with Grey."

"We'll work it out. Our friendship has nothing to do with my job."

"Really?"

He pointed at the half-finished wall. "We going to get this painting done? Or will I have to wait longer to do my place?"

She knew he was teasing, or trying to, but Annabelle pushed the roller up and down her section of the wall. "Shadow always says Grey is stubborn but that you take it to a whole new level, and she's right."

"Two against one," Finn muttered.

Another swipe of the roller put her even closer to the closet door. "I'm not kidding. You should figure out why you're so determined to nail Derek for the hardware robbery."

"Burglary," Finn murmured. "Robbery is when a person is being stolen from."

As if he was reciting from the policemen's playbook.

"Oh." Annabelle felt tempted to back off. She didn't want to ruin one of her last times alone with Finn. "But if—heaven forbid— Derek *is* Emmie's dad, I'll have a hard decision to make myself." Annabelle swiped the roller down the last swathe of wall on her side even closer to the closet doorframe. In spite of her best effort, her hand trembled and blobs of paint slopped onto the woodwork. Annabelle jerked back as if she'd been slapped.

"Steady," Finn said. "Take your time. You need to feather that in." Then, "What happened? You hurt yourself?"

"I'm fine." Her voice sounded sharp. "Would you like something from the kitchen? Coffee, tea, water? A beer?"

"Don't run off. I'm good." Finn set his roller in the paint tray then did the same with Annabelle's. "I can see you're not."

Her shoulders hunched in self-protection. "I don't…this will sound silly…like this closet. The door is locked now and I never go in there. I don't use it for storage because…" She couldn't go on. *I'd have to open it again.*

In her mind she was back inside, curled up

in a ball, trying to make herself as small as she could, trying not to make a sound. Filling her head with images of far-off places. Telling herself she'd be all right, that someday she would go there.

She glanced at Emmie's toy boat, which belonged in her room but had been left on the floor. "That was long ago, but I've always thought one reason my parents never liked Sierra was because she didn't care if they put her in the closet."

"But you did care. So they shut you in. Didn't they?"

She said, "They knew I was afraid of the dark. In fact, my father used to tease me that the gremlins, the ogres, the monsters were waiting for me."

"I wouldn't call playing on a child's fears teasing. How old were you?"

"Small," she said, "Emmie's age at first." Finn winced and she risked a glance at the closet. "Makes no sense to still be afraid of something that can't hurt me now."

"You believed it could then, and your parents used that to keep you in line whenever you disobeyed, which I can't even imagine."

Annabelle looked away. "We don't need to talk about it."

"I think you should."

Her voice shook. "It's too painful."

"Try, Annabelle."

She swallowed but her mouth was dry. "I used to beg him not to, but the only person who would help was Sierra when she came to visit. She'd creep to the closet, open the door my father had warned me not to, bring me something to eat, a drink, a doll to comfort me." She tried to move, but Finn grasped her shoulders, lightly holding her in place as if to give her strength.

"Annabelle, we all have...secrets."

She wondered what his might be but couldn't ask. "It doesn't matter now. My parents stopped using the closet when I was about twelve. Sierra never got caught or they would have found a way to punish her, too. She may not have been the best person, but I'll always owe her for that."

"And you felt you owed her enough to take in Emmie. To put your own plans aside." He added, "I can't blame you for wanting, no, needing, to get out of Barren, away from the diner and this house. You were more a servant to them than a daughter, Annabelle."

"I don't mean to sound like a victim."

"No, you're a strong woman and I admire

you more than I can say. In spite of that mistreatment—emotional abuse—you grew into a fine, loving person." He half smiled. "Even Emmie knows that."

"Not that she doesn't test me every day."

"That's what being a parent involves," he said with that touch of sadness she always saw in his eyes.

"I'm not Emmie's parent."

"No?" he said. "I think you're as much her mother—maybe more now—than Sierra was. You don't leave her alone in some strange hotel room. You find ways to make sure she's cared for—you're even looking for her father. You've taken responsibility for her." His gaze fell on the closet. "You have a key that opens this door?"

"In my junk drawer in the kitchen, but—"

Finn went there and, after she heard a brief scuffling sound, came back with it. "Let's take a look," he said. "Together."

Standing behind her at the door, he put the key in her hand then covered it with his bigger, stronger one. She felt the heat of his body, not quite touching hers, but…there. "I…can't," she whispered. "Finn…"

"Do it. Open it. Let's see what's inside."

Panic rushed through her with the blood

in her veins, but his arms stayed around her, his voice low in her ear. For a second she feared she might faint. Her pulse thundered. Her palms went slick with sweat. And all the while Finn stayed at her back, his hand around hers, guiding her as she fumbled to fit the key into the lock. When she couldn't go any further, he reached around her to pull the door open. Wide.

"What do you see?" he asked, his head bent close, his cheek brushing hers.

Annabelle peered into the darkness. After her parents died, she'd hired a cleaning service, and they'd cleared out the closet while she stayed in a different room. Now she saw…nothing. Not a piece of doll's clothing on the floor, not a crumb of some snack from Sierra, not a single object in the musty-smelling closet. An empty space. "It's so… small," she murmured.

"And you were right. There's nothing to hurt you now." Finn stepped closer, easing Annabelle toward the open door. *Together*, he'd said, and they were. Taking a deep breath she stepped inside, Finn right behind her. "There, you see? It's only a closet. You don't need to be afraid." For a long moment they both looked around at the narrow little room before he turned her to him, his gaze holding hers, his arms around her again. Her pulse began to steady as Finn lowered his head and his mouth met hers in a few teasing, testing kisses, featherlight until he deepened the contact. Unable to resist, she melted into his embrace. "I'm here," he said, and Annabelle had never felt so safe, or cherished, in her thirty-one years.

WHAT IS THIS really about?

Finn was still pondering Grey's question—and Annabelle's sad reaction to the closet where she'd been punished, probably for doing nothing at all—when he went to talk to Derek the next day. He'd had no chance before Derek got out of jail.

The barn at Wilson Cattle was nearly empty except for a few horses that had stayed in their stalls rather than be turned out to enjoy the sunny afternoon. Dusty Malone didn't seem to be around, and neither was Grey. The first snow that had fallen was gone, but Finn hunched his shoulders against the chill in the air that remained. He found Derek in the tack room, his head bent over a fancy bridle studded with silver conchos, his gaze intent. "Moran?"

Derek's head jerked up. Absorbed in what he was doing, he must not have heard Finn come in. "Well, Sheriff, nice seeing you from the other side of those cell bars."

Uninvited, Finn took a seat on a tack trunk across from Derek. Finn had run this by Annabelle first and they'd agreed the timing now seemed right. "I'm here about Sierra Hartwell. According to a reliable source, you once had a relationship with her. True?"

"Sierra?" He shook his head then returned to his task. "Piece of work, that one. She 'bout ruined me for other women." He smiled. "Took me at least a week to get over her. Some kind of record."

Finn didn't think that said much about their relationship. He couldn't picture Derek being brokenhearted.

"Man, I wouldn't come anywhere near Sierra Hartwell again." Curiosity sparked in Derek's eyes. "Even if she suddenly came to life again. Whatever you were told, I didn't do it."

"How about fathering her child four years ago?"

Derek's eyes flashed then met Grey's gaze. "Me? A daddy? I don't care what anyone told you, Sierra and I went out a couple of times, had a few beers, that was all. I wouldn't call that a relationship. In my wayward youth, I might have wanted more, but Sierra treated me as if I was still a kid. Guess I was good enough to drink with, dance with—until she threw me over for some older guy." Derek spat on the rag he held, wiped it across one of the silver conchos then fell silent. In his law enforcement career Finn had learned when to keep quiet and let the suspect do the talking. He waited Derek out. "She had a baby—you need to see that guy. Not me." After another moment, he said, "Wait a minute. You mean the kid who's staying with Annabelle Foster?"

"Yes, and Annabelle would like to find Emmie's father."

Derek laughed. "Man, you gotta love small towns." He rose from the tack trunk, the bridle's hardware jingling in his hands. He ambled over to the wall; other bridles hung there, some plain, some elaborately worked in silver. "Show bridles," Derek explained as if they were having a casual chat. "Most of 'em belong to Olivia. Grey gave me this job to shine them up. Seems she's planning to return to competition after her baby's born. I don't pay attention to kids," Derek was quick to add, "but I sure know someone who should." His gaze bright, as if he liked someone else being on the spot for once, he named a man whose identity set Finn back on his heels. Someone right here in town. "I can't wait till this hits the fan," Derek said.

Finn stared at him. Was he telling the truth?

CHAPTER NINETEEN

WHAT IF DEREK had steered Finn and Annabelle to an innocent man? She was about to find out, and since this was not a criminal matter she'd eliminated Finn from the equation for now. Showing up with the sheriff didn't seem like the best idea and Annabelle had come alone to test the waters. *This is my problem.*

She pulled into a parking spot at the Barren Community Center, which housed the seniors' meeting space and various civic offices. When Finn had stopped by the diner to tell her what he'd found out, she'd been as incredulous as when Nell had told her about Derek.

I know I stood up for him before, but I can't imagine Derek turning the spotlight on someone—anyone—else, she'd said. *Knowing your history with him, he could have been tweaking you about this.*

Which wasn't her only concern. *I'm here,*

Finn had said last night, changing her view of their relationship—whether or not he wanted one—changing her feelings about the closet, and from the moment she'd laid eyes on him at the diner today she'd felt shaky. What if their relationship *could* become more? What if he wanted her and Emmie? Finn had made her feel safe but also capable. What did *she* really want?

Forcing her doubts from her mind, Annabelle got out of the car. She couldn't decide whether she hoped this man, like the one connected to Vegas, was Emmie's dad or not.

She strode up the walk to the front entrance then took the stairs to the second floor. As she opened the door onto the suite of offices, she fought an urge to flee. She'd never had the courage to do something like this before. At the receptionist's desk she gave her name then said, "I'd like to see the mayor, please."

"Do you have an appointment?"

"No, but I think he'll be interested in what I have to say."

In hushed tones, the receptionist spoke briefly to him over the intercom, and Annabelle was soon shown into the mayor's inner sanctum. Seated behind his broad desk, Harry Barnes studied her before recognition dawned in his sharp gaze. "Miss Foster. Did my assistant fail to thank you for your generous donation to my last campaign?"

"No, I received a note, and you're welcome. I was happy to donate this year on behalf of Annabelle's Diner." *The last year*, she thought.

He waved her toward a chair in front of his desk. Its surface was bare except for a thin stack of papers, and she knew that wide smile, which he wore in any photograph Annabelle had ever seen of him. Of course his meals with his staff at her diner were legendary, too. Townspeople often stopped by to greet him or to catch the mayor's ear about some pet project. "What have I done?" He grinned. "Committed a fund-raising violation? I didn't realize you were on the county election commission."

"Nothing like that." Getting to the heart of the matter before she lost her nerve, Annabelle squared her shoulders. She hated having to do this. "It's about Sierra Hartwell."

She watched Harry's expression change. A small crease formed between his eyebrows. "The name sounds vaguely familiar, but...

ah, yes. The woman who was killed in that accident."

"She was my cousin."

He cleared his throat. "Yes, I remember the newspaper reports. And of course, considering my position in the community, I made an appearance at the gravesite to pay my respects. A tragedy like that doesn't often happen here, thank goodness."

Yes, he'd shown up at the cemetery, but as if it was another campaign event. He'd given Annabelle his condolences but was there more, it seemed, to work the crowd.

"Did you know Sierra personally?" she pressed.

In the light coming through the office windows, his skin seemed to turn a sickly gray. "I never met the woman." He looked at his watch. "Now, if that's all, I have a meeting with the town planner. You've heard about my hope to develop the park by the creek?" It was a worthy cause, the spot where Emmie had fallen. "The playground is inadequate for our young people, and we need a better picnic facility, perhaps with a pavilion—if the voters approve." He glanced toward the door to the reception area.

Knowing she'd run out of time, she

reached into her pocket for the photograph she'd brought with her of Sierra and Emmie. Annabelle had found it among Sierra's things when she and Emmie made the collage. "This is my cousin's daughter," she said, holding it out.

He barely focused on the image before handing it back. "A pretty child. I have a three-year-old son."

"He and Emmie are friends at day care," she said.

"Elizabeth did tell me that. It can be a delightful age until it's not." He tried another smile that fell flat. "What does this have to do with me?"

Annabelle tried to sound...tactful. "I think you did know Sierra, and quite well. A few years ago, four in fact."

His gaze shifted. "That's absurd. What are you implying? I'm a married man." As if that protected him from scrutiny. And for a second, it did. She knew and liked Elizabeth. Annabelle didn't want to hurt her, but she could see beads of moisture on Harry's forehead, and his obvious discomfort gave Annabelle courage. His voice sounded strangled. "Why on earth would you come here like this—into my office as *mayor*—

and make this accusation? Do you have any idea how important I am in this town?" He went on, his face red, "Do you know anything about Sierra Hartwell? She was a *man-eater*."

Annabelle leaned forward. Harry was giving himself away with every word. "I thought you didn't know her."

"All right, I did. She had this way about her of charming, enticing, making promises, leading a man on, but it took no time to see what she was."

His tone was harsh and there was building anger in his eyes, yet he also looked trapped. She would confront him as she'd never dared to challenge her parents. For Emmie's sake. "Did you or did you not enjoy a romantic interlude with Sierra—"

"This is not a court of law, but please, say what you really mean," he said, his hands shaking. He lowered his voice to a near whisper. "I'll ask the question for you. Am I the father of Sierra Hartwell's child?"

"Are you?" Annabelle said, trying not to blink under his stare.

"How dare you accuse me of that, too? If a rumor like this gets around—and that's all it is—my political career, my life, would be ruined!" The mayor rose then rounded his desk, pushing his face close to hers, the invisible cloak of his office and its power crumpling like the Wicked Witch of the West into a puddle, but only for a moment. "*Why* would I have done such a thing? Have an affair that would risk the wife I love and three children I adore?" He stalked to the door. "This conversation is over. You will say nothing to the receptionist or anyone else on your way out." But he hadn't finished. "I hope this is the last of this, *Miss Foster.* I'm sure you don't want a visit from the county Health Department in violation of some ordinance relating to your diner." He jerked open the door then turned to grip her shoulder. Through his teeth, he said in a low, menacing tone, "One more thing before you go. I've seen you with Finn Donovan and I have no doubt he was part of this *charade.* Tell the sheriff if he gets involved any further, I'll have his badge."

He waited for Annabelle to leave and slammed the door behind her.

Her pulse thrumming in her ears, she rushed through the waiting area, down the stairs and out to her car, wondering if she should have let Finn handle this after all. Or dismissed Derek's accusation without proof? Certainly Finn doubted him, and though she wanted more than anything to find Emmie's father, she knew Derek could have lied.

But the mayor had certainly reacted, and he'd been right about one thing: he *was* a powerful man in town, even in the surrounding county, and furious, or scared, enough to retaliate now. If that got around, Annabelle would have an even harder time selling the diner. She'd have to cancel her course a second time, try to keep on running the place—and hope it didn't fail after all the gossip. She'd have to stay in Barren.

In her determination to help Emmie, she might have just made everything worse.

FINN STARED AT ANNABELLE. "You wandered into the mayor's office and accused him like that?" Luckily, he hadn't left work for the day yet, and as usual, Sarge was snoring on the floor by the front window. Finn didn't seem to hear him though the sound could hardly be ignored.

Annabelle tried to catch her breath. "I'm sorry. I didn't mean to involve you."

"Never mind me. I've been threatened before," Finn said. From the set of his mouth and the blaze of heat in his eyes, Annabelle knew he must be furious. With Harry, but also with her. "When I told you I thought he could be Emmie's dad, I didn't think you'd act on it yet. We don't have proof, just Derek's word. I needed to get to the truth first. The mayor's not an enemy you should make."

"I know that now." She rubbed her shoulder where she could still feel the imprint of his fingers. "Whatever he does next, I'll deal with it."

To her surprise Finn smiled, then contained it. He perched on the corner of his desk, his jeans taut over his thighs. "I have to admit, that took guts. I'm not worried for myself, but he could make life difficult for you and Emmie. Did you think of that before you barged into his office?"

"Of course I did."

"Then why do that? What's your hurry?"

"I was there for *her*." This wasn't the time to tell him about her trip to Phoenix. "I know I shouldn't have acted so quickly, but I'm—"

"Hoping for what? Harry's not about to move Emmie into his home with his wife and children and announce, even in this enlightened age, that—surprise—she's their sister." He added, "I expected you to mull over what Derek said while I dug deeper. Then if we were convinced he was telling the truth, to figure out the best means of approaching Harry. But now, I need you to keep away from him."

With their talk apparently concluded, Annabelle gathered her bag. She bent down to pat Sarge still sleeping in the sun. Except to cock one ear, he didn't move. When she straightened, she caught Finn studying her. He said, "Let's work on this later. Why don't you bring Emmie to the farm tonight? I'll get us dinner on the way home."

Annabelle couldn't resist teasing him. "From the diner? The special is shepherd's pie."

"Or the café," he said with a light in his eyes. "Jack could be making coq au vin."

Although she'd started it, Annabelle couldn't respond to his teasing; she knew Finn was right about Harry, and she might have ruined everything. Yet for once in her life she'd stood up for something. "It will be hard to talk with Emmie there." And she wasn't sure another evening with Finn was a good idea.

"I know what will keep Emmie busy," he said.

"I RIDING, FINN!" Emmie called down to him from the back of Freckles, the spotted pony.

"Yes you are." The saddle Olivia had donated was big for her, but Emmie couldn't have been happier. At least now, courtesy of his few lessons with Olivia, he could give Emmie some basic pointers.

"Go faster," Emmie insisted.

"Nell was right. She's already a cowgirl," Annabelle said, her first words since Finn had boosted Emmie into the saddle. Her fretful look reminded him of Caro keeping a close watch over Alex to the last second of her life. If Annabelle didn't think she was a mother at this point, she was dead wrong. If only she would realize that, change her mind about leaving town and…then what? Was he really interested in a long-term relationship, even with Annabelle? He'd certainly acted like he was in front of that closet door.

He led Freckles in a last loop around the yard then back to the barn.

By the doors the pony's ears pricked up and she tried to turn a walk into a trot. Finn pulled her up short, and the bay whickered a greeting from down the aisle. Freckles let out a whinny in return.

Emmie laughed. "Pony wants me to ride all the time!"

Finn's arm ached from the hold he'd kept on the lead rope so Freckles couldn't run off with Emmie. "Maybe not *all* the time…"

"Tomorry," she said, her word for *tomorrow*.

"We'll see what Annabelle thinks."

Emmie clapped her hands. "She says yes!"

"Now wait a minute." Annabelle was following them through the dim barn, keeping a safe distance from the pony's rear end.

As he showed Emmie how to unsaddle Freckles, wipe down the pony's hide and brush until it gleamed, he could feel his insides begin to unwind. All afternoon he'd pondered what to do about Harry Barnes.

He'd also asked himself why he had invited Annabelle to dinner. Where had his first inclination to keep her and Emmie away gone? His feelings had gradually changed. Now he enjoyed hearing the bell-like tinkle of Emmie's laughter, seeing her light up as Alex used to do, her joy in simply being… alive. Did that also mean he wanted Annabelle to be a permanent part of his life?

"Okay, short stuff. Let's get some dinner."

"Pony wants to eat."

"Yes, she does, and so does her friend."

"While you finish here, I'll go up to the house," Annabelle said.

Finn nodded. "We'll be right there."

He walked Emmie down the aisle to the feed room where they prepared meals for Freckles and Brown then delivered them to the stall. With the two horses munching away, Emmie finally agreed they could go to the house for their own dinner. By the time she'd finished her fried chicken, smashed potatoes and coleslaw, Emmie was practically asleep in her plate. Finn carried her into the living room—a habit he could get used to—then covered her with an afghan on the sofa. When he straightened, Annabelle was there holding two cups of coffee.

"Thanks," Finn said. "Let's take this outside."

That sounded as if he was challenging someone to a fight. He hoped tonight wasn't going to end up that way, but the thought, plus his uncertainty about Annabelle, hovered in his head like the splash of stars above in the night sky.

BUNDLED IN HER JACKET, Annabelle sat on the top porch step beside Finn. In the cool December night, their shoulders touched, and the quick rush of need that flowed through her threatened to overwhelm her. From the barn she could hear the horses shuffling around, occasionally "talking" to each other. She didn't want to think about Emmie's future tonight, or her own stay in Phoenix. "I wonder if Olivia would consider giving Emmie lessons."

"She has her hands full trying to teach me." Finn sent her a sideways smile. "I have to admit, getting on a horse isn't the worst thing I've ever done. Not that I've decided to buy myself that black Stetson."

She thought of her meeting with the mayor. No matter how that turned out, did she really get how hard it would be to part with both Emmie and Finn? To leave here? Because of them, her worst memories of Barren didn't seem quite as bad as they once had. Neither did the closet.

He reached for her hand. Finn must have sensed what she was thinking. "We'll get through this without hurting Emmie."

We? Could there be a happy ending for them? Somehow? Those sweet moments at the paddock, watching Emmie ride with Finn's gentle guidance, had made her vision blur. What if that could be part of every day? But Annabelle wasn't sure. And once Finn learned about her course in Phoenix… "I can't see any way out," she murmured, "that won't hurt her."

She shivered and Finn tried to draw her closer, but Annabelle resisted. He rose from the step. "I'll get you something warmer to wear. Be right back."

Instead, she stood up too. "No, finish your coffee. This has been quite a day. I could use a minute to myself. Tell me where and I'll find it."

He hesitated. "Well, okay. I'll check on the horses in the meantime."

Finn had sent her upstairs to find a sweater, trusting her to invade his privacy. With a cursory glance at his bed's navy blue comforter, the simple but masculine furniture, Annabelle went straight to the bureau against the far wall—then stopped. Finn hadn't told her which drawer to look in.

Annabelle opened the top one then caught her breath.

Even that quick glance told her these were Finn's most personal items. And they broke her heart.

"Not that drawer," she heard him say. He must have suddenly remembered where she might look. Finn crossed the room and reached around her to shut the drawer, but the images she'd seen were engraved on her mind. Valentine's Day cards. The invitation to Finn and Caro's wedding. Alex's birth announcement. The blue hospital bracelet he'd worn and his baby shoes. A sonogram picture... Finn's voice was low and husky. "That closet in your house, this drawer...we both had secrets."

"You helped me face my fears," she said. "That helped a lot. Will you show me what's in here, Finn? Talk about them?"

"I can't," but then he opened the drawer and picked through the items until he came to the sonogram. "Caro was pregnant when she died," he said in a hoarse tone. "The last thing she said...she couldn't wait for me to see what Santa was bringing."

"Another baby," Annabelle murmured. He'd lost his wife and son, and he'd also lost their unborn child. "Finn, I shouldn't have pried."

"No, that was my fault. You weren't pry-ing. Maybe I wanted you to see all this even when I'm not ready," he said, closing the drawer then turning her toward him. Finn had let her glimpse the deepest part of his heart, and she saw that in his eyes, though he didn't go on. The baby was an additional loss for Finn, but what else did he not want to share with her?

No matter what it was, she owed him the same honesty he'd just given her. She'd stalled long enough.

"I can't imagine how you feel," she said. "I can't imagine how *I'll* feel when I have to leave Emmie. I know that's not the same, but... I'm taking that first step. I'm going to Phoenix." The rest of the words didn't come easily, and when she'd finished explaining, Finn's expression remained impassive. He'd already challenged her for meeting with the mayor, but his reaction to the course wasn't at all what she expected.

"A different school? Huh. I can see why you wanted to confront Harry so quickly." Finn asked about the dates she'd be gone then took a breath as if he were about to plunge into a deep pool but couldn't swim. "While you're away I could watch Emmie if you want, take her to day care, pick her up when I leave the station. She'd love being at the farm with Sarge, Freckles…maybe she wouldn't miss you quite as much."

Shocked, she said, "Is this the same man who once wanted nothing to do with her?" She glanced at the closed bureau drawer. "Are you sure?" Clearly, that would remind Finn of Chicago, Caro and Alex and the baby, but after another moment he nodded.

"Mostly sure. I think Emmie would be fine."

"Finn—"

"I know this thing with the mayor isn't easily resolved and you've spent most of your life feeling isolated because of your parents, feeling as if you need to escape—but you don't have to go it alone."

Annabelle's throat tightened. He'd already helped her with the closet. "I really appreciate your offer, but we're talking about a first, short trip for ten days—not Emmie's entire future. And if I could keep her with me…forever, I would. But that's not the right choice. For her. It's not practical."

Finn's tone hardened. "And you're always practical."

"After I get my certificate, I'll be building

a business. I'll need to put a lot of effort into finding clients." Her voice gained strength. "I'm thinking of doing a mix of adult and student tours—like their class trips on spring break to Washington, DC—but other people would want to see Europe or Asia. Remember, it's a twenty-four-hour job. It would be too difficult to take Emmie with me. Once she starts school—"

"All of that could be worked out. I've watched you with her. If you can't see the love in your eyes for that little girl, just look in a mirror—I can. My role as a father was taken from me. You have the chance I'll never have with Alex. You can watch her grow up and become a good person, provide the kind of secure home she never had with Sierra. That's not simply a matter of place, Annabelle. Or time. So what if Harry Barnes *is* Emmie's father? He might not accept her, but *you* can. You can give Emmie what she needs. You already have."

She almost wavered. "I'm not the person you think I am. My parents didn't show me how to be a good mother, and I won't risk ruining Emmie as they did me."

"That's not true. Maybe you didn't know

at first—no one does—but you're better equipped now. Your bad experience doesn't mean you can't give her a good life."

"You don't understand. I have to—"

"What?" Finn shot a look at the bureau drawer. "Get away from here? Well, let me tell you something. You can travel the world, but unless you make peace with your parents, they'll always control you—even if you never come back to Barren. You still won't find what you're looking for. I should know," he said. "I fled from Chicago, hoping to make some kind of life here, trusting that Cooper would help find justice for Caro and Alex, that I'd find some way to forget—" He shook his head. "It doesn't work. Your memories will go with you. Even after you found the courage to look in that closet."

"Maybe they will, but I need to do this. To try."

"I turned my back on my father years ago," Finn went on. "He never had time for me, yet he still crowds into my thoughts. But when my uncle died, then I lost Caro and Alex, I never even had the chance to say goodbye. My uncle was shot on duty and I wasn't there. With Caro and Alex, I was, but everything happened too fast. I couldn't stop their bleeding. The cops didn't get there for eleven whole minutes, the longest minutes of my life, and the ambulance came behind them. You told me there was nothing I could do, but there is something you can do for Emmie."

"I'm not coldhearted, Finn." Her voice thickened. "It will be hard to let her go, but I feel that's what will be best for her."

"Or easiest for you?" With his back to her, he walked across the room to the door. "We don't always get what we want, Annabelle. I should know that, too."

"Yes you should," she said. "But that new life you wanted?" She gestured at the bureau though he didn't see the motion. "Those mementos are heartbreaking, Finn, but you've all but buried yourself here just as you tried to shut away your memories in that dresser drawer. The way you keep hoping to find justice for your family when that may never happen."

He turned around. "Even from here, with those killers still loose in Chicago, I'll *find* a way if it takes the rest of my life."

"And turns you into a bitter man?"

A muscle ticked in his jaw. "If it does, there'll be no one else to suffer. But, you, Annabelle? I can't believe you'd just walk away from Emmie."

CHAPTER TWENTY

FINN STARED OUT the window at the driveway, the falling snow and the last wink of red taillights from Annabelle's car. Minutes ago she'd walked past him through the bedroom and down the stairs, roused Emmie from sleep then left him to regret what he'd said. He knew she'd never leave Emmie with the wrong person, which apparently included him because he couldn't see Annabelle letting him keep Emmie now even for ten days.

Just when he'd been feeling better about things, even his past, and tempted to give in to his feelings for Annabelle, he'd blown it.

Finn turned from the window as his phone rang. Wondering if it might be her, he saw the caller ID and tried not to feel disappointed. "Hey, Cooper."

"Donovan?" A different voice sounded harried. Why did he have Cooper's cell?

His stomach tightened in dread. "Yeah. Who's this?"

The man identified himself as Jimmy O'Neill, Cooper's current partner. "I thought you'd want to know. His new 'informant' for The Brothers turned out to be a setup. I warned him—"

"So did I." Fear pounded through Finn's veins. Eduardo Sanchez's face, his dark eyes blank and soulless, filled Finn's mind like a bad movie. "What's happened?"

"We got caught in an ambush. You'd remember the site." O'Neill mentioned the old building used as the gang's clubhouse where Cooper and Finn conducted the raid that had led to his family's deaths. "When we went to talk with this woman who claimed she had evidence, all hell broke loose. We were surrounded by those punks, heavily armed." He said, "Cooper's in surgery now. I had his cell phone with your number in his contacts. Before they took him to the OR, he asked me to call."

Finn's hands felt clammy. "How bad?"

"I'm praying he'll beat the odds, but he's pretty torn up, gut shot in fact." Which Finn knew was often a fatal wound. "The bullet spiraled through all kinds of places and it wasn't the only one. Cooper's a tough guy—you know that—but I don't want to get your hopes up. If that was me, I'd already be dead."

Jimmy O'Neill promised to keep Finn in the loop, and after they hung up Finn gave himself a pep talk. The hospital was top-notch and had saved more than one cop in its time, but all he could think about was Cooper on the operating table fighting for his life.

Safe in Barren, Finn had let his partner do the heavy lifting in Chicago, just as his family had paid the price for that raid, and the vicious gang was still in business. Finn wanted to strangle the woman who'd betrayed Cooper.

Ten minutes later, Finn had a plane ticket to Chicago. His heart rate must be in the danger zone, but he couldn't sit on the sidelines any longer. He had lost Caro and Alex and the baby. Even if Finn died trying, he wasn't going to lose Cooper too.

"HEAR YE, HEAR YE." At the end of the large table in the center of the diner's main room, scattered with the remnants of their dinner, Olivia raised her water glass in a toast. "How excited are you, Belle?"

The other members of the Girls' Night Out

group lifted their glasses in honor of Annabelle's upcoming trip to Phoenix, yet she detected a general lack of enthusiasm.

"Very," she said, though that wasn't quite the word. "I'm really looking forward to the course." Outside, the snow kept falling, weighing down the branches of the trees and piling up on cars parked along Main Street.

Annabelle hadn't heard from Finn. She'd finally called the station today only to learn he'd left town on "personal business," and after last night at his farm, she kept turning over his words in the darker shadows of her mind. *I can't believe you'd just walk away from Emmie.*

Annabelle regretted their argument, but on both their parts the words had been spoken and couldn't be taken back. Still, Emmie's welfare preyed on her mind.

Tonight she was with Grey and Ava who planned to watch movies, play games and make popcorn. The little girl who'd come to Annabelle, fearful and alone, who'd mourned her mother in silence, had become a social butterfly with her friends on the Circle H, at Wilson Cattle and with Seth Barnes in day care, which Emmie now seemed to love. Even her temper tantrums were becoming less frequent, and her language development seemed to be improving.

Annabelle smiled. "Emmie's been so cute. Last night she talked to me for what seemed like hours, reporting everything that happened that day at what she calls her 'school,' and after riding the pony at Finn's place, she likes *Janie Wants to be a Cowgirl* even better."

Shadow groaned. "Please don't mention that story. If Ava and I read it once, we've read it a thousand times. Whenever Emmie comes over, they read it together."

"She's going to miss you, Belle, even for a short while." Olivia ran a finger around the rim of her glass, and Annabelle felt another twinge of guilt.

She would miss Emmie too. She'd even almost miss cooking every day at the diner. Who would she share a meal with in Phoenix? Strangers, when right here she had Blossom, Shadow and Olivia who knew her, really knew her. She and Grey's stepmother Liza had become friends too, and from across the table Liza sent her a probing look.

"Are you sure about this?" she asked. "You're taking a big step. I don't simply

mean your course. Are you really committed to selling this diner, your house, then
moving away from everyone you know, including us?"

Yes, she wanted to say—and *not* feel
guilty—but she couldn't seem to voice the
thought. She already missed Emmie, and
the little girl was only fifteen minutes away
at Wilson Cattle. How would she feel when
Emmie was here, and Annabelle was sitting
in a classroom far away, preparing to leave
her for good? Would Emmie cry when she
left? Would *she*?

"The diner has been shown—thank goodness—several times now," she said, "and
wonder of wonders today Jack Hancock
came to see it."

Shadow said, "I thought he was happy
running the dinner service at the café."

"But he doesn't own it. He'd also like to
have his own restaurant, and apparently he's
been considering the diner since my sign
went up in the front window."

"Has he made an offer?"

"Not yet. My asking price seemed high
to Jack—when I'm practically giving it
away. He'll get back to me after he's talked
to Wanda." She added, "He'd have to make

any offer through my Realtor, hopefully by the time I get back."

Olivia took a last sip of water. "After that, things may move fast." A short silence fell over the group. "Well," she said at last, "it seems you've made up your mind."

"The longer I wait, the older I'll get, the bigger Emmie will be, and sooner or later making that choice will seem like too much change. I'll be stuck even deeper in my rut." Annabelle flushed. "I don't mean you guys or Emmie are part of *that*—"

Blossom shifted. "But we are, Belle. I'm getting uncomfortable." Did she mean with their conversation? Blossom pressed a hand to her chest. She'd left her baby at home with Logan who couldn't provide any nourishment. "Sorry, ladies. I have to leave."

"Stay a few more minutes." Olivia cast a worried glance at the others. "We need to say our goodbyes before Annabelle takes off— her first time away from us—and shed some tears. I wish Nell was here."

"She couldn't make it," Annabelle said, a growing lump in her throat. These women were her dearest friends. She'd watched Blossom fall in love with Logan—the right man for her this time—shared their joy when the baby was born. She'd been Shadow's confidante more than once about Grey. She'd seen Olivia through her divorce then her reunion with Sawyer. Every significant moment of her life had been spent or shared with these people, in this place. And some with Finn who'd helped her through Sierra's last days, stood beside her at the cemetery until he couldn't stay, not to mention being with her when she opened the closet door. He'd let her see into his heart, and known how to handle Emmie when Annabelle could not.

The others murmured their agreement. Blossom rose from the table, looking regretful. "I really hate to cut this short—especially tonight—but, Belle, you know I wish you the best. I love you like a sister," she said, folding Annabelle into a tight hug. "I wish you were staying though I understand why you're not."

Olivia's tone turned gruff. "As Sawyer says, I hope you're leaving for the right reasons. Your parents aren't here to make you unhappy now—and I can't help wondering if this has something to do with our hunky sheriff, too."

Everyone's eyebrows shot up in unison.

"Of course not." But her pulse tripped at

the mention of him. She missed him, despite their quarrel about Emmie.

Olivia's mouth tightened. "Grey thinks Finn more than likes you, and I speak for all of us when I say we've known ever since he moved to Barren how you feel about him. It's in your eyes whenever he's mentioned. Like now. Why not stick around? See where that can go?"

Annabelle began to stack their dinner plates. "Before he left for Chicago, Finn and I…" She trailed off, wondering what business he had there. Did it have to do with Caro and Alex? Maybe he'd gone to see about his storage unit. "I can't say we broke up when we never went that far, but…whatever it was, it's time for me to do what I've always wanted to do." *Escape*, he'd said. "I have to go."

Every face fell. Olivia's eyes filled with tears and Shadow pressed her trembling lips together. Blossom busied herself, taking a last sip of tea, fiddling with her coat and gloves. Liza toyed with her turquoise-and-silver necklace.

"My dear friends…" Annabelle couldn't go on.

No one seemed able to speak. Instead, they drew her into a group embrace.

"Well." Blossom pulled away first. "No more of this or I'll be drowning in tears the whole way home. I know you'll be back—for a while—"

"Give Logan a hug from me and a kiss for Daisy," Annabelle said.

"I will. Thanks." She added, "Thanks, too, for being my friend. When I came to Barren, I didn't have anyone here and you've always been so kind."

"I love you all," Annabelle managed to say, watching Blossom walk to the door and open it, letting in a sharp blast of wintry air. "Drive safely."

"I will." But Blossom didn't leave. She closed the door. "Belle, have you decided who will care for Emmie? Logan and I would be happy to have her."

"So would Sawyer and I. Nick would get to practice being a big brother." Olivia fussed with her napkin. "I know you'll be back after the course to tie things up here—and if the trial run has worked for everyone, we'd certainly have room for her in our home and in our hearts. We can decide then."

Liza stepped in, sadness in her gaze. "I'd love another grandchild to spoil."

What were they saying? She couldn't imagine better people to care for Emmie, but all Annabelle would have then was her broken heart. "You all mean...permanently?"

"Yes," everyone said at once.

Shadow added, "If you're determined to leave, we won't see her with strangers. Grey and I would love Emmie to join our family. I don't even need to ask him."

"Go," Olivia said, a tear tracking down her cheek. "Enjoy Phoenix. Emmie will be fine with us. Maybe we'll let her spend a few days with each family in turn. How would that be?"

"She'd like that. She adores Nick, Ava and Daisy. She's never really had a family. Or a home."

"Until she came to you," Shadow pointed out.

As they all hugged one last time, saying goodbye, Annabelle fought back tears. Crying in front of her favorite people wouldn't accomplish anything, and as everyone started for the door, chatting and managing a laugh or two to cover emotion, she held herself in check.

From the doorway Annabelle watched each woman get into her car, the headlights come on, the cars turning away as they headed down Main Street. The diner, the house, the town, even Finn, would be in her rearview mirror soon enough. With everyone gone, she locked up, hung the closed sign on the door and drove off herself to put the last of the clothing and toiletries in her suitcase. *Soon*, she thought.

FINN DISLIKED HOSPITAL ROOMS almost as much as he hated accident scenes. Which was why, half an hour ago, he'd headed from the hospital to Cooper's apartment, which was situated on a quiet side street.

Finn shivered. The heat was off, but it was the sight of his partner lying helpless in his hospital bed, tubes and monitors everywhere, that had chilled Finn. He turned on the heating system then prowled the apartment like a beat cop on patrol, from its small living room to the kitchenette then down the short hall to Cooper's room. He'd left the double bed unmade. Dishes in the sink. A bachelor pad or signs of a man who'd been in a hurry to meet his fate? To sacrifice himself for Finn?

The memorabilia in this room told Cooper's story. On the dresser stood a bunch of awards for high school and college football teams, a 4-H trophy for a calf he'd raised, a few junior rodeo buckles that reminded Finn of the posters in Jared Moran's room and, more disturbingly, of Annabelle's intention to travel, her one-way trip away from Barren.

The mementos and photographs of Cooper with his parents touched him, Cooper on graduation day from the police academy, a rangy teenage Cooper with his booted foot propped on a fence, his arm around a girl, against the view of a flattened landscape. Kansas, no doubt, and the family ranch outside of Farrier where Cooper had grown up—and was that girl Nell Sutherland? In all the pictures he looked the model of a healthy boy then a strong man in his prime.

During his brief visit, Finn was grateful that Cooper had been able to talk. He suspected nothing would shut Cooper up as long as he could draw breath.

What are you doing here? his friend had asked, voice slurred from painkillers. His hair, the color of sun, was dull and lank around his wan face. *Get your kicks watching a man when he's down?*

You'll be on your feet...in no time. The doctors weren't that optimistic.

He'd groaned. *First nurse who tries to get me out of this bed before I'm ready will find out why they call me Mr. Case Closed.* He'd lifted a hand. *Bam. Out for the count.*

Right now I'm betting on the nurse, Finn had said.

Cooper had eyed Finn a little while later, as if he could see through him. *You still here? Should be on your way home. I know the pull that place has on a man, the open space, the lowing of cattle, the wind through the cottonwoods...* He'd closed his gray eyes. *Don't worry. I'll be back in the saddle. So to speak.*

Home, Finn had said. *As soon as you're good again, come see me.*

Cooper had tried to straighten, but fell back against the pillows with a grunt. *Kansas has been good for you. Your eyes don't have the same look they did and your shoulders aren't tensed up around your neck.* He'd offered a weak smile. *You're already a happier man than the one who left here.*

I will be, Finn had agreed. He didn't mean

with Annabelle or Emmie, though. Not after what he and Annabelle had said to each other.

Cooper's gaze had sharpened. *Let it be, Finn. Caroline and Alex are gone and look where I am. Don't want you to end up the same way.*

I won't. Finn had touched his partner's good shoulder, the one without a gauze bandage. *Sure wish I could have you with me when—*

Cut it out. With a softer moan, Cooper had eased away from his touch. *If you'd been there last night maybe things would have ended differently, and sooner or later someone in that gang will mess up, but another cop will have to seal this deal. Not you,* he said. *For both of us, it ends now.*

Finn hadn't answered.

In Cooper's empty apartment now he picked up a photo then set it down. Cooper was a big guy, taller than Finn with more muscle, a guy who could take care of himself. But in the ambush at the gang's clubhouse, that had worked against him. Cooper always thought he was invincible. Now he lay in that hospital bed, eyes closed, face ashen, with half a dozen wounds, most of them serious. Looking as bad as Sierra had.

This was Finn's battle to win, not Cooper's. Always had been. And he'd nearly gotten his old partner killed. Well, with the ambush, that had changed. Even his quarrel with Annabelle finally fled from his mind. She'd accused him of becoming a bitter man, and what had he said? *There'll be no one else to suffer.*

If this was the last thing he ever did, Finn had a score to settle.

WHEN ANNABELLE CAME out of the day care center a few days later, she found Elizabeth Barnes waiting for her in the parking lot. Annabelle's step faltered. Was this to be a day of reckoning? She hadn't seen Elizabeth since she'd gone to the mayor's office; in fact, today she'd purposely brought Emmie a bit later than usual. What kind of reaction would his wife have?

Elizabeth approached her. "Can we talk?"

"Of course." She followed Elizabeth to her car, a shiny high-end model. They sat in the front seat behind the tinted glass of the windshield, but Elizabeth's gaze remained on the parking lot outside.

"I feel like I'm in some kind of spy novel," she said, her eyes not meeting Annabelle's. "But I don't want any of my husband's constituents to see us."

Annabelle's heart hurt. "No one would know what we're talking about," though Elizabeth must surely think everyone would. Obviously, after her husband's betrayal, she felt exposed. "Most of the other parents have gone." Annabelle saw only a few cars parked nearby, and she recognized most of those as belonging to Mary Whitman and two of her staff. "I'm so sorry about all of this. I never meant to hurt you."

Elizabeth ignored the apology. "I've spoken with Harry. At length," she added with a rueful glance at Annabelle. "He's agreed to take a paternity test—if you'll also provide a DNA sample from Emmie."

She started to say I'd be happy to, then thought better of it. That would sound flippant and there was nothing lighthearted about this situation. Also, she really liked Elizabeth Barnes. She'd hoped they might be friends. She could even see her as a new member of the Girls' Night Out.

"Yes," Annabelle said about the sample. "That—at least—won't be a problem."

Elizabeth focused on the building that housed the day care center. Her expression was closed. "I can already guess what the results will be."

Annabelle understood. "You mean, because Emmie and your Seth look so much alike."

"And took to each other right away that first day."

"It's as if they sense some connection."

They exchanged a solemn, knowing look. "I don't want this to hurt either of them." Elizabeth didn't seem concerned about herself, only her family's shattered privacy. "As long as we use discretion, no one else has to know."

Did she think Annabelle would spread the word all over town? Annabelle wondered if Elizabeth was trying to protect Harry Barnes; or if her statement was meant, after Annabelle had confronted him, to thwart her from saying anything more.

"I don't think the mayor's reputation should be the first consideration," she began but she didn't get to finish.

"No, I worry about the children." Elizabeth twisted her hands in her lap. "But I don't intend to leave my husband either. This may be hard to understand... Harry made a dreadful mistake that has damaged our marriage, yet I do still love him. He's agreed to see a counselor with me to talk about his infidelity. We're spending next weekend in Kansas City to meet with her. I suppose we'll have to see how that turns out, too."

Annabelle laid a hand on hers. "You're a fine person, Elizabeth. I don't know that I could be that forgiving."

"I haven't forgiven yet, but I have three children," she said. "I owe them an attempt to put things back together again with Harry."

Annabelle's voice shook. "I wouldn't do anything to harm your family. Or my... Emmie." She reached across the console to hug her. "I really am sorry."

After a moment Elizabeth drew away with tears in her eyes. "You're not to blame. This was bound to surface sometime. The only people at fault are Harry—and Sierra Hartwell." She paused. "If he really is Emmie's dad, you may be sure my husband will provide support for her. I'll see to it."

And Annabelle felt like crying too.

ALONE IN HER BEDROOM that night Annabelle added her toiletry bag to her suitcase. What had she forgotten?

From across the hall came Emmie's soft voice. She was playing both parts in some drama costarring her lamb Finnie. Emmie hadn't spoken to her since breakfast when Annabelle had told her she'd be staying with Blossom and Logan. Emmie had pondered what that meant. "You too?"

"No, sweetie. I'm going away. Remember, we talked about that?"

The light dawned. "To you school?"

"Yes," Annabelle said. "I would have taken you with me, but—"

"They don't like kids?"

"Of course they do. It's just…" She ran out of words. "You'll have a better time at the Circle H."

Annabelle hadn't really slept much since the last Girls' Night Out meeting, and after seeing Elizabeth earlier she doubted she would tonight. Yesterday Nell had come into the diner briefly to say goodbye. Then only last night, while Annabelle and Emmie were reading *Janie,* Jack Hancock's offer for the diner had come in. Without countering the lower price, she had accepted his offer.

Faster than she'd ever thought, everything

was falling into place. She should feel better about that than she did.

As for Finn, he was still in Chicago, which worried her. Had he gone, not about a storage locker, but because of that gang? Was he putting his life at risk? Annabelle didn't have his cell phone number and wouldn't see him before her flight to Phoenix, and maybe that was for the best. Still, if their quasi relationship was now over, she hated to leave without trying to make amends for her unkind words.

The voices in the other room stopped talking, and Emmie appeared, hair tousled, thumb stuck in her mouth. Her expression reminded Annabelle of her own mother, disapproving of whatever she did. *Your place is right here. Don't even think of going anywhere. Your father and I worked ourselves to death so you could have this diner.* Annabelle had been too afraid to tell them that wasn't what she wanted.

Emmie eyed the suitcase as if it were about to explode. "You go now?"

"Not yet," she said. "Tomorrow. You can help me pack your things."

In the morning Annabelle would drive her

to the Circle H where Logan was keeping Finn's dog and the horses in his absence.

"I see pony and Finn?"

"Um, not Finn."

Emmie's face clouded. "Where *he* go?"

"To Chicago—for a while—where he used to live." Annabelle needed to put a more positive spin on this. "Freckles and Big Brown will be at the ranch," she said. "You and Nick can ride."

She'd expected Emmie to jump up and down when she learned her equine friends were waiting for her. Instead, she retreated to the door, keeping one eye on Annabelle's suitcase.

"You don't come back," she said.

"Emmie. I'll be back before you know I'm gone," Annabelle said, wondering how she would explain the permanent separation that would follow. Emmie must still feel afraid of being left alone, as Sierra had often left her. Before she could run across the hall to her room, Annabelle caught Emmie in her arms. Kneeling on the wooden floor, she held her close. "Not like your mother. I promise, I'll be home soon."

But once Jack signed the papers for the

diner and the house went on the market, events would happen even faster, and Emmie would be moving, too. She'd be fine with any of Annabelle's friends, a much better solution for her than even Harry Barnes...

The DNA samples were now with the lab, but after his reaction Annabelle had wondered why Sierra extracted her promise to find Emmie's father. Now she decided it couldn't have been for emotional reasons. Sierra must have wanted his financial support for Emmie.

She kissed the top of Emmie's head. By now she'd hoped to feel over the moon in her eagerness to start this long-delayed adventure. Yet that also meant leaving other people behind, her friends, who were like family to her. And Finn. She wished she hadn't parted with him on bad terms.

How could she make this first journey less painful for Emmie? She had no way of knowing things would work out.

Emmie seemed a split second away from throwing another legendary tantrum and Annabelle braced herself. "I'm sorry you're unhappy with me, sweetie. I don't ever want to hurt you. I...I do love you, Em."

She searched Annabelle's face then nearly knocked her over with a hug. "Lub you too, A-bel." Emmie pressed her face close. "We stay."

CHAPTER TWENTY-ONE

BEHIND A THICK cover of bushes, Finn crouched in the darkness. His gun drawn, he double-checked the area, making sure Jimmy O'Neill, Cooper's new partner, and the rest of the task force the department had formed were in place. The cars and the SWAT team van had parked out of sight near another warehouse. There was more firepower on scene here than ever before. There wasn't a cop in Chicago who didn't want to bring down the gang that had so grievously wounded Cooper. After talking his way into the action for tonight, Finn had been deputized and given the go-ahead to serve as point man. They were all waiting for his signal—

A car pulled up, then a second, a third, and the members of The Brothers spilled out, laughing and talking among themselves as if they hadn't a care in the world. As if they didn't gun down innocent people like Finn's family and Cooper without a thought.

He didn't take his eyes off them. Adrenaline flooded through his body, and his heart slammed against his rib cage. The gang filed into their clubhouse, taking their time, and as they passed mere feet from him, Finn held still in the shadows. Tonight, probably not expecting trouble, they weren't wearing masks, but he had no doubt they were as well armed as the day Caro and Alex died. Or the night Cooper got shot. His breath held, Finn watched their leader walk by so close Finn could have throttled him before he reached the door. *Eduardo Sanchez.*

Finn couldn't move. He saw Jimmy O'Neill pop up and his questioning look from the bushes on the other side of the door, the tilt of his head toward Sanchez as if to say *now*?—but still, Finn felt paralyzed. There'd been a time when he would have given the signal with no more thought than Sanchez had of Finn's family. If he didn't act now… All he could think of was Annabelle, Emmie and the way he'd left things between them. Yet even that wasn't what held him in place as if his feet were glued to the spot. If Sanchez turned and saw him, he would certainly try to kill Finn. In the next few seconds he could *die* here. Once, he'd thought that wouldn't matter. He'd already lost his wife, his son, the baby. *There'll be no one else to suffer*, he'd told Annabelle.

But that wasn't true. *She* would suffer. Emmie would, too. A few angry words from Annabelle—most of them on-target about Finn—didn't change the fact that he cared about her, about Emmie. Even cared about himself again.

Finn had a choice to make. He could either signal the task force to move or stand here frozen as he had the last time he met up with Eduardo Sanchez. He'd never told Annabelle that. He could lose his own life.

Yet he'd come this far. He had to finish what Sanchez had started. As the last guy entered the clubhouse, Finn caught Jimmy O'Ncill's eye.

With no more hesitation Finn gave the hand signal then exploded from his hiding spot and kicked in the door. Sanchez whirled and Finn leveled his gun at the center of Sanchez's forehead. "Freeze! Police!"

Everything happened fast—a burst of shots from the other members of the gang, returning gunfire from Finn's men and the SWAT team. A few seconds and it was over. One dead, two others hurt, all bad guys. Finn headed straight for Sanchez's girlfriend, the one who had pretended to be Cooper's informant and gotten him shot. She'd never been Sanchez's ex. In her ear, he growled the Miranda rights as he snapped on handcuffs. "This is for Cooper Ransom."

Next, he crossed the warehouse to where Jimmy had his gun trained on Sanchez. "Give me a second," he told the other cop.

"Careful, Donovan."

Finn's pulse thundered loud enough to be heard. He snatched another pair of handcuffs from Jimmy then jerked Sanchez's wrists behind his back, hearing the satisfying clink of the cuffs lock into place. "And this is for Caroline and Alex."

Sanchez only stared at him over his shoulder, his dark eyes blank. His gaze didn't flicker, and Finn thought in shock, *He doesn't even remember who they were.*

WITH A DETERMINED squaring of her shoulders, Annabelle turned at the bottom of the Circle H's porch steps. Like the diner, the house and Barren, the ranch would soon be out of sight and out of her life for the next ten days. As she got into her car, she snapped a mental picture of Emmie standing in the door to the house, holding a Popsicle. Who knew it would be *this* hard to actually leave this defenseless child, even though she knew Logan and Blossom would take great care of her?

Lub you too, A-bel. After hearing that simple statement last night, Annabelle had sat on the floor of the hallway holding Emmie in her arms, wanting to never let go.

Blinking, she tooted the horn, gave a last wave then pulled out onto the long driveway that led to the road, to her future. She wouldn't look back. Wouldn't cry. *Stop those tears*, her father would say. *Or I'll give you something to cry about.* Usually, that had meant locking Annabelle in the dark closet. But thanks in part to Finn, that space had ceased to hold such terror for her.

Half a mile down the country lane, she pulled over, telling herself she'd only braked hard to avoid a rabbit leaping across her path. After the bunny disappeared into the thick grass by the road, Annabelle leaned her head on her crossed arms against the steering wheel. Despite the memory of her father's words, she wept.

I can't believe you'd just walk away from Emmie, Finn had said. Sierra had done enough damage to her daughter, and Annabelle didn't want to add to that. For too long she'd seen Sierra as her champion, her protector, but if she'd been wrong about Sierra, what else was she wrong about? *Stay*, Emmie had begged her. So what if Annabelle wasn't the most experienced person to parent that adorable little girl? She was learning, and she would get better. As Olivia had told her, *We all learn by doing*.

No one criticized Annabelle now in the house where she'd grown up or in the diner she now ran on her own. She even missed the diner this morning, the clang of pots and pans, the hiss of bacon frying, the cinnamon scent of fresh pumpkin pies, the daily sight of her regular customers coming in for breakfast, lunch or dinner and, often, conversation. The ladies from the library auxiliary, Nell and even Harry Barnes. She knew them all, cared about them, too, as she did her other friends.

You can travel the world, but unless you make peace with your parents, they'll always control you, Finn had said. And he was right.

She couldn't do this. She couldn't leave Emmie. Or—if there was some way to make amends—Finn. Might as well admit it. She loved him.

FINN HAD TAKEN the red-eye from Chicago to Kansas City. There, in the airport parking lot, he'd picked up the new Dodge Ram he'd bought to haul hay and equipment at the farm then drove just above the speed limit toward Barren. As he blew past the town sign that read "Population 5,265. A good place to call home," he decided to look for a used horse trailer. If he had to take Freckles or Brown to the vet, he didn't want to call Logan, Sawyer or Grey every time. The realization that Grey had turned him into a cowboy of sorts didn't make him flinch.

After bringing in The Brothers and Sanchez, Finn had asked himself some serious questions. Did he want to bury himself here, as Annabelle accused him of doing, remain focused on his past and the tragedy that had taken his family from him?

Through the court as well he would find the justice he'd sought for Caro and Alex at last, but that wouldn't bring them back. He didn't feel the sense of peace he'd hoped for in the wake of the raid. Would he spend the rest of his life becoming like his father, fixated on his job, keeping the people of Barren safe, while letting the rest of him wither away? Did he want to lose Annabelle and Emmie, as he had Caro and Alex?

He ached for every one of them, but *could* he love again? Marry a second time and have more children? He was getting way ahead of himself, but he envisioned a little girl with Annabelle's rich brown hair, her clear brown-to-green eyes and the sweet smile that caught at his heart. Her generous spirit, and how he'd ached for her whenever, because she felt uncomfortable, Annabelle turned away to serve other people. The love he knew she felt for Emmie even when that went against her plans for her future.

Finn made the turn onto Main Street, sped two blocks to the corner of Cottonwood then pulled into a space in front of the diner. As he shut off the engine, his spirits plummeted. The red-and-white sign in the window had a new diagonal strip across it that read Sale Pending.

In his absence Annabelle had sold the diner—exactly what she'd been waiting for. Finn jumped out of the truck, jogged to the restaurant door and pulled it open. The early-bird crowd was finishing breakfast, and the rich aromas of Annabelle's western omelet, bacon and sausage wafted through the warm, cozy space. People talked, laughed and clinked coffee mugs with each other. Well-worn Stetsons hung on the end posts of every booth, and at the large center table a group of ranchers seemed to be debating falling cattle prices. A few heads turned. Several pairs of eyes homed in on Finn. At the counter he saw Sawyer and Doc Baxter eating huge pieces of what looked like Annabelle's huckleberry pie, cups of black coffee beside them. "Hey, Doc. Sawyer. A gathering of the local medical society?"

"We're bachelors today." Sawyer sipped his coffee. "Big women's meeting in progress. Olivia got a new shipment of rugs from Kedar, and her local consortium is planning their Christmas fund-raiser for the cooperative over there. Doc's wife is one of her helpers. They're hoping to sell out for the holidays."

"We don't expect to see them until New Year's," Doc muttered, but his sharp blue eyes twinkled like Santa Claus. "You looking for someone, Sheriff?"

"Annabelle." There was no use hiding his intent. Somehow, he would convince her they had a good thing going; he'd known that before he arrested Sanchez.

"You're looking in the wrong place," Doc said.

Finn hoped she was in the kitchen or her office. "What do you mean?"

Sawyer told him, "Yesterday was her last running the diner." He added, making Finn's heart sink toward his boots, "I imagine she's already left town."

ANNABELLE MADE A quick U-turn then headed back to the Circle H.

To her astonishment—and delight—Emmie was still looking out the storm door at the driveway, her melting Popsicle dripping down one arm, Finnie the lamb in the other. As soon as she spied Annabelle's car, she dropped the Popsicle, pushed out onto the porch and flew down the steps shouting, "A-bel! Here I am!"

Annabelle stopped the car. In those few moments by the side of the road, she had missed Emmie until her heart did break. She shoved the gearshift into Park, switched off the engine then flung open her door. Annabelle hadn't stopped crying since she'd avoided the rabbit. In a few running steps, with more tears streaming down her face, she had Emmie in her arms again. They clung to each other, Emmie's arms around her neck, face buried in Annabelle's jacket, the silk of Emmie's hair against Annabelle's lips. "Baby, I'm sorry."

"You don't go to school?"

"I don't know," she said around the hard lump in her throat that she couldn't seem to swallow. "All I know is I couldn't leave you. I'll never leave you, Emmie. I promise. Wherever I go, you'll come with me." Somehow she would make that work for both of them.

Emmie raised her head. Her blue eyes met Annabelle's. "I like it here. I like it at you house." She held up her lamb. "Finnie does too."

"We'll think of something. Together."

For another moment she envisioned the years ahead watching Emmie learn and grow, as Finn had said she should. Annabelle's mother had been wrong; she could be a good parent. She would be, beginning now. Or had she started the night of Sierra's accident?

She eased back, put her hands on Emmie's narrow shoulders. "For now let's go—"

"See Finn?"

Annabelle felt another wrenching sense of loss. "Maybe later." If he came back from Chicago, if he let her into his life, but after their quarrel that was far from certain and she couldn't tell Emmie. "Let's go home. I'll make lunch. Scrambled eggs," she said. "We can play Chutes and Ladders all afternoon. What else would you like?"

Emmie grinned. "Read *Janie*?"

"Yes. Three times if you want."

She clapped her hands, smeared with red Popsicle juice, then glanced toward the nearby barn. "I ride Freckles today—Blossom said—with Nick." She paused. "But I go home with you."

Annabelle took her hand and started for the porch. "We'll get your things, tell Blossom. You can ride next time."

To her surprise Emmie didn't object. She skipped all the way to the steps then jumped up each one onto the porch. "I stay with you, A-bel!"

"Yes you will. Forever." Annabelle finally swallowed. "You're my little girl now."

She was smiling through her tears when Blossom appeared in the doorway holding her baby. She looked down at Emmie then up at Annabelle. And grinned. Neither of them had to say a word.

But of course Emmie was chattering as the door opened and they stepped into the house. "What else I want," she said, "is a doughnut."

FINN HAD LEFT the diner with his head down. Disappointment swamped him. He'd have to wait until Annabelle finished her course. At least that gave him time to plan what to say, but he felt as if he'd already lost her for good.

And where was Emmie staying while she was away? He put his truck in gear then drove by her house just in case, but, clearly, no one was there.

Finn headed next for Wilson Cattle. When his flight had landed in KC and he took his phone off airplane mode, he'd found a message on his voice mail from the judge on the Derek Moran case. The news wasn't what he'd once hoped for. He was going to have to eat some crow.

Derek was no choirboy, and he'd stepped out of line often enough, but caught up in the loss of Caro and Alex, Finn had made Derek into a scapegoat. In his mind he'd confused him with Eduardo Sanchez, a far more dangerous character.

The chain saws, it turned out, had nothing to do with Derek. While Finn was gone his deputy had arrested Derek's former roommate, Calvin Stern, who still lived—conveniently—in the apartment above Earl Morris's hardware store. Finn hadn't questioned his fingerprints being all over the place, but Calvin had taken the saws and tool chests hours before Derek showed up.

Finn found Derek in the barn talking to one of Grey's horses. "C'mon, sweetheart. You don't want to give me any trouble. Lift that pretty leg so I can see the problem." The well-trained horse complied and Derek, bent over a hoof, said, "Picked up a stone, that's all." He reached up to stroke the horse's side. "You'll be ready to ride by tomorrow."

His easy manner, his gentle tone, surprised Finn. "Derek?"

He spun around, his gaze immediately wary. "Thought you were out of town."

Finn walked toward him, remembering the care Derek had taken to polish Olivia's bridles, seeing the obvious affection he had for these horses. "Heard the news," he said.

"I suppose you did too. Judge says you're in the clear."

"Except for some community service, yeah. He thinks I'm 'redeemable.'" Holding a hoof pick, Derek stooped to pry the stone from the horse's foot. "I'm kind of busy, Sheriff. Grey's in Farrier with Dusty to meet a shipper with some new cattle he bought, so I'm the boss till they get back." His mouth twisted. "And no, I don't plan to steal any cows. You come up with another charge?"

"No charge," Finn said, clearing his throat. "I came to apologize. I've been too hard on you, Derek." He thought of young Joey Foxworth and the boys' club, and what Annabelle had said about helping Derek. "The only excuse I have is my own blind spot." He looked at the ground. "We don't know each other well, but I need to say this anyway. My family—" Finn broke off.

"—got killed in Chicago," Derek said. "Yeah, I remember."

"And I remember how you taunted me about that. Made me mad as could be when you even dared to mention Caro and Alex."

"I shouldn't have said that."

"I reacted badly." Finn ran a hand through

his hair. "The Brothers and Sanchez—the gang that shot them—are in custody now, and the justice I wanted so badly for my family will finally come. But I'm sorry I let my hatred for those thugs spread to include you."

"Huh." Derek didn't seem to know what to say. "Well, they're off the streets now."

"For a long time, I hope." Finn felt as if a huge weight had been lifted from him. Still, he couldn't let Derek completely off the hook. "I have to tell you, if it were up to me, I'd have pursued those rustling charges, but the court has made its decision. You got off easy this time."

Derek straightened. He unhitched the horse from the cross ties then led it to a stall. He slid the door shut then turned. "I'm clean, Sheriff. My first mistake was coming with my brother Jared that night to this very ranch—where he died. I still can't walk past that front porch without seeing the whole thing, but I'm working on it."

Finn stared at him. This was a first, Derek taking responsibility for his actions. "I know what you mean. Grey says that, too." He held out his hand. "Apology accepted?"

"Long as you don't chase me down Main Street for showing off my truck."

"If it's against the law—"

Derek laughed. He took Finn's extended hand. "Lighten up, Sheriff."

"Finn," he said. "As long as you stay on the right side of things, we'll be fine."

To ANNABELLE'S RELIEF, as soon as she pulled up to Finn's barn, she saw he was home. She'd heard from Sawyer and Doc that he'd returned, and after spending the afternoon with Emmie she couldn't wait any longer to drive out to the farm. With his back to her, he stood in the barn aisle grooming the bay gelding. For a moment she sat watching the play of muscle in Finn's broad shoulders and back, his lean but well-built frame, the glint of the late day sun off his dark hair.

"You're back," she said, getting out of the car.

With a brush in his hand, Finn turned and she saw his eyes light up. "This morning," he said. "I stopped by the diner, but you were gone." His gaze seemed to drink her in—or did she just want to think it did? A sleepy-looking Sarge loped around the corner of the barn, tail wagging, and Annabelle stooped to pat his head. "Logan drove him and the

horses home," Finn said. "I thought you were
on your way to Phoenix."

"I couldn't go," she said. "I mean, I can't."
She told Finn about last night with Emmie.
"How could I leave her, Finn? Even for ten
days, never mind forever, no matter how well
cared for she might be. It's just as you said.
I won't have Emmie think I'm like Sierra,
dumping her here and there to do my own
thing." She told him about her conversation
with Elizabeth Barnes, the DNA test, her
promise to provide support for Emmie if,
indeed, Harry was her father.

"And he'd relinquish any other claim to
Emmie?"

"Yes. Olivia's sitter is with her now so I
could come talk to you."

He walked toward her, passing the grooming brush from one hand to the other.

"What about your course?"

"I had my priorities mixed up. I'll take a
course another time. When Emmie came to
me, my life changed too. I'm keeping her,
Finn."

His gaze flickered. "What I hear, you've
sold the diner."

"To Jack Hancock. And I put the house
on the market today. It's not where I want

to live. So, we'll be moving, but I'm thinking…somewhere here in town." Where she could at least see him.

With Sarge behind him, Finn wandered back into the barn, and for a moment Annabelle thought she'd been dismissed, and that, as she'd feared, Finn didn't care what she did or where she went. She couldn't blame him. Annabelle followed, pausing in the doorway to let her eyes adjust to the dimmer light. "I shouldn't have said what I did to you, Finn. I truly can't imagine losing everyone I loved as you did."

"Not everyone," he murmured.

Annabelle wasn't sure what that meant. "How can I fault you for wanting to be left alone?"

"No, actually, that was what I needed to hear." As he tacked up Brown, his movements sure and confident, Finn said, "I didn't want to get close to anyone, Annabelle, but you made me see how wrong that was. So did Cooper—my partner—from his hospital bed."

"Something happened in Chicago," she guessed, a look of horror in her eyes.

Finn told her about the shooting. "I was able to join the task force there to round up The Brothers. I made the arrests with the help of Jimmy O'Neill and the other members of the force, but then I realized that wouldn't be enough. I'm ready now," he said, "to look at those mementos in my dresser drawer. Maybe—like I was with your closet—you'd like to be there for me."

Annabelle blinked. The tears brimmed anyway, threatening to spill over. "Of course. That was something I needed to do and so do you. I'll help with your storage unit too if you want." And settle for friendship if she had to.

"Good," he said. "Because I'm not buried anymore, Annabelle—I'm alive. Let's talk some more. You can ride double with me."

Annabelle half smiled. "So you're taking Grey's advice?"

Finn flushed. "About ready to buy myself that hat," he said, then led the bay past Annabelle out into the fading light. "It'll be dark soon, but we have time for a short trip around these five acres. My little kingdom," he added, his gaze sliding away from hers. "Funny, how getting on a horse really can cure whatever ails you."

Despite her lack of experience with horses, Annabelle didn't refuse. Finn helped her up into the saddle. He rode behind, his tanned arms around her. Annabelle gazed down at his hands loose on the reins, remembering how it had felt when he touched her. How she'd felt when he kissed her. They went through the new gate into the pasture with Sarge trotting along, having befriended Big Brown, then took a few laps around the fenced-in area while Annabelle tried to calm her nerves. There was no denying how good it was to have the horse under her, the sway of the gelding's body in a slow walk then a lazy lope, to watch the setting sun across the meadow and hear the birds roosting for the night in the trees. Peaceful. She was no rider, but it seemed Finn had learned quite well. So could she—another, different adventure.

"Olivia's a good teacher," Finn said as the sky turned a deepening blue with gorgeous wisps of pale pink and the sun finally slipped below the horizon. "I'm not the best student, but I'm coming along. Maybe I ought to buy another horse."

Annabelle's pulse tripped. Did he mean— "For Emmie? She's not ready, is she?"

"Not yet, but I hope—since you're not going anywhere—you'll bring her over again. A lot." He slanted a look at her. "I meant a horse…for you."

She couldn't say a word. Hours ago she'd been on her way out of Barren, away from the memories of her childhood—and from Emmie. She'd thought her fantasies of Finn would remain just that: dreams that could never come true. "You were right when you said my parents would control me unless I put *them* behind me instead of Barren. I don't need to let those bad memories—of that closet, too—define me."

She heard the smile in his voice. "When I was in Chicago, I stayed at my old partner's apartment a few blocks from where I lived with Caro and Alex. Cooper's still in the hospital and he has a long road to recovery ahead of him, and maybe some other issues to deal with, but at least he's on his way. I thought I'd drive by the old house before I left, worried I wouldn't be able to even look at it," he said. "But then, I left without going past because it's part of yesterday, and I'm already looking ahead to tomorrow."

Annabelle held her breath. "The trip was good for you, then."

"Yeah, and I'm glad I went—except for seeing Cooper busted up—but the justice I found for Caro and Alex isn't all I want, or even what I need most anymore." Finn tightened his arms around her.

While he told her about his talk with Derek, Annabelle stared at the space between the horse's ears. And her pulse leapt in her throat. When he finished, Finn gestured at the far side of the fence and said idly, "There's some adjoining land over there I might buy, turn this into a real ranch."

"With cattle?"

"Maybe so. Grey does well with his Black Angus. I can get a few chickens, as you said." He grinned over his shoulder. "Why not? Raise some hay to sell…"

Leaving Annabelle speechless astride the horse, Finn stopped Brown, swung down to open the gate then led the bay through. After closing it again, he walked them toward the barn, his head up, his shoulders back, every line of his body seeming to belong right where he was.

Ducking her head, Annabelle followed him into the barn on Big Brown. In the aisle Finn held up his arms and she slid out of the saddle and down into them, his body warming hers the whole way to solid ground. "That was fun," she said and meant it, although her legs felt shaky.

Finn's hazel eyes turned somber, searching. "A lifetime kind of fun? I can believe in that again—if you can too."

In the cross ties Brown shifted, one iron-shod hoof clanging against the other. Dust motes drifted through the overhead lights, and along the aisle Freckles whinnied for her companion. Sarge sprawled in a heap against the opposite stall, and Annabelle stayed in Finn's arms. Was this where *she* really belonged?

"A big part of my wish to travel as far as I could get from Barren really had to do with my parents—and not even the diner. Now I'm free to live my life as I please and—what did you mean by...a lifetime?"

He took a breath but didn't hesitate. "I tried pretty hard not to see how special this could be, you and me and Emmie, but I missed you both like crazy when I was gone. When I stopped at the diner and heard you'd already taken off for Phoenix, I thought I'd lost you." He waited a beat before going on. "Finding justice for Caro and Alex, and forgetting my pain, were my only goals. Obviously, I can't forget them—I never will—but now bringing the gang to justice doesn't seem like an ending to me. I hope it's a new beginning."

"I think Caro would want you to be happy."

"I know she would. I'm still a young man, and it's quieter here in Kansas. I don't have to risk my life every day like I did in Chicago." Finn cupped her shoulders. "I want you in my life, Annabelle. *All* I want now is…you. And Emmie."

Her breath caught in her throat. "That's a big commitment, Finn."

"I'm ready. Maybe, instead of coming over all the time, you could consider moving in with me. I know the house isn't much right now but we'll make it better, add on a wing or two." His eyes clear, Finn said, "If you want to travel we can do that, too, show Emmie the world. While you're doing a tour, and she's in school, I'll be here. I never want you to give up your dreams, Annabelle."

"I've found my dream," she said. "With you. But I have another idea. Instead of becoming a tour director, while Emmie is small I can work as a tour guide instead, which means I can show up to narrate at a site of interest closer to us, then be with you and Emmie each night. I never thought, never imagined I should have children of my own—"

"But you already do."

"Yes," she said, breaking into a smile. "I certainly do. I love Emmie so much." For the rest of her life, Emmie would bring them laughter and frustration and joy. "And I love you, Finn."

"I love you too. I expect that will take us—and Emmie—a long way."

She raised her face to his. "Maybe to Kedar next spring with Sawyer and Olivia?"

"As far as you want." Finn kissed her. "Sounds like a plan."

* * * * *